Hurricane Baby

Hurricane Baby

Stories

Julie Liddell Whitehead

Madville Publishing

Lake Dallas, Texas

FIRST EDITION

Grateful acknowledgement to the now-defunct journal *China Grove Press* for publishing earlier versions of the stories "Holding On" and "Ave Maria" in their March 2014 and August 2014 issues.

Permissions
Madville Publishing
PO Box 358
Lake Dallas, TX 75065

Cover Design: Jacqueline Davis
Author Photo: Julie Liddell Whitehead

ISBN: 978-1-956440-95-9 paperback,
978-1-956440-96-6 ebook

Library of Congress Control Number: 2024931059

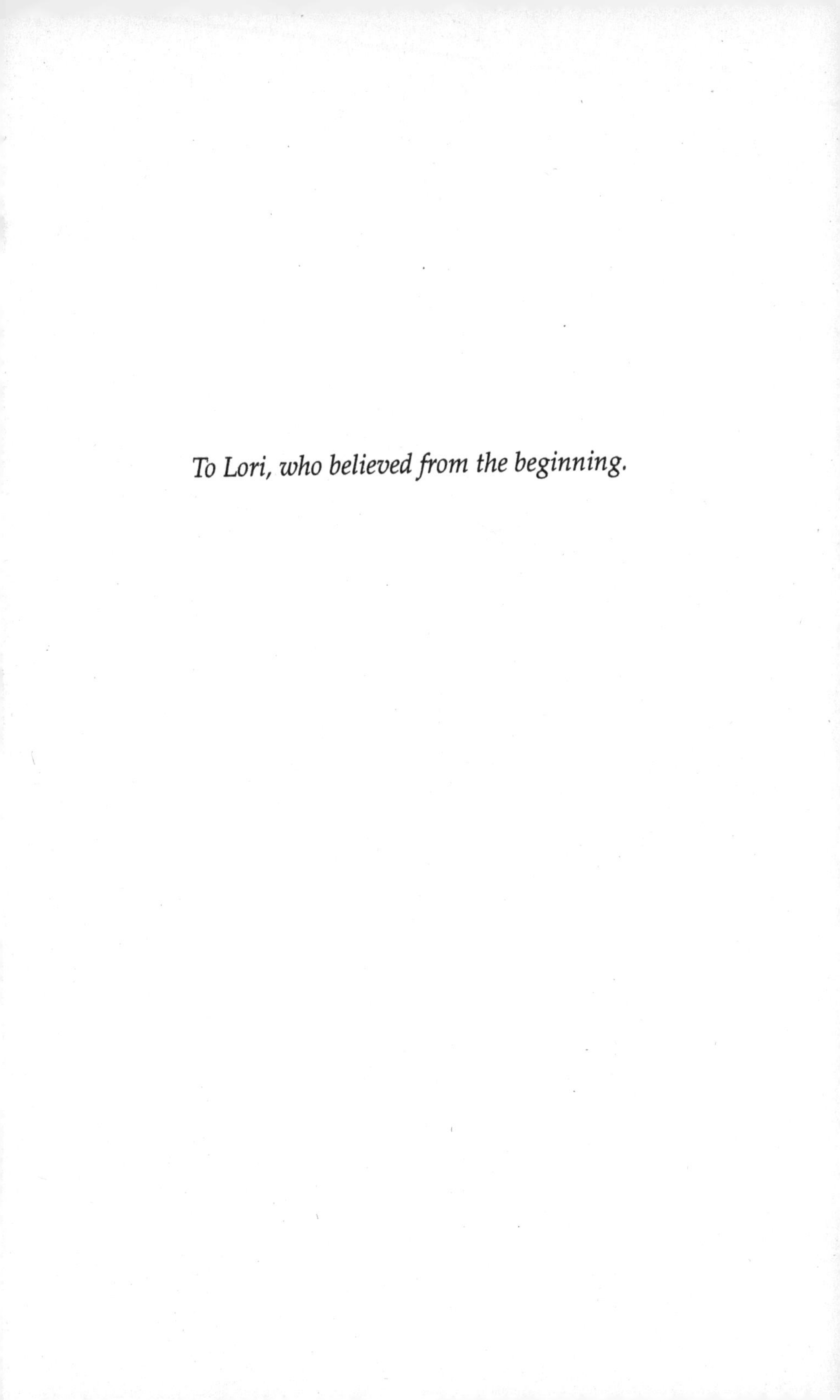

To Lori, who believed from the beginning.

Table of Contents

Still Waters

Wendy didn't know but that it was better way back when. Now you can hear all the weathermen talking about it on TV, but all you can do is wait while she builds up steam. Hurricane Katrina crossed Florida as a Category 2 storm and was spinning around again in the Gulf, and no one knew what was going to happen next.

Her older sister Rosie and her three kids drove the seventy miles upstate to Hattiesburg on Friday morning while Lee stayed down in Gulfport to take care of the house. Rosie said she heard going up the next hundred miles to Jackson was worse.

The kids watched TV and Rosie cooked while Wendy was down at the hardware shop helping her husband, Ray. Some folks from Gulfport came and bought them out of plywood, but Ray was still selling generators, flashlights and batteries, and power cords. People from as far north of the coast as Picayune were ordering the generators from him as the supply on the coast dried up.

Judd McKay brought in a load of generators from the supply warehouse further up in Jackson, dropping them off to all the dealers in the area that afternoon. Wendy never could figure out how he always looked so well-turned out in flat-front khakis and white golf shirts, considering how much time he spent in hardware and mechanics' shops all over south Mississippi and the coast. He was good-looking enough that you'd think he'd have a girl in every town he traveled through, but even as gossipy as their trade was, Wendy'd never heard much up that line about Judd. Where Ray was beefy and muscular, Judd was shorter and thinner but still strong as an ox, lifting parts and engine boxes like they were full of air.

On Friday afternoon, Judd was worried about getting back to his wife in Mandeville before the hurricane hit. "I want her to get out before the traffic gets so bad," he said. "But my boss wants all the generators out he can move before Monday."

"So how many more you got to do?" Wendy said.

"Well, there's another truck coming in from Shreveport, and they say that's it."

"So you're on the road 'til then?"

"I suppose so," Judd said, looking like a kicked dog.

Judd came back in Saturday afternoon with twenty generators. "If you want them, they're all yours, Ray," Judd said. "Jason down in Slidell was asking me how much they were and if I'd take them back if they didn't sell, and I told him too many people were begging for them."

Ray took ten, and Judd was heading back to the truck when he turned around. "Any hotels you know of still open? My wife's already headed out to her mama's, and traffic's bad all the way to Grenada."

"Hattiesburg's booked solid as of last night, according to the TV. How about you stay with us until she blows through? The shop'll be closed since I'll be on duty at the Hattiesburg Firehouse, but Wendy and Rosie'll take care of you and fix you up a bed on the couch. That okay?" Ray said.

Judd blinked his bright blue eyes, always such a shock in someone with such dark hair. "You don't have to do that," he said. "You've already got a houseful."

"It'll be no trouble at all," Wendy said. "I've got a big pot of red beans and rice on for tonight, and Ray's promised us all steak on the grill after she's over if they don't need him at the firehouse or here at the shop."

"Then I'll see y'all tonight. I'll run these others over to Maxey's."

Some rain was already moving in that night, and that kept Rosie's kids inside after dinner. The baby boy took a liking to Judd, toddling after him around the house and climbing into his lap after Rosie let him down from the table.

"You want to go home with me after all this is over?" Judd said, bouncing Bubba on his knee. "I could use a big boy like you around the house."

Bubba looked at Judd and then at Rosie. "Mama."

Judd gave him a hug. "Okay. You go on to your mama then," he said.

Wendy knew Judd had bounced around in the business some; all the heavy equipment dealers knew him from back when he sold chains and bars for saws right out of LSU when Ray started the business ten years ago. Ray still called him "Coon-eye" from when he got two black eyes from a drunk Cajun who thought Judd was admiring his wife a little too much. She'd always heard Judd, with his own buck wild streak, gave it right back to him and broke the Cajun's jaw.

After the kids went to bed, Ray and Judd started talking. Wendy could hear them from her galley kitchen while they talked in the den. "I heard you outran Ivan last year, Judd," Ray said.

"My boss sent me down to Orange Beach with generators in his Explorer. I thought about staying and waited just about too long to change my mind. I got off onto some back road. As long as the GPS said north or west, I kept driving."

Wendy came to the kitchen door. "Where'd you wind up?" Wendy said.

"Meridian."

Ray shook his blond head. "I'll tell you—I'd rather work a fire than a storm. A fire you can put water on and get taken care of. I can deal with that. A storm just don't stop."

That Sunday, Wendy could feel the air closing in. She watched through the kitchen window as Rosie's kids ran around outside. Ray watched the news in the den while Judd talked to his wife on the cell phone out on the front porch.

She heard Ray going to the door and calling out to Judd. "Looks like the eye's going to miss New Orleans and come over Biloxi instead," Ray said. "They're looking at hundred-and-forty-five mile-an-hour winds."

"What's the storm surge going to be like?" Judd said back.

"Saying it might make twenty-five feet."

Wendy came in the den to see Judd looking startled. "They're saying Category 5?" Judd whispered.

"Yeah," Ray said.

Judd let the door slam behind him as he went back out on the porch. "Hear that?" Wendy heard him say to his wife.

Ray sat down in his recliner and started pulling off his tennis shoes. "You getting ready for bed already?" Wendy said.

"I'm going on down to the firehouse," Ray said.

"Why?" Wendy said, brushing her black bangs out of her eyes. She resolved to chop off her long black wavy hair next time she went to the beauty shop in a couple of weeks—it was just getting too unmanageable in the humidity.

He didn't answer, just got up from the chair and headed to the back to start packing to spend the night. Wendy went into the kitchen and poured two steel thermoses full of coffee like she always did when he went on duty.

She heard him going back outside and rumbling something to Judd in a low voice. She heard Judd say, "Are you sure?"

Another low rumble from Ray. Wendy realized he was trying to keep his voice down.

She heard both men come back in off the porch and turned. Ray was coming towards her through the kitchen door, carrying his duffle bag, and she heard Judd settle into the recliner and turn up the news some—all the work with saws years ago had hurt his hearing, she figured.

Wendy followed Ray out to his red Ford Explorer. He turned to her before he climbed into the cab, concern in his eyes. "You get those big girls to gather in those deck chairs and get them into the garage. Get Judd to help you with the wheelbarrow and the gas grill, too. We don't need nothing else flying around the backyard, and I want you and Rosie and the kids inside with the TV and the radio on listening. Don't forget the—"

"Batteries for the radio. I know the drill—we went through all this with Dennis. Though I don't know why you're worried about the deck chairs. You don't worry."

"I can't help it—Wendy, this one's bigger that anything they've ever seen in the Gulf. Camille was bad—this one's going to be worse."

Wendy felt her stomach drop. "You don't know that."

Ray shook his head. "I know you don't like hearing this—it might be a while before I'm home again. The wind, the rain—it just doesn't look good. Judd may be here for a few days because he won't be able to get out. He says he'll help you all he can. But I know how you get, and I need you to hold yourself together. Okay, hon?"

Wendy nodded, not trusting herself to speak.

Ray hugged her, and she squeezed his strong chest extra tightly. "See you in a while," he said.

"All right. Love you."

Rosie was just getting off the phone with Lee when Wendy went back in. Her graying hair was sweaty from the kitchen heat from all the cooking she had done. "Lee says she's knocked out the buoys in the Sound, and the wind is really getting up there."

Wendy heard Judd from the den; she turned and he was watching the Weather Channel guys in Mobile on the beach. "They're damn crazy. Standing out there in that wind. No one with the sense God gave a billy goat needs to be told to stay off the beach!"

She'd never heard him sound so rough, not even when talking with the guys in the shop when he thought she couldn't hear.

Wendy went in the kitchen, and she heard Judd follow behind her. "I want to thank you for letting me stay over in all of this, Mrs. Wendy," he said, his voice smooth and easy and back to normal.

"I appreciate you saying that, Judd. We usually have someone in whenever one of these storms comes through; if it's not Rosie and them, it's someone else. I'm used to it."

Wendy and Rosie heard the little boy fussing and started back for him at the same time, but Rosie waved Wendy back. "I'll take care of him. It'd be a help for you to finish cleaning up in there."

Wendy turned around to see Judd grinning with eyes sparking with mischief. "Bossy older sister?" he said.

Wendy nodded, not taking the bait. "I was just trying to help her not have to worry so much about them. But she's right, I can help in here."

"You like having those kids around, don't you?" Judd said, still grinning. "I saw you smiling while I was messing with him earlier."

Wendy felt herself smile in spite of the old emptiness that rose inside her talking about kids for herself. "Yeah. I love working with my three-year-olds at the daycare, but babies are something else. Since we don't have any, I have to get my baby fix when Rosie comes up."

"She's sure got her hands full," Judd said. Then he looked at her with a question in his blue eyes. "Can y'all not have any?" he said.

Wendy's chest and throat tightened, and she turned away. She didn't think he meant any harm by asking, but still—"I don't know. We just don't," she said, her voice pitched high.

She wasn't hiding anything from him, she guessed. "I didn't mean to upset you by asking," he said as he touched her shoulder.

"You didn't," she lied. "It's just not something I think much about anymore. Ten years is a long time to wait—and soon I'll be thirty." She licked her lips. "What about you—y'all have any kids?"

"My wife says she's not much for that kind of thing," Judd said. "I'm trying to change her mind—we waited a bit to find each other and now been married five years, and no one's getting any younger in my house either."

Wendy nodded absently as she finished wrapping up the last of a leftover chocolate cake she'd bought on sale before the storm warnings. She concentrated on the smell of the German chocolate cake frosting, Ray's favorite.

She hadn't touched on the idea of trying harder to have them to Ray lately—money was always so tight, and it seemed like whenever they got a little money together, something happened to wipe it out: car repair, fixing the roof, an order falling through. Truth be told—she knew they might never have one, and that was why she'd taken the daycare job in the first place.

Rosie got all her kids down on quilt pallets in the floor of the back bedroom before she went to bed herself around midnight. Wendy had pulled out a sleeping bag for Judd the night before to bed up on the couch, so that's where he slept again.

That night, Wendy sat up in bed taking deep breaths to stop the pounding in her chest. *Not again.*

The dreams were back full force—she'd dreamed she'd opened the door to Roger Timms, the fire chief, tall and thin and bald, hat in hand, coming out to tell her Ray was gone and wasn't coming home ever again.

She got out of bed and went up front to the kitchen.

She was pouring orange juice into a glass when she thought she heard Rosie behind her. "You need something?" she said.

"I'll take a glass of that, too, if you would," Judd said.

She reached up for another glass and filled it before she turned around. He was sitting at the table in khaki shorts and a Bob's Bait Shop t-shirt.

"Sorry I woke you up," she said. "I tried not to turn too many lights on."

"You didn't, really. I just heard you stirring around—thought Ray came in."

She handed him the glass and sat down across from him.

"You look like you've spent a long night," Judd said.

She shrugged without looking at him. "Ray works forty-eight hours on and seventy-two hours off at the firehouse. I've gotten where I can handle that. But when it's a storm, he's gone for as long as it takes, depending on how bad it is." She propped up her chin on her hand. "Sometimes I have nightmares that he doesn't come home. That's all," Wendy said, willing her voice to stay flat.

She saw his eyes soften. "Oh, man. That must be tough." He shook his head slowly. "I don't blame you much for worrying with this one. All the Weather Channel guys are saying no one's seen anything like this before."

"Oh, that's all I needed to hear," Wendy said, staring at the back door Ray had walked out of that afternoon. "I told myself I am not going to cry tonight. So don't make me."

"God. Wendy, I didn't think about what I was saying," Judd said as he reached across the table for her hand.

She looked at him and felt heat creeping up her throat at the stricken look on his face. "It's all right—you didn't know any better."

"You keep saying that—but I should have, though," Judd said. "That's twice tonight I've upset you."

Wendy shrugged. *What does he want me to say?*

They sat in silence for a bit, Wendy sipping at her orange juice and Judd leaving his untouched, staring at the table. *He's probably used to something a little stronger this time of night.*

"You know what my daddy used to say to my mama to make her smile?" Judd said to her with a sidelong glance.

"What?" Wendy said, putting her glass down.

"You're too pretty a girl for me to make want to cry like this," Judd said.

Wendy felt her cheeks heat up, and he must have realized

he went a step too far. He dropped his eyes. "Sometimes it works," he mumbled so low she could barely hear him.

"Maybe you have to be married," Wendy said, holding her voice steady.

"Maybe," he whispered.

He looked so hangdog she didn't know what else to say. He always carried himself in a friendly way that you couldn't help but like, but the night and the storm and her fear and the quiet of the house made her feel longing for Ray, but he wasn't there.

And Judd was.

Then she felt him squeeze her hand—tight. "I'm sorry. For trying to make light of Ray being out in this mess and for—saying something so incredibly stupid."

She looked over at him and saw his eyes were wet. She let go of his hand, got up, stepped over to him, put her hands on his shoulders, and squeezed them. He patted her hand lightly, like you might a baby's—

I've got to get out of here.

"I'm going to go try to get some more sleep," she said.

"Me, too." He let go of her hand, sat back in his chair, and downed the orange juice as she left him there, feeling a little shaky as she walked.

Wendy woke up at six Monday morning to hear the wind whipping around the house. As everyone else got up, she passed out donuts and coffee with one ear to the TV. The drumbeat of the news was clear—this hurricane wasn't going to be any ordinary storm, and she had to shut thoughts of Ray out of her mind to keep from falling apart. *I thought my nerves were better than this.*

At around nine, Judd walked in the kitchen looking like he'd seen Death on the corner eating Lifesavers. "WLOX says the eye's about halfway between here and Biloxi and it's still a Category 3."

Just then the wind kicked up another notch, and the lights went out. Wendy handed Rosie a flashlight. "Let's get those kids and you settled in the back bedroom," Wendy said.

They pulled out all the play-pretties Rosie had packed for the kids for the trip—coloring books, crayons, flat puzzles, and picture books. Wendy felt her stomach settle some at the familiarity of the routine but wondered what to do with Judd and herself. The baby was too big and active to be in a bouncy seat like he had been last year for both of them to fit back there with them—it would be too cramped.

She finally settled on where she went when tornado winds threatened and she was at the house by herself—the big walk-in closet off of hers and Ray's bedroom.

Thirty minutes later that's where Judd and Wendy sat with the Eveready light shining up from the floor after they kicked all the shoes and boots in the closet out into the bedroom so there would be room to sit. He fiddled with the battery-powered radio while she stowed away their cell phones, wallets, and Judd's laptop into one of Ray's backpacks.

The wind was starting to whistle by now, and Wendy remembered her mom talking about hiding under the couches tipped over in the living room when the Inverness tornado went over. She shivered.

"Scared?" Judd said.

She nodded.

"If it makes you feel any better, I am too," he said.

"Have you tried to call your wife this morning?" she said.

"I'd just hung up when the news came on saying the eye would be here by ten."

"You say everything you needed to say?"

Judd ran his thick fingers through his hair and inhaled. "Yeah. You and Ray, too?"

"Before he left," she said. "As much as we ever do when he's out in these."

So they sat in the dark with the flashlight casting strange shadows and listened to the rising wind and the radio bulletins. Hours passed. The storm moved up the state bit by bit—thunderstorm warnings in Pearl River County, funnel clouds sighted in George County, extremely high winds moving into Forrest County, reports of thirty deaths already in Harrison County.

Wendy swallowed hard. She glanced at Judd and saw him chewing his fingernails. "Do you drink?" she said.

"Right now I wish I did," Judd said.

"Yeah."

Then she heard the wind come howling in, cracking trees and shaking the house. Judd grabbed Wendy's arm and pulled her over beside him, wrapping one arm around her and holding the flashlight with his other hand.

She heard the porch swing banging on one of the posts where the wind ripped out one of the chains. She couldn't tell if she heard Rosie screaming or if it was the wind. *Not even Elena sounded like this. God, help us.*

Wendy shut her eyes and started whispering some of the only Bible verses she knew from way back in Bible school when her mama made her go. "The Lord is my shepherd. I shall not want. He maketh me lie down in green pastures. He leadeth me beside the still waters—" she said.

Wendy heard glass shattering from up front. She buried her face in Judd's shoulder and dug her fingernails into her palms to keep from screaming.

"Stay with me, baby. Stay with me. It'll soon be over. You're going to be all right," Judd said in her ear as he rocked her back and forth. His arms felt strong and safe, just like you would imagine in a man like him. She felt her body start to relax with the motion, so much like how Ray would hold her when she was crying. Then she heard something smash into the garage.

"We're going to die here, aren't we?" she said.

Judd didn't say a word, just started moving his hand up and down her back. Another crash. *That was the back bedroom. That's the only blood kin I've got.* She tried to get up.

"I told Ray I'd take care of you, and I meant it! Now get back down!" Judd said as he yanked hard on her arm.

On her way down, she knocked the flashlight out of his hand, and it went out.

She landed in his lap, and he put both arms around her as she tried to sit up. The wind kept getting louder and louder. *This is really going to be bad.*

Another crash sounded like it was just by the other side of the wall, and this time, Wendy couldn't help it; she screamed. Judd pulled back from her and clapped his hand over her mouth. "Don't start that!" he hissed, mouth close to her ear.

I can't breathe. Oh my God, I can't breathe. Oh God. She licked his hand.

He yanked it away as if she'd bit him and shoved her backwards into the wall. She heard his breathing turn ragged as the winds rose even higher.

Now what and I going to do? I don't want to die alone!

"Judd?" She reached back out in the dark. "Judd?"

Her hand touched his arm, and he grabbed onto it and pulled her back to him. He put one hand behind her head like she was a baby and pressed her face into his shoulder again. Another window blew out, and Wendy put her hand up to her mouth and bit down hard on the back of it.

Judd pulled her hand loose from her teeth and held it tight against his chest. "I've got you—I'm not letting go," he said.

She thought about Ray at the firehouse. It'd be just like him to decide to haul the flag down out front before it got ripped apart. She let out a sob before she could stop it. She felt Judd turn his head towards her, then he started to kiss his way to her mouth.

She could feel the wildness in him, like a stallion that had never tasted a bit. His kisses lapped up her tears, and she heard him growl low in his throat.

Wendy knew she could pretend it wasn't happening—try to keep her mind safe from what might happen between them—but suddenly she didn't even care, letting her feelings flow throughout her mind, her body—everywhere.

It seemed like forever until they both finally fumbled for his belt. Their hands touched. Judd twisted his fingers into hers and raised her arms above her head and held them there as he eased her onto her back in the floor. The wind eased down to a low whistle as the eye started to go over.

"I shouldn't do this," Judd said. Wendy could feel his breath on her face.

"I know."

He let go of her left hand and ran his fingers through her hair. Wendy turned her face away and sobbed at his tenderness. "I shouldn't be doing this," he whispered again in her ear.

"But you don't want to stop?"

"No." He tangled both his hands up in her hair. "Do you want me to stop?"

Wendy knew that she could say yes and he would stop.

But wait—did she know that for sure? Could she pull away and run out into the house, risking the storm's fury? They were in a safe place, with no walls to the outside and no windows.

But was it safe? No one could hear her scream over the wind—

But could she let him down easy? Let him kiss and touch her in ways that were already sparking in her in spite of her fear, then tell him to please stop—that she couldn't do this to Ray, her husband and his friend, who trusted him to take care of her while he was gone.

But could she tell him she was on her period? That her periods were heavy and bloody? She could lie convincingly; that she knew. But wasn't it close to her period? Maybe it wouldn't be a lie—maybe she already started bleeding out her fear, her pain, her wanting.

But did she want him to stop? It was too close to her period to be safe; she imagined holding her baby for the first time....

"Wendy?" Judd said, his voice hungry.

She squeezed her eyes shut even though she already couldn't see a thing. "No. I don't want you to stop."

She arched her back under him once he got back to where they'd left off with his belt.

Cramped quarters weren't new to him—he showed no trouble maneuvering at all as the other side of the storm seemed determined to take down everything she'd left standing outside before.

In a corner of her mind, Wendy was waiting for when the roof was finally going to come down on them, and then for a few long seconds—she wished it already had.

Judd stayed laid down on top of her, breathing hard. After a final kiss, he rolled off her, and she pulled herself together, clothes and all, without looking at him and sat up with her head between her knees and her back to him.

"I'm sorry, Wendy," Judd whispered. She could barely hear him through the rain.

"So am I," she said.

"I started it—"

"I let you," she said. She crossed her arms over her head.

As the storm blew itself out, she could hear him whispering to himself in low bursts of common talk and Cajun, spitting out words she didn't have to know to understand. She tried to listen for Rosie or one of the kids, but the rain was coming down harder even as the wind was finally starting to let up. She put her hands over her ears to try to block it all out.

When she couldn't hear the wind anymore, she left Judd there and went out in the house calling for Rosie, stumbling through the bedroom and the hallway full of dustcatchers knocked loose from their places onto the floor.

The kids came out of the bathroom crying, and Rosie staggered out, looking teary-eyed but smiling. She hugged Wendy. "We're here! We made it! We're alive!" she laughed. "Isn't God good?"

Wendy hugged her back without a word, then looked out the window through the rain. One tree landed on the garage where Ray's truck would have been if he'd been home; it rested on the frame of the garage while the branches came in through the roof.

The north wind blew trees all over the backyard. The front room's windows were knocked out when the porch swing finally tore loose. Wendy pushed it back out the window frame, and her and Rosie taped up some Visqueen over the windows while Rosie's biggest girl fixed sandwiches from what they'd put up in a cooler.

When Wendy went back into the kitchen, Judd was walking toward the front door with a sandwich in his hand. "I'm going out to check on your shop. If I can help out there, I will. Do you think I can get out?"

"I don't know. You can try. Your truck's okay as far as I can see."

"Thanks for checking." He started to say something else and stopped. Finally he said, "Can I come back here tonight and sleep?"

Wendy nodded. He reached out to touch her cheek, and she flinched away.

"I'll see you then," he said and went out.

He pulled out with his wipers going full blast on his big white diesel pickup and picked his way around the branches from all over the driveway. Wendy watched him go as she picked glass up out of the front room floor while Rosie tried to keep the kids occupied. Lee called Rosie's phone to say he was okay.

The radio said that the storm should be in Jackson by five. She walked through the house looking for any other limbs or broken windows.

She came back in the living room and sat down in her favorite blue chair that her mother had given her before she died and opened her mouth wide and screamed at the ceiling, eyes squeezed shut.

Rosie came out running. "What's wrong, Wendy? What happened?"

I can't even tell Rosie. "I'm scared. I'm scared for Ray and everyone else. I'm just scared to death, Rosie, and I want to—"

"Wendy, we all just went through hell. We're all scared. But get it all out of your system before Ray comes home because God alone knows what he's having to do now."

"He might not come home!" Wendy cried.

Rosie grabbed her arm. "I prayed for him and Lee during the storm and asked the Lord to save them both. He's saved Lee; He'll save Ray. Do you believe that with me?"

Wendy nodded, blubbering nonetheless. "Then let's pray," Rosie said.

Rosie prayed for Ray, all the guys at the firehouse, Lee and all the folks on the coast, and everywhere in between to be safe. Wendy looked at the floor with eyes wide open, trying to blank out her mind of the past few hours.

Wendy stopped crying, and Rosie patted her arm before she went back into the den with the kids. Wendy turned on her cell phone in case Ray called and sat there.

She was still there when Judd came back at ten o'clock that night. She heard the rain coming down hard as he opened the door she'd left unlocked. He looked startled when he came through the house and saw her sitting there with a candle burning and a flashlight in her lap Rosie gave her before she went to bed.

"Did you eat?" Wendy said.

"A little bit back at dinner time," said Judd.

"Okay." Judd sat down on the couch. "How is it out there?" she said.

He shook his head. Wendy looked down at his feet and saw how muddy his shoes were, then how filthy his shirt was. "I saw Ray," Judd said.

"He's all right?"

"Yes ma'am, he is, and he's working. I told him y'all were fine and the house was pretty good except for the windows and the garage." He shifted on the couch to look at her. "He said for me to tell you if anyone comes to the house that's hungry to feed them. But if they come to take something that isn't theirs, for you to shoot them."

Too late for that.

Judd said he and one of Ray's guys pulled tree limbs out of windows at the shop and tarped them up. He couldn't get in to check on any of the other dealers, and that's when he'd found Ray at the firehouse and told him if they'd get him gas for his power saw, he'd help cut trees off the roads.

He saw folks congregating at the big Baptist church, which fired up their kitchen with generators. He saw a fireman leading dogs he'd found up the street, trying to get them into the pound to get stitched up, and he saw ambulances stop with the paramedics and firemen walking in to dig someone out from under their house.

He stopped talking suddenly and leaned his head between his knees.

"You been able to call your wife?" Wendy said.

"I can't get through," Judd said. "The circuits are busy."

It took Wendy a minute to realize he was crying. She moved over next to him and put an arm around his shoulders and a hand on his knee. "I should have gone on upstate Friday," she heard him say through gritted teeth.

"I don't know what to say to you, Judd."

He turned and wrapped both his arms around her and held her. Her hands were shaking as she smoothed his nasty, matted hair and rocked him back and forth.

Judd lifted his head off her shoulder. He kissed the corners of her eyelids and moved down the side of her face to her mouth. As he moved his hands down her back, she squeezed her eyes shut and thought about Ray climbing into his truck to leave. She pulled away from him. "Please stop."

She could feel his fingers under her jaw as he lifted her chin up and brushed his thumb across the tears on her cheek. "It seems like all I can really do for you is make you cry," he said.

"It's not you I'm thinking about when I cry," Wendy said.

He let go of her, and she stood up. She was halfway to the door walking out of the room when Judd said "Wendy?"

"What?" She didn't mean to snap, but it was all she could do to talk.

"Do you love Ray?"

"Yes."

"Have I changed that?"

"No."

"Do you hate me?"

"No."

"You hate yourself?" Judd said.

"Right now? Yes," Wendy said.

"Don't."

She turned around to look at him. "Why not?"

His eyes were bleak in the weak light. "Because you'll hurt yourself worse that way for no good reason."

"I don't want to hear it, Judd. I just want to go to bed."

"We need to solve this right now, or it'll eat us both up for the rest of our lives. It was all I could do to walk out and leave you this afternoon, and I'm heading out in the morning. I can't stay here another night with you, not after what happened today. But I've got to know you can forgive me and yourself."

Wendy couldn't give him what he wanted so she didn't say anything.

She heard what sounded like a chopper overhead and hoped that whoever was in it knew what they were doing.

"Wendy—were we good together?" Judd whispered.

The look on his face in the candlelight was more than Wendy could take. She could see fear, and hurt, and something else she couldn't identify. She sat down in the floor as she went weak in the knees. "Yes."

"Why?" he said as he moved to sit in the floor in front of her.

"How do I know? Judd—"

"What were you thinking about then?"

He put his hand up to her face. She made herself look him in the eye as she answered. "Nothing. Except you."

"Same here," Judd said. "We forgot about the storm, the wind, and everything."

Wendy shook her head back and forth slowly. "I didn't just

forget what was happening, Judd. I forgot who I was, and now I remember, and it hurts."

He dropped his hand and looked down at the floor. "Then try to forget about me. Maybe that's the best I can hope for."

Another spatter of rain hit the window plastic as they sat.

Judd said, "Wendy, I—"

Wendy bolted for the door and ran back to her room. She threw herself onto the king bed, picked up her pillow, stuffed it into her mouth so as not to wake the baby, and cried herself to exhaustion.

She woke up again when Ray came out of the shower at two. "You're here! What happened?" she cried.

"Chief sent me back and told me to hug my wife and get some sleep," Ray said, so tired he sounded like he was drunk.

He sounds half-dead.

All Wendy knew was that she was desperate to get Judd's touch and scent off of her. Ray's familiar smells and tastes helped—but not enough.

After they were done, Ray wrapped his arms around her as she cried herself to sleep.

Feeling Judd's hands under her clothes and his mouth on hers. His fingers tangling her hair and pulling her head backward to run his tongue down her neck—

But when Wendy got up again with Ray at five, Judd was gone. Ray said he was packing up when he came in. He'd finally got through to his wife upstate, and he wanted to try to make his way to Mandeville to check his place. If he couldn't get through, then he'd turn around and go to Jackson to start running generators again for his boss.

Wendy tried to get out of bed, and the room spun around her. She felt like she was going to get sick. She got to the bathroom, looked in the mirror over the sink, and splashed water on her face to get her color back. Then she saw where she had a little mark right where her ear met her jaw. She reached for concealer to dab over it but dropped the container into the sink as she started sobbing quietly. *Marked me for good, he did.*

Neighbors Helping Neighbors

Tommy Hebert woke up the morning after the hurricane landed on Louisiana feeling bone tired, sore in every muscle, and sticky hot with sweat to a text from his girlfriend Cindi Delafosse. "hey" it said. "how you doing"

She included a picture of herself and their five-year-old Marilee smiling at him, both with long blond curls, which gave him a bit of a lift he needed that morning. Tommy looked at his watch. It was five forty-five a.m., he'd been sleeping the sleep of the dead. "ok" he sent back.

He spent most of yesterday afternoon and night once the storm passed through out on his airboat, loading people, children, and pets out of their homes in Metairie and taking them to the shelter on higher ground. He'd sent Cindi and Marilee up to Baton Rouge to stay with her grandmother and get them out of the storm. He stayed to ride it out because that's what his people always did. But no one ever expected it to be as bad as this.

He remembered the heavyset guy he'd seen losing his temper in the shelter when one of the workers asked for his drivers' license. "I ain't got no driver's license! I ain't got no insurance cards! All I got is the clothes on my back! My house is gone; my car is gone; and my babies is gone. I ain't got nothing left!" he'd shouted at the girl sitting behind the long cafeteria table. "You gonna help me out or not?"

Tommy walked over to the guy who'd turned his back on the shelter worker who looked like she was trying not to cry. Tommy always carried a hundred dollar bill on him for emergencies, and he judged that this was about as bad an emergency as he was ever going to see. He shook the big man's hand and passed him the bill in his palm, then turned and walked away so as to not embarrass the man any further.

He saw a flurry of texts asking for more volunteers throughout the night on the group text he and his neighbors set up before they'd knocked off the for the night, with most updated that people were saving people. He was drinking a bottle of water he'd put up in a cooler before the storm hit when his buddy Mark Showalter texted him. "you need anything" the text read.

Tommy texted back. "im good you"

Mark's text back said, "ok trees down in front"

Tommy nodded to himself. His backyard trees came down, too, having smashed his shed full of fishing equipment flat. But his shed of lawn equipment—lawnmower, trimmer, saws—was good, and his garage with the cars was in good shape too as well as the house. He'd spent the night fighting the floodwaters some more in his dreams, but even there, everyone got out. He texted. "mines in backyard we cut up mine today and yours tomorrow"

Just then another text came in on the group text, asking for any able-bodied men with chainsaws to go out to the Thompson place north of town by thirty miles in Mandeville. Tommy shook his head. *The only way anyone's getting to Mandeville was by boat.*

He changed into shorts and a t-shirt, and scraped his scraggly dirty-blond beard-growth away, looking in the bathroom mirror—he'd been trying to grow one to look older, but it was too hot now for that mess.

As he was getting dressed, another text on the same chain came in, all caps. "PLEASE HELP THOMPSON PLACE

EMERGENCY SOMEONE BURIED IN THEIR HOME PLEASE COME"

He checked the group text and discovered no one was responding. He texted back. "911 responding"

The number immediately sent "NO ONE RESPONDING AT 911 OR FIREHOUSE ACCORDING TO NEIGHBOR" back to him.

Tommy swore at the phone. He texted, "on my way by boat keep calling 911 until someone responds coordinates"

After a few minutes, the text came back with a location. Tommy pulled up his text chain with Mark, who drove an ambulance for Metairie. "alert someones buried in their house in Mandeville try to raise hospital 911 whoever on your radio" and sent the coordinates.

He went out to the boat trailer and was glad he left it tied to his yellow 1985 Chevy Silverado and filled it up with his spare gas can before turning in last night. He drove to the waterline separating high ground and flooded areas and turned due north to the far side of Lake Ponchartrain. He unloaded his boat and sped out onto the water.

He did a lot of veering and steering to avoid debris cluttering up the lake surface. He didn't want to think about what might have already sunk down to the bottom of the lake—he imagined there'd be bodies washing ashore throughout St. Tammany Parish for a long, long time.

About halfway across, he got a text from Mark. "911 having to cut their way through im on the way approaching fontaine bleu sp meet you there."

So Tommy angled his position to the left and saw several boats approaching the pier there, same as he was. He finally saw Mark's boat back aways behind his; he pulled up to the pier, almost swamped from the lake's risen waters. He dropped anchor and waited for Mark to pull in beside him.

Back behind the main building was a pair of cop cars with lights flashing. Tommy and Mark climbed out of their boats and walked over to them along with about four other men in various states of disarray. Some looked like they'd been out all night; others looked fresher but still haunted around their eyes. The first cop popped his door open and climbed out. "You guys must be some of the Cajun Navy we're hearing so much about."

Tommy glanced around at the other guys, who looked too beaten down to answer. "I don't know about that," he said. "I just got an alert about somewhere called the Thompson place and saw no one was responding. So I came out."

Mark spoke up. "I'm the one that got the hospital alerted about the same situation, sir. Last I heard they were about three miles out cutting their way through."

The cop nodded. "We got your message about the place. It's what passes for a hill in these parts with one house near the top. A neighbor heard screaming this morning and put the word out. I'm to get you as close as I can to the house with the roads as they've been cleared so far. We've got other men coming from other parts north, but nobody much is moving very fast."

Tommy looked around the group, and to a man, they looked like they'd already seen enough of the storm. But if there was someone else needing help, it looked like they were the ones to do it today. He nodded to the cop, and they started making their way with their saws and other equipment to the cars.

Tommy stowed his chainsaw in the trunk of the cop car and came around to sit in the back seat. He was having bad memories of being a teenager and seeing the inside of a cop car from the back after wrecking his red 1984 Camaro against a tree. He'd been sober, but the cops didn't believe him and brought him to the station after the hospital cleared him of injuries. He didn't know who was watching out for him that night to keep him alive, but a night in the drunk tank kept him off the sauce for the rest of his life thus far.

Twice the men climbed out of the cars and cut limbs off roads to get through. They heard the radio reporting the ambulance was almost there with a firetruck behind it for good measure.

Tommy heard the siren of the ambulance as it crashed through the brush on a cross-road of what they were traveling on. The cops turned to follow it as it ran over a bunch of smaller branches; the woods were opening up to an area that once was a manicured yard; now it was covered in building waste—loose shingles, insulation, splintered wood.

Tommy looked over at Mark riding beside him. "We're going to have to watch our step out here so we don't get lockjaw before the day's out."

"I hear you, brother," Mark replied.

They rounded a turn and were on the house before they knew it. The cop screeched to a stop in front of a house flattened to the ground; the way it was oriented, nothing protected it from the winds. As soon as the car stopped skidding, Tommy heard a girl screaming.

Everyone seemed to freeze at hearing that scream.

A man came running around the side of the house, pointing to the center of the woodpile. Tommy figured it was the neighbor who tried making the original report. Tommy looked down at the waterproof watch he never took off—he'd gotten the original text at around six in the morning and now it was seven-thirty.

The guy was wearing long cutoffs, a lawnmower ball cap, and a torn red t-shirt. "She's somewhere in here!" he shouted. "She's getting weaker and weaker by the minute!"

The cry was enough to end Tommy's paralysis—he reached for where the door handle should have been and started banging his fist on the door looking for it. The cop unlocked the doors and turned himself out after popping his trunk from the inside. Tommy and Mark raced for their saws and ran up to the neighbor. He led them around the wreck of the house to the back where the bedrooms likely were.

The screams were coming from an area where it looked like the roof ridge collapsed in on itself. Tommy turned to the neighbor. "Was this a one-story or two?"

The guy said, "Two-story in front and one-story in the back. But she's under all that roof."

Suddenly she screamed out again—no words, just pure pain. Tommy looked at Mark. "Let's get to cutting this roof into pieces we can move."

He raised his voice. "Me and Mark'll cut up the roof and you pull it away behind us and maybe we can burrow our way down and pull her out. That sound like a plan?"

The men nodded. But just before Tommy cranked up the saw, they heard another sound: a weak, weak little cry. Then the girl again—"Save my baby—please save my baby!"

Every hair on Tommy's body prickled in the heat, and he felt a chill run through him. Mark looked like he'd seen the walking dead go across his path. They both cranked up and got to cutting.

After slicing through several pieces of roof, they moved back out of the way for the other men to lift it. The ambulance driver, the firemen, the cops, and the neighbor pitched in, too, trying to clean off the smaller pieces of house from around the edges of the pile.

After every run of the saws, the neighbor hollered. "Amy! Can you see any light up top of you?"

And she would cry out. "No—please hurry!"

After a long twenty minutes of cutting and digging, one man reached down in the hole they'd created. "Can you see my hand?" he shouted.

Progressively her cries weakened. But Tommy heard her say, "Yes, but I can't reach it."

The man started digging furiously, flinging scraps every which direction. All the men took an edge of the hole and started moving the debris off the pile. Tommy finally saw the handle of a baby seat—one of the bucket styles. "I found the baby!" he yelled.

Suddenly the pile shifted to the right. Tommy and Mark shut off their saws in a hurry and tried to keep their footing. But

Tommy knew where to start digging next, so he went at it with his hands. Finally he was able to touch the handle. He shifted another piece of roof and saw the girl for the first time.

She had the look on her face of a spotlit deer—her eyes were glazed over and staring, her blonde hair was matted with a mix of sweat, dirt, and blood, and she was bleeding out of her nose, her scalp, and the corner of her mouth. He shifted another piece of roof and saw the whole baby carrier with a small baby in a dinosaur t-shirt and diaper in it, covered with clods of dirt and insulation.

His eyes darted down the girl's body; his view of it ended abruptly when he saw a beam across her bare legs. She wore a pink top and blue jean short-shorts and was covered in splinters and carpet padding and God alone knew what else.

He willed his face to not show emotion as he reached for the handle of the baby carrier. "Here, hon. I'll take the baby and take him to the ambulance. Then we'll work on getting you uncovered and out. Sound good?" he said in what he hoped was a reassuring voice.

Her eyes focused on his for just a second, then they darted to the baby carrier as he gingerly tried to pull it away from her. Her voice found a new urgency as he worked to free the carrier from her grip. "Don't take my baby! Give me my baby! Don't take my baby away! Do you hear me? Don't take him!" she cried.

Tommy remembered the neighbor calling her Amy. "Amy, I'm Tommy. Tommy Hebert. I want to help your baby. I need you to let go so we can help him. We still need to cut away part of this roof, and you don't want him to get full of splinters from the saws," he said, making lines up as he went along. "Just let go, and I'll take care of him."

"No! I want my baby!" she screamed again.

Tommy closed his eyes. "I swear, lady, on my daddy's grave, we'll give him back after we get you out," knowing he was lying. He just hoped his daddy didn't come back to haunt him for saying it.

Tommy tightened his grip and finally pulled the carrier loose after the girl couldn't stretch her arms any longer. "Promise me I'll see him again," she said.

"I promise," he said, feeling his face go scarlet. "But first I'll take him to the EMTs."

She never took her eyes off the baby as she said, "Bye, Avery. Be good." She fell back against the ground and closed her eyes.

Tommy stood up and looked around. His eyes found one of the firefighters. "C'mere," he said.

Tommy gave Mark a look. Mark got the message immediately and cranked his chainsaw back up, trying to cut away more roof to get Amy Thompson out next.

Tommy spoke into the ear of the fireman so Amy couldn't hear over the sound of the saw. "Can you drive this baby to the hospital? We can't wait on them to get his mama out—that's going to be a bit."

The fireman made a face. "I can't hold him and drive, too."

"I can hold him. I'll carry my saw so that if you get in a jam, I can cut you out. Deal?"

The fireman nodded. He went and said something to his supervisor, who nodded as well.

Every time the chainsaw slowed down, he heard the girl screaming again. "I want my baby! Give me my baby!"

Tommy put the baby carrier handle in the crook of his elbow and went on a dead run and beat the fireman to the truck. Tommy swung up in the passenger seat, and the fireman did the same on the driver's side. He looked at the deathly-quiet baby in Tommy's lap, then looked up at Tommy. "I'll step on it."

"Yeah," Tommy said.

And the fireman did indeed step on it, flying back down the road the way he came. When he got back into town, he cut the siren on, and traffic started pulling over for him. He radioed ahead to the nearest hospital. The baby stared at Tommy with his blue eyes matching his mama's but didn't make a sound the entire way. Avery reminded Tommy of when his baby Marilee had been so sick and too weak to even whimper when she was born.

They got to the hospital, and the firetruck got as close as the fireman could get it to the emergency entrance. The ER people were waiting, and the fireman told them about the situation, how the baby had just been pulled out from under a destroyed house. Tommy sat in the truck until the ER people took Avery Thompson inside the doors.

The fireman came back. "I'm going back to the station."

Tommy sighed. "I need to get back to my boat."

"Where is it?"

"Fontainebleau State Park pier."

"I'll ride you by. You sure you can drive it back across?"

"I guess I'll have to," Tommy said, feeling his adrenaline drain away, replaced by a soul-numbing ache in his bones.

They were quiet on the trip back. They saw an ambulance driving past with no siren and moving too slow. Tommy's hands started shaking as he remembered the girl's face.

The fireman dropped him off at the pier, and Tommy saw Mark standing beside where their boats were docked. He shook the fireman's hand silently and climbed down out of the truck, stumbling his way down and almost face-planting off the last step.

He looked at Mark. "Did the girl make it?" he said.

Mark shook his head slowly. "The beam crushed her legs. They couldn't move it, even sawed down. They started talking about cutting her out, and the EMT said there wasn't no use in that. She gave her a knockout shot. I got out of there. I ain't never seen anything like that in my whole life."

Tommy felt his stomach drop on his insides.

He started walking over to climb into his boat. Mark followed him, and they started back to Metairie together.

Tommy's stomach was growling by the time they got to Metairie, and each went to his own truck after agreeing to meet at the Waffle House, which was the only place on their side of town still operating. Tommy drove home, unhitched and stowed his boat and trailer, and turned off his phone before heading back to the Waffle House.

They ate in silence. It was hard to talk over the place's generator without shouting at each other. Finally, as Mark finished off his plate of bacon, he said. "You still want me to come over and cut up wood this afternoon?"

Tommy nodded. Mark said. "I've got to stop off and fill my can with gas for the saw if I can find a gas station open."

Tommy felt tongue-tied. He forced out an "Okay," before falling silent again.

They finished their food, but Tommy still felt his stomach calling out for something else to fill it. After he and Mark went in different directions, Tommy pulled into a gas station himself to get a candy bar or something.

He walked by the beer cooler. Then he stopped. A cold drink would probably do him a lot of good right now.

He started to walk to the soft drinks but saw them pretty much picked over. On the other hand, the store stocked plenty of Budweiser. *Mark drinks that. I'll grab him some.*

He paid for the six beers and a candy bar and hightailed it out of there. He ate the candy bar before it could melt more in the heat.

He beat Mark back to the house and sat in his dark kitchen with the beers in the sack. His stomach growled again as he sat waiting. The longer he sat, the more the girl's screaming echoed in his ears.

Tommy realized he was so thirsty.

He'd gotten down to three cans left when he heard Mark pull up. He got up to greet him and felt the room lurch around him. He sat back down. He took another long drink and felt his stomach settle after the sudden motion.

Mark came in the unlocked front door carrying his saw and stopped. Tommy looked up at him. Mark sat the machine on the floor and sat down at the kitchen table with Tommy.

Tommy reached and cracked open his fourth beer. "You that thirsty?" Mark said.

"Not really," Tommy said.

He expected Mark to reach for a beer himself. But he didn't. "Too much of that and we're not going to get anything else done this afternoon," Mark said.

"I don't care," Tommy heard himself say. "I'm done in. It can all rot down where it sits as far as I care."

"Okay," Mark said. "Cindi might not like that."

Tommy was quiet. Then he said. "I hope I never have to take a saw to another tree as long as I live."

"It's like that, is it?" Mark said. He stood up.

Tommy looked up. "Where you going?"

"I'm going to work on my house," Mark said.

"Have a drink," Tommy said. "I bought enough for you, too."

"I think I'll just leave you to it," Mark said.

Tommy stood up to see him out the door. The room lurched again, but Tommy was able to steady himself by imagining he was on a boat. "You be careful," Mark said.

"You, too."

Tommy watched as his best friend banged out his front door and spun out of his driveway.

All he could think to do was reach for another beer to try to drown out the girl some more. So he did.

What a Man Has to Do

Thirty hours after the hurricane blew through Slidell, Mike Seabrook stood on the loading dock behind Slidell Memorial's emergency room at six a.m., gripping the iron rail for support with his left hand as he vomited the last of his hurried lunch break while bent almost double. He stared out at the muggy August air without really seeing the spectacular sunrise in front of him. All he saw were the tree limbs, leaves, and debris littering the loading zone he was standing above. "God, you've got to help me out," he whispered.

"Dude. What's got into you?"

Mike turned around to see JD, his assistant, looking at him from the door leading onto the loading dock of the hospital. His buzzcut gray hair was plastered to his head with sweat. Mike imagined he looked much the same as JD, except JD had more gray than him even though he was younger. "Saw where someone tossed through my stuff and pulled out the Salems, and Simmons told me you'd gone on break, but I didn't see you in the breakroom. So, I thought I'd come out here and smoke some myself."

Mike didn't answer. JD Carson walked over and lit up.

Mike leaned over the edge of the dock and retched again, but nothing came up. He was acutely conscious of the puddle of urine between his legs and of his wet black scrubs but hoped JD wouldn't notice.

"Menthols still make you sick?"

Mike nodded, wiping his mouth with the back of his hand. He put the cigarette back up to his lips and took it down to the filter in one last drag. He spit over the side again. "Can I have another one?"

JD looked at him. "I asked you a question. What's got into you?"

"And I asked you if you could see your way to giving me another one," Mike said, his voice sounding rough and unfamiliar to his own ear.

JD handed the pack over, and Mike shook one more out. "Thanks," he said.

"Thought you swore off these years ago," JD said.

"Oh, I did," Mike said.

He handed the pack back to JD and lit the last one with the embers left on the filter. *I swear, God, not another one after this.*

"Have you ever thought about just how much paperwork we fill out around here?" he asked JD.

JD whipped his head around and stared. "What did you just say?"

"Well, have you?"

"No, I haven't," JD said. "I fill it out and get on with my job."

After buttoning his lip for so long inside the hospital, Mike felt a rush of relief at finally being able to talk. "About four hours ago, the new triage nurse—Whatshername Baxter—noticed a guy sitting over in the corner of the waiting room looking like he was asleep. She about decided he'd been there for a long time because she didn't remember signing him in. Suddenly he fell off the chair into the floor and didn't move."

"Wait a minute—slow down," JD said. "You're not yourself, Mike."

"You're damned right I'm not," Mike said, feeling the bile coming up again. This time he swallowed it back down.

J.D.'s eyebrows jumped up. Mike felt his face go scarlet; he wasn't used to swearing but felt like if there ever were an occasion to do it, now was the time. "She went and tried to shake him awake, but he just lay there. She hollered for me to come out with the a-fib paddles to try to shock him back. I came out, took one look, and told her to go get a doctor."

Mike noticed his hands were shaking. "I pulled his shirt up and shocked him twice. I was getting ready to shock him again when Rick Randolph came out on a dead run. He pushed me out of the way, then just stood there."

Mike stared at the hand holding the cigarette, trying to will it to be still.

"I said what's the deal? Let's get him back." Mike said. "Rick looked at me and said there wasn't any use. He pointed around his eyes and tried to bend one of his fingers. He said he'd probably been dead for two hours already. Told me to go back and get the death paperwork started."

Mike turned his head and looked at JD whose face blanked. "You're talking about that guy on the gurney out in the hall, aren't you?" he said.

Mike nodded.

"I just got through calling his wife and telling her what happened," JD said. "She said he'd been working since the storm came through, trying to clean the trees off their roof by himself. She said he'd started throwing up and came in because he couldn't stop and was shaking really bad. She'd convinced him to go to the hospital to see what was wrong."

"Sounds about right," Mike said. "Rick said it looked like they triaged him as a case of heat exhaustion at 7:30 p.m., and with all the other injured we've gone through, it looks like they kept putting him off and putting him off. I'd called his name at about four in the morning but no one answered, and I assumed he'd gone back home after waiting so long, and now he's in there dead when all he needed was electrolytes and fluids."

JD shook his head. "Not the first we've lost working a double shift, and likely not the last either," he said, puffing again on his cigarette.

Mike smoked in silence. *Doesn't mean it doesn't hurt.* "How'd she take it?"

"About like you'd expect," JD said. "She's on her way and going to wait here for the coroner and the funeral home people."

Mike shook his head. "Who's going to talk to her?"

"Probably Rick since he's the one who declared him dead," JD said.

Mike sucked in another drag, then spat over the rail again.

"Get Rick to give you a Phenergan for that," JD said.

Mike didn't answer.

They stood in silence.

"You did everything you could," JD said.

"That's where you're wrong," Mike said.

JD cocked his head at that.

"It's the last one I've lost, and I'm not losing any more. I'm going to pack it in," Mike said.

"It's not time for your shift break yet," JD said.

"I'm not talking about going to sleep. I'm talking about going home."

JD looked at him. "You likely can't get there yet. You live kind of off-the-grid."

"Nope. This time it's for good."

"Aw, man, you don't mean that."

"Hide and watch me," Mike said. "Where's Hatchett?"

"Probably in his office," JD said.

"All right," Mike said. He threw away the last of his cigarette and stuck out his hand. "Been nice working with you, and I mean it."

J. D looked at his hand like it was a snake. "You're not serious. You've been working here too long—what? fifteen years?—to throw it all away like that. You're the best head of nursing I've ever worked with," he said.

"Was," Mike said. "I was. Get it right."

He made a move towards the door, his hand still extended to JD.

JD grabbed his hand and pulled him close until only a few inches separated them. "I mean it. You can't go. Not like this."

Mike looked JD in the eye. "Do me a favor."

"What?"

"Stop talking."

JD nodded slowly and pulled away.

Mike let him, then stepped back. JD looked at the ground. "Give Dinah my best," he mumbled, kicking away the cigarette butt Mike dropped.

Mike nodded, then moved toward the door, his head down. He pulled it open and went back inside without another word to JD Carson, one of the best friends he'd ever known.

He made his way through the halls, head down and trying not to hear the alert buttons sounding off in the various rooms of the hospital. People were working double shifts tonight taking care of the ones the hurricane wounded—Mike envisioned a lot of tetanus shots and broken bones from people caught in Slidell, unable to leave before the storm.

He got to Cecil Hatchett's office and walked right through the open door, ignoring a receptionist that was angling to head him off. He stood in front of his desk while Hatchett was filing something in a cabinet behind the desk chair. Hatchett finally turned and looked at Mike, standing there with his arms crossed. "Seabrook," he said. "What are you doing here?"

"I quit. Bye," Mike said, pulling his lanyard with his name on it from around his neck and dropping it on the desk and turning to go. But his way was blocked by the receptionist who stood in the doorway.

Hatchett looked at the lanyard, then back up at Mike. "Wait just a minute."

Mike turned back to him.

"You can't just leave. Your contract calls for three weeks' notice and input to hire your replacement," Hatchett said. "Get back into the ER."

"Nope. Keep my next paycheck if that's what you want to do. I'm not coming back up here," Mike said.

"What? What's got into you?" Hatchett said.

"I'm dead on my feet, and I'm not up to arguing. I'll get my stuff out of my locker and get out of your hair."

"Where are you going? If you've gotten a better offer somewhere else, I'm sure we can work something out," Hatchett said calmly.

Mike wanted to grab him by the shoulders and shake him hard. "I don't have an offer. I'm going to work for FEMA. Help people. A lot of people."

"You are helping people—"

"I need to find a new line of work where not every mistake I make means someone is going to die," Mike said. "That's what's on my mind."

"Mike, you can't be serious," Hatchett said. "You can't take that kind of stuff on yourself."

Mike didn't answer.

"You're serious." Hatchett's eyes narrowed. "FEMA? Really? Insurance money?"

Mike met his eyes, stare for stare. *Let him think whatever he wants to think.*

"I thought better of you. Never thought I'd see you chasing the almighty dollar."

Mike shifted his weight to the balls of his feet.

"Amazing what smelling a little money in the air can do to a person."

"Are you through?" Mike said.

"If you're so determined, then get out. Good luck to you, I guess," Hatchett said, picking up the lanyard and tossing it into a trash can by the desk.

Mike turned and stared at the receptionist who took her time moving out of his way. Mike could feel Hatchett's gaze on the back of his neck as he walked out and headed for the elevator.

He walked out of the hospital into the stifling heat of August. He picked his way around all the debris in the lot, heading for his red Chevy Blazer. He stood and looked at it from afar—he saw where flying rocks cracked the windshield in multiple places, but otherwise it looked fine from this side. The hospital was up on a bit of a hill that kept it from being swept away by the surge.

He got to the drivers' side door and opened it gingerly, hoping the windshield would hold for the trip out to his house. He hoped the roads were clear; he thought they might be since the stream of people coming in steadily for the past several hours were under their own power and not in ambulances.

He crunched over the limbs and leaves down as he drove out and away from the best job he'd ever worked.

Mike tried to concentrate on the road in front of him, but that was hard. Familiar landmarks were gone. With the waters mostly receded from all but the most low-lying areas, the most unnerving sights were boats thrown up on dry land from the marinas and waterways and scattered like so many toys in a bathtub—he shook his head at the sight of five outboards piled against the Waffle House further down Gause Boulevard from the hospital.

Every house broken down into matchsticks made his stomach just twist into a little more of a knot.

He kept driving, but as he got to the first parish road, he maneuvered his way around some downed trees that covered it halfway across—he didn't have a lot of traffic to contend with either so he was able to drive down the wrong side of the road here and there, seeing entire rows of trees mowed down.

His place being north of town would be a good thing as far as water damage, but the wind could still have wreaked havoc throughout the property. Mike tried to keep his mind from superimposing images of destruction on his memory of the house he left, but he eventually gave up. He decided to prepare himself for the worst, so that maybe the reality would look better by comparison.

After a few seconds of that, he started whistling a tune he didn't think he even knew the name of to distract his mind again.

Finally, he signaled to turn onto the road leading to his driveway and noticed a road crew driving out for the day's work—he decided to let them turn in ahead of him and follow them as far as they could go until he got to his driveway.

Five Black guys holding chainsaws in their laps sat in the bed of the black diesel truck with a cow-catcher bumper on the front to move the smaller stuff out of the way. Mike followed them down to where he would turn in to his road and waved his hand to them as he turned off.

He drove a little ways and skidded to a stop as he turned the last curve. Branches lay across the road, too high for him to drive over. He put the truck in park and opened the door to climb out.

He started walking around the curve. He saw the gravel driveway covered in branches, trunks, and roots from where the wind lowered the boom on all the trees lining it.

Dear Lord, please let it be safe. Please don't let us have lost everything we have. Please, Mike prayed.

He got several feet closer down the driveway before he let himself look up from maneuvering around the branches.

All five of those big oaks surrounding the house—every one of them down.

Maybe the first floor's okay? he wondered.

Until he saw where the oak that shaded the kitchen smashed the garage flat.

His legs went so weak that he felt like he was walking through cold molasses.

When he came to himself, he was sitting in a puddle of sweat in the front seat of his truck. He didn't remember tripping on anything, but he tore a new hole in the knee of his scrubs with blood oozing from the broken skin.

Mike sat and stared at the steering wheel for a good ten minutes. He resisted the urge to punch out the windshield.

God damn you, Katrina.

He waited for the lightning to strike him where he sat. It didn't.

He started crying, resting his forehead on the steering wheel.

He didn't know how long he sat there. He finally reached down on the floorboard for his phone and tried calling Dinah. All he got was a fast busy signal. He'd tried to call once the storm blew through but couldn't get through—he knew she was wondering if he was alive or dead by now.

He tried again.

Nothing.

He stared at the phone. Then he remembered his neighbor's place back up the road looked in pretty good shape—maybe they had phone service.

He backed out of the driveway and drove slowly back down the road, dazed. He drove past the hidden driveway at first, then reversed and eased backwards, watching for traffic. He saw his neighbor Sammy Landry sitting on a tree trunk wiping sweat from his brow. He was grimy in a white t-shirt, brogans, and ripped Dickeys covered in dust.

Sammy stood up and extended his hand. "Hey Mike. How did you come out?"

"Okay," Mike heard himself say. "I'm trying to call Dinah; she evacuated up to Petal and I haven't been able to get through the phone lines to talk to her. Do you have phone service?"

"Last time I checked we did," Sammy said. "Cell phone not working?"

"Nope," Mike said.

"They say you can text and get through," Sammy said. "But a landline might be exactly what you need. I know she's likely anxious to hear from you."

Mike nodded. His throat felt tight. "Thanks, buddy," he managed to say.

So Mike drove up to the house and went through the open front door. He didn't see Sammy's family and figured they were evacuated, too. He went to the kitchen and reached for the wall phone. He dialed his mom's house, where Dinah had taken Candi. Jamie, and Bracey. His mind started spinning, and his mouth was dry.

Dinah answered, sounding out of breath. "Hello?"

"Dinah?" Mike whispered.

"Oh, my Lord—you're all right!" Dinah said.

"Yeah, honey—I'm all right."

"Oh, thank you, Jesus. I've been praying," Dinah said. "Oh, Lord. I'm so glad to hear from you. The kids have been asking ever since they woke up. How are you doing?"

"Okay," he lied.

"Are you calling from the house?"

"No. From Sammy's."

"Oh, no. That doesn't sound good."

"It's not," Mike said.

He went on to tell her about the place. He heard the tears in her voice as she asked questions. He tried to reassure her—he told her that the second floor looked like it was the most hurt but that he hadn't gotten close enough to really tell anything about the first floor.

"Well, how are things at the hospital?" Dinah finally said.

"I'm off for a while," he said.

"Why?"

"Dinah—" Suddenly his throat closed even tighter.

"What is it?"

"I quit."

"Why?"

"These people—everyone's hurting, even if they're not at the hospital. It makes me want to sell everything we own and give the money away to try to help these people," he said. "We've got our cars and our land, and the house isn't that bad. I want to help the people. I want to help people get back on their feet."

"What are you saying?" Dinah said.

"They're saying FEMA is already here and looking for able-bodied men to help out in clean-up. I can bring my own equipment or use theirs. I feel like God wants me to it," Mike said, playing his trump card.

"Well, if you feel that way, I suppose that's what you need to do," Dinah said hesitantly. "Can we come and move back into the house?"

"I'm not sure yet," Mike said.

"Well, we'll just stay up here until you work out the details. Mrs. Seabrook sure is enjoying playing with her grandkids, so I suppose she won't mind if we stay a bit longer."

"I'm about to head up there after I go to FEMA and sign up to work," Mike said. "I'll see you before sundown."

"Okay," she said. "You be careful coming up here—they say the roads are horrendous."

"I'll go get my saw from the house so I can get from here to there as quick as I can," he said. "Love you, honey."

"Love you, too," Dinah said with a quaver in her voice. "I'm serious. Be careful."

"Yes ma'am," Mike said.

He heard her hang up.

He hung the phone up slowly. He turned and leaned up against the wall. "Forgive me for lying, God," he whispered. "I'm just doing the best I can here. God, help us."

He walked back out and slowly went to his truck.

What's Mine is Mine

That sunny morning, James King was whistling along with his radio as he drove through the streets of Kenner, Louisiana. Most structures in the town suffered wind damage: businesses, houses, power lines. He was off work almost a week now because of the storm; he'd spent the days in Noxapater, Mississippi with his wife's family. Now he was headed down to his place to see what needed to be done now that his neighborhood, next to a police station, received power back after the repairs to the lines.

He'd wanted to see it first before bringing his wife Lori down—he'd already sent her some pictures of landmarks around town over text so she could get a feel for what was going on. He'd almost cried when he saw Mary Mahoney's Restaurant in the newspaper the day after the storm, off its foundation and sitting forlornly on the beach. The owners vowed to rebuild, but of course, it wasn't ever going to be the same. Nothing was ever going to be the same, James was convinced. Except that he still loved Kenner as home and wanted to be part of rebuilding it.

He turned his maroon Ford F-350 into the area his house was in and drove down the main street, trying not to look at his neighbors' houses. They were on high enough ground that they avoided the storm surge, but trees were still down everywhere and blue tarps were spread throughout the street like so much mold. The streets were quiet; it looked like not many folks were back.

He turned onto his street and saw some trees were down in front of some houses but not as many as he expected. One tree looked like it tried to crash into the roof of the Simpsons' house, but it was just sitting there, branches spread out over the tin roof. Someone already cut a way through to his house; he figured that was his neighbor Jack Swindoll, who decided to ride the storm out in his house next door.

Sure enough, he saw a lawn chair with a big orange cooler on one side of the chair and a high-powered rifle on the ground on the other side. A big homemade sign saying, "No Looting!" was posted on the border of their properties, and James guessed that when people saw it and him, they took it seriously. He parked his truck on the side of the road and got out.

The green-and-white chair was tipped over backwards. James went to set it right, and something caught his eye right in front of his garage door. He looked and saw that it was wide open—and someone was lying on the garage floor face down.

James backed away slowly to his truck, keeping his eye on the still figure. He opened his door slowly and found his Glock nine mm pistol under the driver's seat by feel. Then he tensed up and moved slowly to the figure that was wearing a green and white ball cap, khaki shorts, and an untucked red plaid shirt. He carried the gun for protection because Kenner was just that kind of town, but he'd never fired it outside the range after he first bought it.

He got to it and kicked the figure's foot, encased in a dirty white tennis shoe. The figure didn't move.

He moved slowly and leaned over and shook it by the shoulder—and when he pulled his hand away, he had blood on it. Cold blood at that.

He squeezed his eyes shut, shook his head, then opened them again, He rolled the figure over—and it was Jack, his best friend and neighbor since grade school.

He heard a sound and looked up—but saw nothing in front of him. He glanced over his shoulder and saw a squirrel running across the front yard.

He looked around in front of him. Lori's car was gone. He took a few steps, pointing the Glock in front of him. He saw where the front door had been kicked in. He stopped again and listened. Nothing.

He went inside, careful not to touch anything. Whoever looted the place took their time—and been choosy, too. All he could see missing right off the bat were his gun safe out of the utility room and the big TV.

He came back out and looked down at Jack. It would've been just like him to try to help James out and try to protect his place, too. Then James had another thought—someone had to call the police—and Marla, Jack's wife.

He lowered his gun. Nothing more to do here.

He started to walk away, then looked back. "Thanks for trying to help me out, buddy," he whispered.

He drove to the police station, and the rest of the day was a blur—giving his statement, going to the house with the cops and trying to account for what all was gone. The looters towed the boat from back of the house, took the fridge, and stole the freezer full of deer meat and frozen fish, along with the hunting guns.

The place wasn't messed up—they hadn't trashed it, and most of the trees that were down hadn't fallen on the house. It looked like they could move back in whenever they wanted to.

He watched as the coroner loaded Jack up into his vehicle and nodded assent at whatever anyone said to him. Of all the things he'd imagined he'd find when he came down to check his place—he'd been prepared for the house to be flattened, either by the surge, the winds, or the trees. He'd wondered what they would do if they lost everything.

But losing Jack to some thug after his guns?

Something must have changed in his face when the rage

began to rise. He imagined what might would have happened if he had come by just a little earlier, in time to catch them after they shot Jack—cutting them down one by one where they stood—

One of the cops came up to him and said quietly. "How about you come with us to the station so you can help us tell his wife what you found?"

For the first time, James let himself focus his eyes somewhere other than where Jack had fallen. The cop was young, baby-faced, and his eyes and mouth were studiously neutral. But James could see the same heat in his face that he likely had on his own.

All he could think was that he was grateful Marla hadn't been home to find him first.

Then he realized he couldn't stand to wait to talk to Marla. He needed to go back to Lori; he needed to see her and hug her tightly and never let go.

"I'm sorry, sir," he managed to say. "My wife is up in north Mississippi and expecting me back tonight. I can't stay."

"Where is she?" the cop said.

"Noxapater. Right outside Louisville."

"Are you sure you're going to be all right driving?" the cop asked.

James nodded, not trusting his voice not to break if he said any more.

He went and started to pull the garage door down and tried not to stare at the blood on his carport.

The young cop stopped him. "Wait a second," he said.

James turned. The other cop had come up from the police car and was holding a two-liter bottle of Coke. The baby-faced cop pulled his arm gently, and he backed away from the stain. The other cop opened the bottle and poured the Coke on the area, covering it.

James stared. The other cop looked up. "Eats it right off the concrete," he said.

That's one thing I'll never be able to drink again.

"You be careful," the cop said. "Good luck from here on out."

"I'm going to need it," James said.

James drove back up in Mrs. Tucker's driveway late that night and climbed down out of the truck. He noticed that the house was completely dark on the inside and his mother-in-law's Crown Vic was gone from the driveway. *Looks like no one's home—where would they be this time of night?* he wondered.

He used the spare key to open the door and stumbled into the kitchen. He felt his way to the light switch and turned it on. He saw a piece of paper on the counter. "We called the ambulance to go to the hospital," James read in Mrs. Tucker's immaculate cursive handwriting.

Fear stabbed at James' heart. *Something's happened to Lori. Please God, no.*

Lori was four months pregnant; they just finally got around to telling her mother the news. He flipped the light off and ran back to the truck, his tires spitting gravel as he turned around and pointed his front end at the highway.

He got to Winston County Hospital in Louisville in a hurry, speeding through the flashing red lights and praying that no cops were up that late at night or that they were too busy somewhere else to catch him. His luck finally held, and his truck clock said it was two-thirty a.m. once he got to the emergency room. He told the security guard who he was and who he was looking for, Lori Ann King. The security guard moseyed in, and James resisted the impulse to push past him.

He walked him to an older doctor who looked half-asleep himself. The security guard started to talk, but James ran out of patience. "I'm looking for my wife. Lori King."

The doctor nodded. "Room twelve. Can you sit down here for me, Mr. King? While I go get her chart?"

"I want to see her," James said, his voice rising.

"I think I need to talk to you first, son," the older man said composedly.

James looked hard at him but saw only compassion in his eyes. James felt his throat start to constrict.

James sat where the doctor pointed. "Is she okay?" James choked out.

"Now she is," the doctor said.

James felt like he'd been punched in the gut.

"It was kind of touch and go for a few minutes there the morning they came in."

James felt his heart hammering. "What happened?" he whispered.

"Something that usually happens around a hurricane, Mr. King. Your wife went into preterm labor, and we couldn't stop it. I'm sorry, son."

James leaned over with his hands on his knees. "The baby?"

"He didn't make it," the doctor said gently. "He was too small."

James shut his eyes. "Can I see her now?" he whispered.

The doctor nodded. James got up and followed the doctor to room twelve. He hung back as the doctor opened the door. "Mrs. King, your husband's here."

James looked around the doctor to see his wife. Her face was white against her blond hair; her dark blue eyes staring out into space.

James came around the doctor. "Lori?"

Her eyes focused on him. "Hey."

Janes turned his head at a small cough from Mrs. Tucker. He nodded to her. Her face was drawn with worry and concern.

The doctor said. "Mrs. Tucker, let's step out and let them have a moment."

Lori's eyes followed her mother outside the door. Then she looked back at James. The way her eyes were twitching, James figured she was doped up on something. *Maybe making it easier for her to recover.* "Hon. You okay?"

Lori's face was distant. "Uh-huh. The doctor tell you what happened?"

"A little," James said.

Lori's gaze shifted to her feet. "Not long after you left, I was feeling kind of bad ever since the storm passed through—my back hurt a lot. I thought it was from riding in the truck for so long to get here."

"Why didn't you call me?" James said.

Lori looked back up at him. "We did. Over and over and over. But the phone wouldn't go through."

"Why didn't you call the house? Leave a message there?"

"Tried that too," Lori said.

"I wondered why you weren't answering when I texted you earlier today," James said.

"I got yours. I figure you sending those pictures from around the town is why we couldn't get through."

James' heart sank.

Lori didn't say anything more.

James reached over to smooth her hair out of her face. She turned her head away.

"What?" James said.

"You were so worried about the house, and Jack, and the town. I was up here having a miscarriage all on my own and you were so ready to get there, even without me."

James looked at her—her eyes were sparking a dull fire. She was angry, even through all the drugs.

He didn't know what to say. He couldn't tell her what had happened to him that day, not now. If she wanted to be mad, he couldn't stop her.

"Once it started, there wasn't any way to stop it."

James couldn't even muster up the will to comfort her.

She stared at her feet.

Then she took a deep breath and let it out.

"I don't know if I matters to you or not now, but the house is okay. We can go back whenever we want to," James said and instantly realized how cold he sounded. *That's never happened before.*

She lifted her face. "James, I don't know how to say this," she whispered, looking at him.

"Straight out's usually the best way," James said, again hearing it cold. *What is wrong with you, man?*

"I'm not sure it is this time," Lori said.

"What do you mean? You're still here with me and our house is okay. What else is there to say?"

He saw her eyes filling with tears. "I don't want to go back to Kenner," she said.

"Well, there's no great rush. The house will still be there whenever we're ready. That's the important thing," James said.

"James, I don't want to go back ever," Lori said, raising her eyes and looking at him calmly.

The weight of what she said bent his back over, and he put his elbows on his knees and his face in his hands. "Lori—let's not start in on this. You don't know what kind of day I've had."

"It can't be worse than mine!" she cried. "We lost our baby!"

"I'll take that bet," he said.

"What?" she shot back. "You said the house was fine. What could *possibly*—"

All the anger he'd been trying to tamp down came boiling up and out. He couldn't help it; the truth came out. "The house was looted," James said, surprising himself at how calm he sounded. "And they shot and killed Jack for trying to stop them. That's what. I didn't want to tell you now, but you've dragged it out of me. Satisfied?"

Her eyes went round. "Really?"

"Yes, *really.*"

"Marla?" Lori said.

"She should know by now. When I left, they were going to contact her," James said.

Lori's lip started trembling.

"So excuse me for not being up to talking about this right now."

And the whine was still there. "Then you should understand

why I don't want to move back there. I want to sell it and move somewhere else," she said.

"Sell my daddy's place? Where would we live, Lori?"

"We can go anywhere we want to. You can find a new job, and we can start over with the money we get out of it," Lori said.

"Lori—I don't understand. There's nothing wrong with the house."

She rolled her eyes and tried to lift her hand to her face but failed. "I cannot live like this any longer," she said softly. "I don't want the stress and worry about the storms. I can't—I can't go back and see the baby's room. I don't want to live somewhere where we have to evacuate once a year any more. I don't want to live somewhere where everything that ever meant anything to us is gone. That's why."

"You're not thinking straight with everything they've given you. Everything's going to be rebuilt soon; the insurance money is already rolling in to get businesses back up off the ground. I'm making good money doing what I'm doing, and so do you. Your office is still standing, too. They're just waiting for the power to come back on where they are," James said, feeling the anger he'd struggled with all day growing. "Everything'll be back to normal soon."

"Not soon enough. And knowing Jack died there? That doesn't even move you?" Lori said. "Listen to yourself. You don't even believe what you're saying, much less able to convince me."

"I can't just pick up and leave. I've never lived anywhere else but school. The day I was able to come back home was one of the happiest of my life. I was born and raised there. I don't know anywhere else to be."

"Well, maybe it's time to find out," Lori said.

James stood up and leaned in closer to her to whisper so Mrs. Tucker couldn't hear him outside. "What has your mama been telling you?" James said.

"Don't make this about Mama," Lori said. "It's not. It's about you and me and where we want to have a future together.

The coast is as we knew it is dead and gone. There's no future down there. From what you've sent me, it'll take weeks for them to even get back to where we could live. The only reason we have power is because we're on the grid next to city hall. Where are we going to buy groceries? What about water? Did you check that?"

"No," James said. "I didn't. I had my hands full with the cops and Jack."

"Don't you see what I'm saying?" Lori said, tears running down her cheeks.

"No. I don't. They're not going to run me off what's mine—what my family's worked for and what Jack died for," James said with a steel in his voice he wasn't sure he needed. But it was there.

"Why can't we make it together somewhere else? Somewhere we don't have—bad memoires of. We're young—we can start over."

James was silent.

Her face finally crumpled. "I just—can't make myself be happy there. Not after running away to here every summer to escape the storms. It just—makes me miss home even more, and I can't face seeing the nursery, taking it all down—any of it."

James didn't want to start yelling because he didn't know if he'd ever stop once he started.

She must have read his look. "I knew you wouldn't understand," she whispered. "You never have."

Both of them were quiet.

Finally he said, "Look. We can talk about this more later. You stay here for the time being if that's what you want to do. We can wait on getting everything else back to normal and then talk about it. I'll come up here as often as I can. How does that sound?"

"Please don't go," Lori said.

"Lori, I can't—*not* go. There's too much work to be done down there," James said. "I've got to get the place cleaned up with all the trees down. I'll—I'll probably have to handle some legal things if they ever find any of our stuff. There's a lot to do."

"Let someone else do it. I don't want you to leave me again," Lori said.

James sat still as she started crying. He knew he should go to her. But he didn't.

She turned her head away from him as her nose turned snotty, and she didn't even try to wipe it or anything.

James sat and put his face in his hands.

He remembered the feel of Jack's shed blood on his hand and finally just started sobbing himself as he turned to go out the door and let her mother come back in. He cried for Jack, for Marla, for his dead son, and just the thought of leaving his home that he loved so much.

Hurricane Baby

Judd didn't see Wendy at the shop again until right after Christmas when he came in early one Monday morning with a parts order instead of on Friday like he usually did. "Hey, Mrs. Wendy, how are you?" he said.

She turned around behind the counter, and he caught a glimpse of her swollen belly. Her black hair was shorter than he remembered, too, trimmed up to her shoulders. He felt a shiver down his back at how she was looking at him—her eyes were wide open and scared, and her lower lip showed a thin line of blood where she'd bit through it.

"We're fine. How are you?" she said, staring at him.

"Pretty good, I guess. We're getting ready to move upstate," Judd said, trying to steer the conversation to something normal.

"You changing jobs?" Ray said, coming out from the office door behind the counter.

"Sort of. I'll still be working for the same company, but I'm being shifted to another territory," Judd said.

"So that's why you're here early this week," Ray said. "You won't be back down around here anymore, huh?"

"Not unless there's another storm," Judd said.

Ray walked back into the office to get the checkbook.

Wendy said. "Well, good luck in your new job," as she came out from behind the counter.

Judd looked at her big belly with a smile. "I didn't know about this! How far along are you?"

"Twenty weeks. We didn't tell anyone for a while—you know, to make sure everything was all right after waiting so long. Just went and watched the sonogram and found out it's a girl," she said, sounding dead in her heart.

"Wow," Judd said. "After so long."

Wendy nodded, looking stricken.

What the hell is going on here? "So she's due… when?"

"May 30."

Judd looked up. She had gone stony-faced, except her pretty red lips were trembling a little. Her dark eyes were even blacker than he remembered. "Wendy—"

"Don't," she said, so low he could barely hear her.

"But I need to—"

"Whatever you're going to say to me, Judd—don't," she said.

And she turned and walked back into the office. Judd saw the door slam shut.

He closed his eyes. *Ten years without any kids, and now she's due in May.*

He thought about the look on her face when she talked about not having any kids. *What have I done? Mary, mother of God, help me.*

After a minute, Ray came back out, looking grim. His brown eyes were flinty, and his scalp showed red through his buzz-cut blond hair. *What did she say to him*?

He cut his eyes over to the exit and gauged how quickly he could get to it.

"Let me guess—you were stupid and cracked a joke about a hurricane baby," Ray said.

Judd nodded dumbly to cover up his shock. Ray gestured toward the office door. "She's gotten a lot a kidding about it, and I guess it's not funny to her anymore. Hell, anyone can do the math."

He looked at Judd, catching him off guard with a lopsided grin. "At least you didn't ask what we're going to name her. That's the latest joke around here ever since we found out it was going to be a girl."

He leaned forward. "I shouldn't tell this, but it was a hoot. You know Maxey? He knew we were going to have the sonogram, and he came in a few days later and asked Wendy what we found out. She told him it was going to be a girl, and he laughed and said, 'Well, why you don't just name her Katrina, then?' And Wendy was at the register and looked up at him and said nice as you please 'And why don't you just go to hell while you're at it?'"

Ray grinned, showing his teeth. "I tell you, no one else has asked that question again."

Judd swallowed hard. "Have you come up with a name?"

"Yeah, we have. We're going to name her Judy Ray." Ray gave Judd the check. "Guess I won't see you around again. Good luck!"

Judd nodded and walked back out to his truck. He sat in the driver's seat, leaned his head back against it, and closed his eyes, remembering the taste of her mouth on his.

Then he cranked his truck, looked at his watch, and started driving blindly through the streets. He was trying to make his way to Maxey's, but he couldn't seem to steer his way through. Finally he just pulled into a parking lot and cut off the engine.

She did not just say she was due in May. Ray did not just call her a hurricane baby. I'm having a nightmare, and please God, I need to wake up.

He looked up and saw he was parked in front of the liquor store just down the street from Maxey's. He popped open the truck door and went inside, feeling very wobbly already.

The aisles were brightly lit with fluorescents; he wandered around not knowing what he was looking for. He finally picked up two bottles of Evan Williams bourbon since it was the brand his daddy always drank. He made his way to the front and put his bottles on the counter.

The checkout lady came to him, her blond hair piled up on top of her head. She smiled a big smile at him. "Get everything you needed?" she asked.

"Yes, ma'am," Judd answered.

He paid for the bottles, and she put them together in a tall brown paper bag for him to carry out. He walked back to his truck, climbed in, and started the engine. He let it sit there in idle for a moment, looking at the bag he'd just paid for. *You know better than this. You know exactly how this is going to turn out.*

He put the vehicle in gear and drove out to a no-tell hotel out on one of the Hattiesburg exits. He'd stayed there before when he was too tired to drive to the next stop; he liked it because it was clean with free internet, and the staff didn't ask questions.

But that was all it had going for it. No free breakfast, no microwave, no coffee. The towels were that color of brown that just made them look very dirty, as was the carpet, the bed linens, and the curtains. But that wasn't on his mind at the moment. He just hoped they already had something available this early.

Once he had a room, he sat on the bed and stared at the bottles in the bag. He'd pounded his share of beers in college but gave it up when he'd gotten his commercial license to drive. He couldn't get Wendy's last words out of his head.

He finally opened one of the bottles and drank directly from it until he passed out asleep on the bed.

He woke up to Ray Magnum shaking him. "Judd, you better hope I can leave you here for dead because if you're not, there's a long list of people waiting to kill you."

Where am I? Then he remembered and felt his stomach lurch.

"What are you talking about? What are you doing here?" Judd said.

"I'm here because I was the last person your wife could find who set eyes on you today. Your boss saw where you logged your call to me and that was it. So she called me, and we've been busy trying to hunt you up."

Judd squinted his eyes against the lights Ray was flicking on throughout the room. His eyes ached at the brightness. Ray looked around the room and grunted when he saw the unopened bottle. "Well, you were just going to make a day of it, weren't you? What's the last thing you remember today?"

Judd thought back. He hoped he was more sober than he felt. "Walking out of your place to the truck this morning."

"About 8:30 or so?"

"Yes sir."

"Judd, it's nine o'clock at night, and you have no idea what the hell you've been up to since then, huh?"

Judd rolled over on the bed and saw the other bottle of bourbon spilled on the floor. He swore under his breath.

"That's right. Now do I call your wife and tell her what happened or do you?" Ray said.

"I'll call her. It needs to come from me. I'll tell her."

Ray nodded. "You do that." Then he sat down on the bed, jostling Judd's bones with an ache he'd never felt before. "Any part of the truth you need to tell someone other than your wife?" Ray said.

Judd froze just as he was starting to stand up. *This is not happening. I'm having a bad dream.*

"I'm not trying to get into your business," Ray said. "But I know there's things a man can't tell his wife about. I can't talk to Wendy about what happened to me working the storm. It's not something she could do anything about, so I don't tell her about it."

He leaned forward. "Judd, if there's something getting to you so much that you have to check into a hotel and drink to stop thinking about it, maybe you better tell someone. And I'm here listening."

Yeah, I'm going to tell you I think your wife is carrying my baby. "I can handle it," Judd said.

"And doing a bang-up job of it so far," Ray said.

They sat for several minutes. Judd couldn't muster up the courage to look Ray in the eye, scared of what his face might tell him. They'd been business friends for years, longer than Judd had even known his own wife. He'd trusted Judd, and now Judd had done this—and had known better when he was doing it and couldn't have even told Ray why if he asked him straight out. *Damn you, Judson McKay. Lying to Ray like a dog in the road on a hot day.*

"It's your hangover," Ray said. "You ever done this before?"

"No sir."

"Sure you don't want to talk about it to someone who might understand?"

Judd shook his head no and could hear his pulses in his ears.

"I want you to know I'm not planning on telling your boss I found you out here, either. You can try to right that little red wagon all by yourself, too if that's the way you want it."

Judd shook his head. "How you come out to find me here anyway?"

"Well, the police didn't have you; Forrest General didn't have you, and neither did the county morgue," Ray said. "So I played a hunch. Drove around to all the hotels until I saw your truck outside."

He stood up from the edge of the bed. "I'll go and leave you alone and let you get yourself together."

He picked up the bottle Judd left. "You planning on starting over with this after I'm gone?"

Judd felt his guts roll at the thought.

"That's what I thought," Ray laughed. "My advice is to at least cut it some rather than drinking it straight from the bottle, and get ahold of some coffee when you wake up tomorrow morning. But I ain't you, and you're a grown man. Just call your wife first."

Ray started for the door. "Thanks for coming out here. Ray," Judd said.

Fifteen minutes later, Judd was turning off the phone after

talking to his boss when someone knocked at the door. "Hang on," he said.

He opened the door, and Wendy stood there, looking like a cat with a bottle-brush tail. She was wearing a loose-fitting top and bulky jeans, making her look even further along than she had said. "Ray told me you might want this tomorrow morning," she said, holding out a stainless-steel thermos with a red cap.

Judd looked at it, then at her. "Coffee. Like I make for the firehouse. He called me once he got on duty and told me where you were and said that you might could use it in the morning," she muttered.

"I appreciate it." He took the thermos from her and stepped back. "You coming in?"

She hesitated and looked down the hall. "You and me need to talk, Mrs. Wendy," Judd said.

"Ray said you weren't feeling good."

"Nothing a good night's sleep won't help. Mrs. Wendy."

She inclined her head to the bottle on the table. "Is that whiskey?"

"Bourbon," he said.

"I thought you told me you didn't drink."

"I didn't until this morning," Judd said.

She flinched. "I suppose that's my fault," she said, dropping her eyes.

"You seem awfully anxious to take the blame for something I've done to myself."

She started to wring her hands. "I can't talk. This isn't a great part of town, and I need to get home."

"Then I'll climb right back into that bottle when you're gone," Judd said, his voice sounding knife-edge in his ears.

She stepped inside hesitantly, keeping her head down. She sat down in one of the chairs by the table. "What is it, Judd?" she said, staring at the floor.

"I want to know about the baby," Judd said, trying to stay calm against the feeling of doom coming over him.

Wendy closed her eyes and slumped over with her elbows on her knees. "I told you how far along I was and when she's due. The doctor says she's healthy."

"Wendy, look at me."

Wendy didn't speak.

"Wendy, please."

She looked like she was trying to not vomit in the floor.

"I guess I'll just have to ask straight out then. Is she mine?"

"As far as I'm concerned, she's Ray's," she said in a sick-sounding voice.

"What makes you say that?"

She looked up at him then. "What kind of a question is that? You think I haven't slept with my husband since you left? We were in bed making love before you'd packed to go back to Mandeville that night, and plenty more times after that. For God's sake, Judd." Then she clamped her jaws shut and was quiet.

I guess I deserved that.

"Do you remember what you told me that night about forgetting? That you guessed that would be the best you could hope for?" Wendy said.

Judd nodded.

"Well, you were half-right about how that worked. Since you asked me to try to forget you, I thought Ray could help me with that."

She looked at him again. "You asked me to forgive you. I've done that. But forget you—I haven't managed that yet, though God knows I've tried."

Judd found his voice. "I also asked that you be able to forgive yourself."

She stood up and walked over to the other side of the room with her back to him.

"I take that as a no," Judd said.

She wrapped her arms around herself and started crying. He got up and stepped closer to her but stopped short when he saw her raking her fingernails across her bare arms. The scratches were bloody and ragged up and down her arms.

He was staggered. He'd never seen a woman do herself that way. Then he heard what she was saying with every scratch: "Whore. Whore. Whore."

The venom in her voice at herself snapped him out of it. He moved quickly and reached around her, grabbed her wrists, and pried her arms open. "You've got to stop that, Wendy," he said, holding her hands up in the air.

She twisted her fingers up in his and clamped down her nails on the backs of his hands. How he was going to explain those scratches was anyone's guess. "Go ahead," he said. "However it is you want to hurt yourself, do it to me instead if it'll make you feel better. It's all my fault anyway."

"I didn't tell you no," she whispered. "It's mine, too."

She tried to twist away, stomping on the floor and kicking her feet with the effort. He closed the distance between them in two steps and put his face up next to her ear and shook her hard. "Stop it. Stop punishing yourself. Stop hurting yourself. Stop it."

"You don't understand," she whispered. "I can't. And I'll scream if you don't let go of me, Judd."

"No one here would notice. I'm not letting go until I know you're not going to hurt yourself."

He felt her suck in her breath to fight him. But then she let her hands go limp. He still held on tight as she tried to pull her hands away. "Judd?" she said.

"What?"

"Does your wife know?"

Judd dropped his arms down but still held on to her hands. "No. At least I don't think so."

He let go.

She turned. "Judd, I don't know how to say this."

She was crying. He wanted take her into his arms and kiss the tears away again, but he didn't dare.

"When I lost my daddy when I was fourteen, Ray was my

best friend even though he was older, and as soon as I finished high school we got married," Wendy said.

She put her right fist up to her mouth and started biting her bloody nails. "I'd never even looked at anyone else besides him ever—and there I was holding on to you for dear life, crying like a baby. I'm not stupid; I could tell what was happening with you, and I let it."

Fear clawed at him. *Was it that obvious*? "I *did not* come into your house that weekend with that on my mind, Wendy—"

"I know," she said, cutting him off.

She looked past him towards the window. "Whenever you'd come to the shop, I'd always tried to be in the back. Today it was all I could do to speak to you. I just wanted to get away from you before I said anything that Ray—wouldn't understand."

Judd raised his hands—then let them drop. Her tears were doing something to him that no woman's tears ever had—he felt the resolve behind them, and he knew every word she was saying was truth. No arguing or sweet talking would move her from what she knew. She'd had something very precious and good—and had given it up to him for whatever reason. If he wanted to know his baby girl, he had to give back to her something just as good.

Judd took a deep breath and stepped up to her and lifted her chin. "Before you say anything else, there's something else you should know, Wendy."

Her eyes widened.

He hated how his voice came out, shaking and scared. "Until I saw you today, I'd forgiven myself and moved on with my life. But watching you walk away from me this morning with that baby in your belly liked to have killed me. The thought that I'd landed in your life like that—and then just disappeared like I did in the middle of the night after the storm cleared out—"

He stopped and looked at the floor. "I sat in the truck and thought about you and me, and I wound up here tonight."

"Oh, my God," Wendy groaned as she turned away. "Don't tell me that."

Judd heard the traffic going by outside as they were both quiet. *I've got to say it, even if she slaps me in the face. I've got to.* "It's really simple in a way, Wendy," Judd said.

"No, it isn't," she shot back.

"Yes, it is. If you want her to be Ray's baby, she's Ray's. You can walk out of here, put down the fear, and go on with your life. I won't stop you if that's what you want."

"Or what?" Wendy said.

His mouth felt like cotton on the inside. *If only water could wash away my sins.* "Or if you want her to be mine, she can be mine," he croaked.

"Judd, *what* are you thinking?" she said.

"I don't know, Wendy." Judd said. He reached out and touched her belly. He felt the baby move against his hand. "But even if she's not my baby. Wendy—even if all we have is whatever we felt in the storm—if you're willing to chance it, I am too," Judd said.

Wendy stood looking at him, breathing hard. Her eyes narrowed.

"You are still drunk, aren't you?" she said.

Judd closed his eyes and sat back down on the bed. "Probably so."

"That's not a bet I'm able to take," Wendy said. She turned away. "I've got to go."

She walked over to the door, opened it, stepped out, and closed it behind her without a word.

He got up and opened the door to see her walking fast down the hall. "Wendy!" he cried.

She just started running and crashed her shoulder into the door going down stairs, disappearing from view.

Judd slammed the door shut and leaned his forehead against it, taking deep breaths. Every fiber in his body hurt at the thought of trying to chase her down, take her in his arms, and—

And then what?

Judd flung himself away from the door and picked up the unopened bottle, smashed the neck open on the edge of the table and put it to his mouth, turning it up to drink and feeling the glass cut into his lips. *You don't want to do that,* he realized, almost too late.

Maybe I can slit my own throat with it.

He walked back across the room and poured the rest of the glass and bourbon down the bathroom sink, then turned and flung the empty bottle across the room to shatter into the wall.

He walked over to the window and pulled back the curtain. He saw someone walking to the parking spaces under the floodlights. He watched as she slowed down and stopped in the middle of the lot.

She stood still as he watched her. She broke into a run and climbed into her car and drove off.

He sank to his knees beside the bed with his arms cradled to his chest as he felt hot tears running down his cheeks. *She's gone. She's gone.*

He went into the bathroom and splashed some water on his face and then dried it off with the hotel towel. He went back into the bedroom and stared at the bottle on the floor. He picked it up and put it in the trash. Then he got out of his clothes and climbed into bed.

He lay back with his hands behind his head, staring at the ceiling. "Jesus. What am I going to do?" he whispered. "What am I going to do?"

Holding On

Tommy felt Cindi shift in the bed, then he heard Marilee padding up the hall to their room in her pajama feet. "Mama?" she said. "You up?"

"I am now, baby," Cindi said.

She switched on the lamp—and the light felt like it was stabbing Tommy in the eyes. He had a hangover, all right—just like Cindi had said he would when he'd come in the night before.

He felt her get out of the bed, and he rolled over, his stomach complaining with the motion. He felt so bad. He'd just been out with Mark and his friends, and he'd let the amount of beer he was drinking get away from him. It hadn't seemed like so much—until he tried to drive home. Mark had to drive his truck, cussing the stick shift all the way. "Why can't you get with the program and get a new truck like everybody else?" he said.

"When this one finally falls apart, I guess I will," Tommy replied. He heard himself slurring a little. "Until then, just get me home."

Mark had gotten him to the door and had to help him unlock it. He'd tried not to wake Cindi up, but he tripped over himself and crashed into the floor, bringing Cindi out of their bedroom with her nightgown on and his .38 Special in her grip. He looked up to see her pointing the gun at his head. "Put that thing down," he said. "It's just me."

She lowered it, staring at him. "What have you been doing to yourself?"

"I'm okay," he said.

"Not tripping over air," she said, pushing her long blond hair out of her face. "Come on to bed, if you can make it."

So he had—and it was way too early to be waking up now, he decided.

As she went out of the room, the phone on the nightstand rang. Tommy lay there and waited on Cindi to answer it from the kitchen. It rang again, and his head started throbbing. "Answer the phone!" he said.

"I've got to fix Marilee some breakfast. You want any?" she called back.

He rolled his eyes at the thought. "No," he said.

It rang again. He reached over and grabbed the receiver. "Hello?"

"Hebert. Hey, Roscoe Finch. You sober this morning?" he heard in his ear.

He sat up quickly and instantly regretted it. "Yeah," he said with as much honesty as he could muster. Mr. Roscoe had been the owner of the mechanic shop Tommy worked at before it was sold to his current boss. He'd always been good to Tommy, and Tommy missed him badly after Mr. Roscoe had decided to retire after the storm to Brandon, Mississippi, where he'd had a hunting camp for years.

"You got anything planned for today?"

"I don't know," Tommy said. "I just woke up."

"Well, I'm down here in Slidell with Rogers and Daniels from the church helping a fellow clean up his place before he moves his family back in. You think you can run out here with your saw and your mower and trimmer?"

"I—guess," he said. "What kind of cleaning?"

"Trees, weeds—a little bit of all kinds of things. I didn't

bring enough equipment or men to take care of it all today, so I thought of you."

Tommy shut his eyes as the Thompson girl screamed in his ears.

But it was Mr. Roscoe.

He couldn't say no.

"Give me directions, and I'll get over there as quick as I can," he said.

Mr. Roscoe told him what he thought would be the quickest way to get to the place, and Tommy lodged the information in his brain—he knew his way all over south Louisiana, and Slidell wasn't exactly big enough to get bad lost in.

He rolled out of bed and slowly walked to the kitchen. Cindi and Marilee were sharing a plateful of bacon. "Who was that on the phone, Tommy?" Cindi said, her mouth full.

Tommy thought for a second. "Mr. Roscoe," he finally said.

Cindi looked startled. "Goodness, you haven't heard from him in quite a while," she said.

"You're right," he said.

"What does he want?" Cindi asked.

"He's over in Slidell, and he wants to see me," Tommy said, stalling for time to think.

"What for?"

Tommy's muddled brain gave up. "He wants my help with something—he needs my mower and trimmer, and chainsaw."

"What's he up to these days?"

"He's still retired, I think—but he's at a guy's house in Slidell doing cleanup work with his church..." Tommy let his voice trail off. "He wants my help."

Cindi gave him the side-eye. "I thought you were over helping people from the hurricane after the Thompson place in Mandeville," she said.

"But—Mr. Roscoe's been so good to us over the years—and he's never asked for a bit of anything back but a good day's work from me at the shop," Tommy said. "I don't hardly see where I can say no."

"So what did you say?" she asked, still looking at him sideways.

"I told him I'd be there as quick as I could," he confessed.

Cindi's mouth drew up. "Your own shed in the backyard's got grass growing up beneath it, too. When you going to take care of that?"

"Don't remind me, Cindi. I know. But I—want to pay him back at least some. And maybe it won't be like I'm thinking," he said, knowing he was lying.

She shook her head. "Well, next Saturday you can spend cleaning up your own yard, I guess."

"Okay," he said, his head hanging. He'd known she was going to say it, and he had to be a man about it and not blame her either.

"Want me to fix you some bacon? Or toast at least?"

"I don't think I could handle it," he said. "I'm just going to get a Coke and get some aspirin from the medicine cabinet."

Cindi nodded. "Well, that's your business. I suppose you're going to be gone all day?"

"Not sure—depends on how much work there is, I guess," he said.

Condi didn't look at him. "Say bye-bye to your daddy, sugar," she told Marilee.

"Bye-bye!" Marilee said.

"Bye, princess," he said back. "See you this afternoon."

After he got the double dose of aspirin for his headache, he downed the Coke as he went out to load his saw and trimmer in the back of his truck and hitch his trailer to bring the big red mower he'd bought a few years ago for the place. He looked over at his fishing shed, where it was rotting down still from where the storm had smashed it flat. *No watching the games next weekend.*

He drove the half-hour to Slidell slowly; he wasn't used to the new trailer he'd had to buy last year after the hurricane destroyed his other one. But he got to the guy's place out in the country a bit from Slidell itself. He felt his heart lift at seeing a brand-new beige Eddie Bauer 4x4 Explorer with a trailer hitched to it in front of the place Mr. Roscoe told him it would be, along with a big black diesel truck with another trailer. He hadn't seen Mr. Roscoe in months and was looking forward now to catching a few words with him.

He heard the saws going already, with two guys he didn't know cutting up trees with Mr. Roscoe, who was horsing his own saw over the stumps and pitching in right with them.

He pulled in behind Mr. Roscoe's SUV and started to walk up to the house. A guy in denim shorts, a t-shirt, and a Braves ball cap came out to meet him in the front yard.

Tommy saw Nelson and grinned. "Is this Rich Nelson's place?"

"I'm Rich Nelson. You here to see Roscoe Finch?"

"Yes sir. How are you this morning?'

"Pretty good so far."

"Mr. Roscoe chewed you out yet?"

Nelson raised his eyebrows. "No."

"Then he must be in a pretty good mood this morning. That always helps."

Mr. Roscoe had cut off his saw as Tommy had climbed down from the truck, and he walked up behind Nelson. Tommy looked over at him. "Good morning, Mr. Roscoe."

Mr. Roscoe was working in his undershirt and blue jeans; his grey eyes sized up Tommy head to toe. *Some things don't change.* Mr. Roscoe wiped his brow with his fist and stared. "Hebert, I asked you if you'd been drinking before I told you to come out here, and you said no."

Nelson slid his eyes over to look at Tommy, and Tommy had to stifle a laugh at the look on his face.

"You asked me if I was sober, Mr. Roscoe," He felt his grin fading under Mr. Roscoe's look. "You didn't say anything about being hung over. But I've eat some aspirin and a can Coke and I'm ready to help you out if you still want me to."

Mr. Roscoe rolled his eyes toward heaven and shook his head. Then he waved him off. "Mr. Nelson, this here is Tommy Hebert, one of the best Chevy mechanics I've ever seen in my forty years in the car business."

Tommy stuck out his hand, and Nelson shook it.

"We've already got a system going on over here," Mr. Roscoe said. "You do whatever this fellow tells you to do so we can get this wound up."

Nelson looked up at Mr. Roscoe, then back over at Tommy. "Okay," he said.

Tommy shifted a bit over to where Mr. Roscoe couldn't see his face and winked an eye at Nelson. "It's okay," he mouthed.

Nelson nodded. Mr. Roscoe walked back to the other two guys, leaving Tommy with Nelson.

Nelson shook his head. "How long did you work for him?"

"About six years," Tommy said.

"He sounds like he'd've made a fine slavedriver back in the day."

Tommy rolled his eyes. "He's used to getting his way wherever he goes. He's made enough money in his life that he doesn't have to care what anybody thinks about him," he said.

Then he grinned again. "But he sometimes forgets that some people can't be bought and sold quite as easy as he thinks they can," he said.

Nelson looked at him. "He paid you enough to put up with that?" he asked.

"Usually." Tommy cocked his head. "Got to do what the boss man say do wherever you be," he said in a singsong-Cajun way. Then he shrugged. "I liked the work, and when it hits the fan, he'll come through for you no matter what it takes, if he can. So it evens out in the end," he said.

He hefted the saw. "So where you want me to start?" Tommy asked.

Nelson aimed him at the pile of big branches the other crew stacked up already. "I want to save these for kindling for heat," Nelson told him. "So cut them up small."

Tommy went to work slicing up the limbs and letting them fall until the branch was cut up.

He saw Nelson cut his eyes over at Mr. Roscoe, then he went over and started stacking what Tommy already cut up. He cut the saw off, and Nelson looked up. "I'll take care of it. Don't worry yourself," Tommy said.

"No," Nelson said. "You keep cutting, and I'll stack. Then when you've got nothing else to cut, I'll be able to send you back home so you can get on with your day off."

"There's nothing back there you're keeping me from except baseball on TV," Tommy said. "I'm not in any hurry."

They went through the morning like that.

By lunchtime, Tommy didn't know how much more of the work he could take. He started being careless with the saw, wanting to get in as big a hurry as he could to get done. He caught Nelson watching him with scared eyes once or twice and settled down after that.

Noon came with Mr. Roscoe driving his crew off for lunch without a word to Tommy about coming along. Tommy hadn't packed anything because he had assumed Mr. Roscoe would take care of him like he always had. And now he was getting hungry.

He stowed away his saw and asked Nelson, "You want me to start cutting all of this with my mower in front now?"

"I thought we'd take a break, too," Nelson said, wiping the sweat from the back of his neck. "What you got in mind for lunch? It's on me for all your help."

Tommy looked up. "I appreciate that. How's that country-café place just down the road?"

"Best thing about it is that it's quick and hot." Nelson said.

"Suits me," Tommy said. "I couldn't handle breakfast this morning, so I'm ready."

"You want to bring it back here?"

Tommy looked down at his clothes. He was as muddy as Nelson was, covered in sawdust, and already felt about done in. "Sure. We probably don't look fit to stay there too long."

They drove over in silence. Tommy stared out the window as they went. "Parts of this place finally look pretty cleaned up," he said. "Other spots don't, though."

"Some folks never came back and did nothing," Nelson said.

"Same as back in Metairie," Tommy said. "I'll admit it took me a good while to get the trees up around my place."

They didn't say much more until they were on their way back. Tommy was holding the to-go boxes on his lap as Nelson drove. They pulled into the driveway, and he looked over at Nelson. "That swing set out back—that yours?" he asked.

Nelson nodded. "I've got three kids—all boys," he said. "Them and my wife are with my family up in Jackson, Mississippi. Told her the kids must have prayed for it to still be standing—I certainly wasn't bothering the Lord about it."

Tommy nodded. They got back to the house and unpacked their chicken strips and fries. They sat on the kitchen floor eating when Tommy asked, "You ride the storm out here?"

"At a shelter in town. I don't ever want to be that scared ever again in my life. I didn't even get back inside this place until three days later." Nelson sat up straight. "Did you stay at your place and send your family off?"

"Yep," Tommy said. "Spent the time after helping people get out of their homes when the east half of Metairie flooded."

"That was good of you to do," Nelson said, chewing up his food. "Saw a lot of damage?"

"More than I ever want to see again in my whole life," Tommy said.

He realized where the conversation was going but didn't know how to stop it. Something about Nelson made him easy to talk to, and the last thing Tommy wanted to do was talk right then.

But Nelson looked at him with grey eyes that seemed to reach right inside him—he told Nelson about how he took his boat out to a call for help to a house piled with debris.

He told him how trees brought down the walls and

beams of the house. But two people were inside—a mother and baby.

Tommy talked about being on the firetruck that carried the baby back to the hospital.

Finally the compassion in Nelson's eyes was too much to take; Tommy took to staring at the floor the entire time he talked like he was ashamed of the story he was telling.

Finally he looked up. Nelson was still staring at him. "I don't even know why I'm telling you this. I don't know you from Adam's housecat."

"Maybe because you have something inside you about it that needs to get out."

Tommy snorted. "Why would you want to listen to my problems? Seems to me from what Roscoe said you liked to have lost everything you had, and you're just now starting to get back on your feet."

He looked down. "I'd been sober for all my life—busted that all to pieces that night. My girlfriend caught me at it and laid down the law. But that didn't stop me from trying to forget."

He looked back up at Nelson. "And all I see when I go to sleep is nightmares about that girl. They say the baby lived. But the girl didn't make it—her legs were crushed, and she bled out lying there. I wake up with her screaming in my ears. I have to get up and go sit up front and drink or wait for it to wear out."

Nelson bit his lip. "I'm sorry, son."

"Not nearly as sorry as I am," Tommy said.

Nelson was quiet. Tommy started chewing on his nasty fingernails again—there wasn't water back on at the place yet for him to have washed his hands. He spit the dirt into a napkin.

"The way you've been talking, you don't believe that God's in control of everything," Nelson said. "I'll just have to tell you like I tell myself—if I didn't believe that God was in control even though I didn't understand what all he was doing, I couldn't keep going," he said.

Oh, holy hell. A preacherman. "He's done pretty good by you, huh?" Tommy asked.

Nelson nodded.

"Maybe you haven't done the kind of things I've done in my life, either," Tommy said. "Or seen what I've seen."

"Bible says that doesn't matter," Nelson said. "All have sinned and come short of the glory of God."

"Don't see how God could have much use for a guy like me," Tommy said.

"He made you, didn't he?" Nelson asked.

Tommy looked up. "Yeah. I—guess."

"There you go," Nelson said.

Tommy snorted again. He'd gone to his last Mass ten years ago when he graduated Catholic school and never set foot in a church since. "My daddy didn't leave much doubt in my mind as to which place I was going when I died, and I don't see anything I've done in my life since to change that."

"Look, you ever see somebody buy a nice new car then tow it to the dump?" Nelson asked.

"No," Tommy said.

"Jesus bought your soul from Satan," Nelson said.

Tommy looked away. "What if you get under the hood and the engine's busted all to pieces and won't run?" he muttered.

"Don't you fix it?" Nelson said. "He's handy that way, too, just like you are."

Tommy looked out the window. He knew he couldn't take much more of this kind of talk.

Then he heard a truck coming back up the driveway. "There's Mr. Roscoe and the guys," he said. "You'd better see what else he needs to do before he decides for himself."

"Kind of a bull in a china shop, huh?" Nelson said, getting up out of the floor.

"Sometimes," Tommy said.

They walked back outside.

Tommy heard doors slamming on the trucks out front. "Better get back to it," he said.

Nelson nodded. "In case you leave before I get back around to speaking to you, thanks for coming by and helping. Hope I can help you out someday."

He stuck out his right hand. Tommy shook it. "You're welcome anytime." Tommy said. He looked around. "Where to next? Cutting the front yard grass, right?"

"How about you start at this fence line and cut? I'll be along behind you with a trimmer," Nelson said.

"All right."

Tommy moved off toward the fence, then turned around. "Thanks for lunch."

"No problem," Nelson said. He waved and moved off.

After he'd cut the whole front, the day seemed to be over for them all. Nelson had come up to him about halfway through and had given him a good-sized bottled water to get him through the heat of the afternoon. They were all loading up—Mr., Roscoe and his crew to go back home to Brandon, and Tommy to go home to Metairie—when Mr. Roscoe stopped by Tommy's truck.

"You be careful going home," Mr. Roscoe said. "I thank you for coming out."

"You're welcome, Mr. Roscoe."

He saw Mr. Roscoe staring past him. "You know I was kidding when I asked if you were sober this morning."

"Yes sir," Tommy said.

"But you were hung over bad this morning, weren't you?" Mr. Roscoe said.

Tommy nodded.

Mr. Roscoe shook his head. "I don't know what you've got going on, son. But be careful with yourself is all I'm saying."

"Yes sir," Tommy said.

Mr. Roscoe patted him on the shoulder and went and climbed up in his Explorer.

Tommy backed out of the driveway into the road and let Mr. Roscoe out, then followed him out for just a little while—until he saw a store called Max's with a neon Budweiser sign in the window.

He pulled into the parking lot and hoped Mr. Roscoe didn't see him.

He walked in and picked up a case of beer, telling himself it was to add to his stock at home—but he knew he was lying to himself about waiting until that night to drink them.

He didn't even look at the lady selling him the beer—he kept his head down and paid and hefted the case, walking out without even waiting for his change.

He got into the truck, tore open the case, and pulled out a can before he even pulled out of the parking lot. He put the case in the floorboard so he couldn't get to it as easy and set the beer in the custom cupholder he'd installed when he last redid the interior.

He drove slow again back home, not wanting to attract attention. He felt steady enough, after finishing off the first beer, and the clamor in his head had died down a little, replaced with the warm feeling he got in his mind now with booze. He'd tried other brands of beer and couldn't find a lick of difference between them in giving him what he was looking for—and he'd made one attempt at whiskey shots on a dare from one of Mark's friends, only to decide that the buzz was the same and not worth how much worse the hangover was.

He got to the house by sundown, leaving the beer in the truck. He knew Cindi could tell from how she wrinkled her nose at him when he hugged her coming in, but she didn't say anything—maybe she was giving up on talking to him about it.

They went to bed, not speaking. Tommy lay awake as long as he could, feeling the buzz wear off and being replaced with a dread of the night. Then he got up and sat in his recliner and leaned the seat all the way back.

Back in Rich Nelson's yard. Cutting up branches with the saw feeling easy and light in his hands. He could feel the beer buzz in his brain even as he was cutting up the branches. But he tripped jumping over one of the felled tree limbs—and realized the point of the saw was about to cut through a baby carrier—

He sat up in the chair with his eyes wide open. Cindi was standing in the room in front of him, having cut on the lights as she came in. She didn't say anything at first. They just stared at each other.

Finally she whispered, "More dreams?"

He nodded, scared to answer out loud and wake up Marilee—if he hadn't already.

She reached out for his hand. "Come on back—I'll give you one of my sleeping pills. They usually help you, don't they?"

He followed her back to their bedroom, not having the heart to tell her that they didn't anymore.

Do Unto Others

Dinah walked into the grocery store. The kids, all middle-schoolers, were taking advantage of it being Spring Break and sleeping in as long as they could. Dinah enjoyed going to this store for the friendliness and atmosphere—it reminded her of the store her grandparents managed down in Slidell for her whole childhood until they retired—complete with a couple of old men sitting in rockers out front when they came by in the middle of the day. They were the butchers, resting and sometimes playing checkers on their lunch break.

This morning, Dinah picked out her packages—a lot of store-brand box meals and a smattering of fresh meat for the weekends for when she helped Mrs. Seabrook cook proper meals in her kitchen on Saturdays. Sundays, Mike would spend the Sabbath playing with Bracey and reading with Jamie and Candi while Dinah napped or read during the afternoons after they all went to church.

Only one other shopper was in the store this early—a very elderly lady carrying a wire basket as she walked through the store. Her white hair was pulled back into a bun, and she wore a flowered old-fashioned dress that had probably seen better days.

She got to the check-out counter right before Dinah did, and Dinah noticed she shopped for very little—a jar of smooth peanut butter, a box of saltines, some cans of Vienna sausages, and store-brand white bread. The lady slowly unpacked her basket as the teenage-girl cashier waited for her to finish.

The girl rang her up and gave her the total—somewhere in the neighborhood of fifteen dollars. The lady slowly packed her basket back up, telling the girl, "Just put it on my ticket."

"Miss Moss, it's the first of the month. It's time for you to pay last month's ticket total," the young blonde said.

Miss Moss rested her hands on the counter. "How much?"

The girl told her.

The lady sighed and reached for the white purse hanging by a chain from her shoulder. She reached in, pulled out a bank envelope and started counting off five-and one-dollar bills.

Dinah felt a pull in her heart—but she didn't want to embarrass the lady, so she held her tongue until she finished counting.

She turned out to have enough for part of the ticket but not all of it. Miss Moss sighed again and started unpacking her basket.

Dinah spoke up. "Miss Moss, don't unpack your basket just yet," she said, pulling out her wallet. She counted out three twenties and pushed them toward the cash register. "Consider your ticket and your groceries paid today."

Miss Moss and the girl both stared at her. Miss Moss said, "Lady, you didn't have to do that."

"I know," Dinah said. "But let me bless you today, please."

Miss Moss nodded her head. "Thank you."

The girl picked up the bills and looked back at Dinah. "You sure you want to do this, ma'am?"

Dinah nodded, a lump filling her throat. Miss Moss walked to the door of the market, and Dinah heard her humming an old hymn, the tune "God is so Good."

So the girl gave Dinah back her change, then Dinah unpacked her own basket. Dinah got a look at the name tag on the teenage girl's top—it read "Katrina".

Oh, it used to be such a pretty name for a girl, too. Not anymore.

Before she could stop herself, she said, "Oh, you poor child."

The girl didn't even look up. "You mean my name?"

"Yes," Dinah said. "People must have given you a terrible time the past several months."

"It's okay," the girl said. "I'm used to it now."

Dinah was grateful to see she brought enough money to cover that, too, thank goodness. But she saw only twenty-something dollars left after that; she would have to hope Mike got paid good today to have enough to get food the next week.

That night, she boiled pasta and water and mixed up the powder for boxed mac and cheese, a favorite of the kids', especially Bracey. But tonight they all just picked at their servings.

"Are you kids feeling okay?" Dinah said.

"Not really, Mama," Jamie said. 'It's been a long day, and I'm ready to go to bed."

You all slept for half of it. "Well. You can be excused," Dinah said.

Candi and Bracey slipped away from the table, too, and they went back to take their sponge baths for the night. Dinah held out some for Mike when he came home, and she was expecting him any minute.

After the girls bathed, they climbed up to their bunks and read their books quietly as usual. But after a bit, Dinah heard them whispering. "I'm tired of mac and cheese," Jamie said to her sister. "I think Bracey is, too, the way he didn't eat any tonight."

"I know. I am too. I'm tired of everything Mama fixes every week. I wish we could have real mashed potatoes again instead of that instant stuff," Candi answered.

About an hour later, Dinah heard Mike's truck come rolling in. She heated up the leftover mac and cheese in the small microwave and felt reassured when he tore into it and cleaned his plate of it. "Thanks, hon," he said.

"How'd the work go today?" Dinah said.

"Okay," Mike said. "I've got to go back Monday and finish up and get my money."

"You didn't get paid again?" Dinah cried out.

Mike stared at her. "It's okay, hon. We'll get the money Monday when I finish the job."

Dinah felt the tears welling up in her eyes. She confessed how she spent so much money at the grocery store helping Miss Moss and how there wasn't enough to go back Monday morning once the kids got back in school. "I thought for sure you'd get paid, it being almost Friday and all," she said. "I guess I shouldn't have done it."

"Dinah, it'll be okay. Here's another twenty I squirrelled back so you can get lunch things for the girls and you and Bracey. I'll manage without hot meals for a week; you can pack me a lunch too, I guess," Mike said.

"Okay. I guess I'll just have to shop super careful next week. They'll be eating a lot of peanut butter, but they can manage that, I think."

"Don't worry, honey. God's taking care of us, just like he always has." Mike put his arms around her. "Don't ever feel bad about doing a good turn for somebody. You blessed that lady, just like you told her. God'll honor that."

Dinah felt good relaxing in his embrace. He must have felt the tension run out of her; his arms tightened. "It'll take more than a few dollars short a week for me to not trust you and the Lord, Dinah."

Dinah nodded, trying to keep the tears held back. *Haven't we been through enough, God?* she thought. *How much more will we have to take?*

The next day came and went, with Dinah making the kids another of what was their favorites—a box pasta casserole that she added pouch tuna to, jazzing it up a little. They came to the table again with long faces and ate even less than the night before.

But Dinah prepared a secret weapon this time. "Now look here," she said. "I've got a surprise for you for dessert if you eat good tonight."

"What is it, Mama?" Candi asked.

"You just wait and see," Dinah said. "You'll like it."

The girls ate slowly. Bracey, like any boy, was the only one who cleaned his plate completely; the girls left a few bits of tuna and pasta when Dinah stood up. "Well. I guess Bracey's the only one who gets dessert tonight," Dinah said. "That's just more for your daddy and me after you've gone to bed, I guess."

She went over to a Tupperware bowl she'd borrowed from Mrs. Seabrook and brought out soft chocolate chip cookies she'd made from one of the refrigerator-cookie-dough rolls Mrs. Seabrook kept on hand for special occasions. She was hoping that seeing the cookies would encourage the girls to finish their plates.

Jamie looked at the bowl after Dinah brought it to the table and set it in front of Bracey. "Are they homemade, like Great-grandma used to make? Or are they those stupid slice-and-bake from Mamaw next door?"

"What's wrong with those?" Dinah said.

"I don't like those," Jamie said. "I'm not hungry anymore, anyway."

She started to get up from the table, and Candi moved to follow her. "Sit down," Dinah said. "Both of you."

She gave Bracey two of the cookies and took two for herself. "Bracey and me are going to enjoy them, and you two are going to sit here until I tell you that you can be excused."

She took a bite, and Bracey did the same, and the next thing Dinah knew, Bracey put his cookie down. She looked at him, and he took the bite out of his mouth and wrapped it in a napkin. "Yuck," he said.

She looked back to Jamie and caught her smiling at Bracey from her seat at the table. The cookie in her mouth turned to so much sawdust to her, and Jamie's smile unlocked a voice she didn't even know she could make.

She stood up. "You kids ought to be ashamed of yourselves."

"But—" Candi said.

"But nothing," Dinah said, hearing her voice rise. "You kids haven't done anything the past few nights but fuss and whine and complain. You've got a roof over your heads and food on your table. Your daddy goes every day to help people who don't have even that because the hurricane took it all away. They have nothing. You could be sleeping in a sleeping bag in some motel room in Houston or Atlanta and living off the Red Cross and Salvation Army food. How would you like that?"

Both girls sat and stared at her without a bit of repentance in their faces. Bracey stared at the floor.

Fine. "I have never seen three more ungrateful brats in my entire life!" Dinah yelled. "You'll eat what I give you and be happy for it! You can think anything you want. I don't care anymore! But I'm not going to listen to another word of it. Next hateful thing I hear come out of your mouth, I'll be washing it out with soap. Be brats, be whiners. But I'll be *damned* before I try to fix something nice again for three children who have the audacity to put their feet under my table and then complain about what they're served! Get up and go to bed right now. All of you. I don't want to hear another word out of you until morning. Do you understand?"

Jamie and Candi nodded, their faces red. Bracey cracked his knuckles, a sound Dinah hated, and he knew it. "Go. *Go!*" Dinah said.

Bracey went to his pallet on the floor. Candi started to bring her book out from under her pillow, and Dinah said, "No ma'am. You're going to lie there and think about how you've acted today. You and Jamie both," she said as she snatched the books out of their hands.

"But Mom—" Candi whined.

Dinah reached over and grabbed Candi's arm. "What did I *just say*?" she hissed as she dragged Candi over to the kitchen area. She grabbed a washcloth and soaked it under the sink faucet. She put a drop of dishwashing liquid on it, and Candi started screaming and struggling to get away. Bracey was hanging back, eyes wide. "Mama, stop!" Jamie cried. "Just stop!"

And that's when Dinah slapped Jamie in the face.

Bracey moved to stand between Dinah and Jamie. "Mama—" he said.

Then Mike came in the door on a dead run and froze when he saw Dinah and Candi at the sink. Jamie couldn't stop blubbering. Dinah let go of Candi, who ran behind her daddy, tears running down her cheeks.

When Mike spoke, Dinah could tell how he felt from how carefully he started talking. "What in the Sam Hill is going on in here?"

"Mama cussed at us, Daddy," Candi said from behind him. "And hit Jamie."

As soon as she said it, Dinah felt the red creep up her neck. Candi was right, and there was no help for it.

Mike stared at her. "I think we all need to settle down in here and get ready for bed."

Then Bracey made a retching sound and threw up his dinner.

Dinah moved towards him, and Mike spoke again. "I'll take care of him, Dinah. You go outside and—*cool off*."

Dinah walked outside slowly. She wanted to defend herself immediately, to argue with Mike. But from the look on his face, it was all he could do not to start cussing a blue streak himself. *Plenty of time to talk it out once the kids are down.*

Dinah sat outside for a while in the night air, trying to figure out where everything went so wrong. She was old enough to know better than to act to the kids that way if you looked at it from that point of view.

The load of worry and fear and pain was just too heavy for her tonight, and she started crying silently in the night. *Forgive me for my anger, God. They're just kids*, she prayed. *Help me.*

Mike finally came out, smelling like bad tuna and sweat. He sat down next to her, and Dinah held her breath against the stench. "What exactly did you say to the kids tonight?" he said.

"I didn't cuss the kids," Dinah said. "I cussed myself."

"That's not what I asked you," he said.

"I told them I'd be damned before I fixed another meal for ungrateful kids."

Mike closed his eyes. "And why in the world did you hit Jamie?"

"I told them not to say another word if they did I'd wash their mouths with soap. Candi did, and as I was getting ready, Jamie started screaming at me. So I taught her a lesson, too."

"Yes, that hitting people solves problems. I ought to slap you myself and see how you like it."

She turned to stare at him. He'd never said any such to her, not in twenty-five years together. His face was shadowed by the moonlight, making him look menacing and not the man she knew. "I'll scream if you do—"

"And I can keep hitting you until you stop. How would you like that?" Mike said.

Dinah cowed down, realizing where this was going from the venom in Mike's voice.

"And what would we all learn from that?" Mike continued, sounding deadly serious.

Dinah felt the sobs shaking her body that she didn't dare vocalize. They'd never fought like this.

Both were quiet for a long time after that.

Finally Mike exhaled slowly. "You apologize to them tomorrow. Do you hear me?" he said.

She nodded, biting her lips to keep them closed.

"And I know this is hard, Dinah," he went on. "Me gone all the time, barely bringing in money, us all being away from home. It's enough to make a saint swear. But I need you to be strong for them, but I need to be straight with you. I don't want to come home to another scene like this. It's just made a bad day worse."

Somehow Dinah knew. "You didn't get paid again today, did you?"

"No, I didn't," Mike said. "I got another check I'll have to hold."

Dinah started sucking in air through her nose, willing herself not to scream at him. He seemed to sense her feelings, talking fast. "We'll get through it. I swear we will. We've got to hold on for the kids and each other. We can do this."

He didn't sound angry anymore; he sounded beaten down and very, very tired. Dinah swallowed the words she wanted to say and finally let the tears go silently and turned her back on him.

"I love you," he said.

"And I love you, too," she lied.

No Going Back

Lori King was sitting outside Boyce Watson's Louisville office in early May waiting for James to show up. The front room was decorated like a living room—two long couches ran along the walls with overstuffed armchairs next to them and coffee tables full of magazines in between. All navy and hunter green and maroon with shiny brass accents—Lori decided it was decorated in the eighties and not touched since then.

Just don't let him be late.

Lori was jolted from her thoughts an hour later by the sound of the bell jingling on the front door. When she looked up as James came in the front door, she knew. His blond hair was tousled, his razor hadn't made it all the way to his lower jaw, and the circles under his green eyes were darker than usual. Her mouth tightened.

"The least you could do is show up on time to work out your own divorce," she said.

"I'm here now. Maybe I'm late for a good reason—not that it's any of your business."

"Like I said."

Boyce opened the door. "Y'all come on in."

The back held individual offices and two conference rooms, one of which was where they planned to meet. It wasn't anything special—a room lined with bookshelves on every wall and a table seating eight right in the middle. The carpet was worn under the table, and Lori could feel her boots wearing a new hole under her chair as she kicked her feet and waited for James to say something else. But he didn't; he just sat on the opposite side of the table and stared at Boyce, waiting for him to get started.

Boyce pulled out his papers and started ticking off points for them to sign.

It all held together until they got to the house. "Both houses remain jointly owned and on occasion of sale, proceeds are split equally," Boyce said.

James looked up. "Bull."

Boyce looked at Lori. She tossed her head. 'My name's on both deeds, James."

"No ma'am," James said. "My share of equity in the house in Louisville is worth more than your share in Kenner. I'm giving it to you to pay for your equity down there, and I'm paying you alimony to cover the payments here. You agreed to that—and we're supposed to take these documents over to the bank tomorrow and get it done."

Lori tapped her foot impatiently. "Whatever."

James looked at Boyce. "We'll come back when you have those new papers filled out," he said.

He slammed his pen down on the table, got up, and walked out.

Boyce looked at Lori. "Are there any other surprises in here I need to know about?"

She shook her head. "Just get it together and I'll pay you myself for it," she said.

She saw Boyce shaking his head as she walked out.

James was pacing outside the door when she came out. "You—" he said.

"Shut up, James."

"I put your name on that place because I loved you. But it's mine from my daddy—."

"Hire your own lawyer next time, James."

"I don't have a lawyer because I'm *giving* you a divorce, Lori," he said. "If I wanted to, I could have filed for one back home for abandonment and put you out on the street with nothing."

"Keep your voice down, James," she said.

He spun around and headed for the door. He banged the hall door open, crossed the lobby, and didn't even look back when the glass door to the outside almost hit her in the face as she followed him out to the parking lot. "Where are you going?" she said.

"Away from you. Isn't that what you want?"

She stopped. "No. It isn't."

He stood there staring at her. "Then what are we doing here?"

"What I want is the James King that left Kenner that August. He never came back to me. You did."

He came back towards her. "Lori?"

She turned her back. "Answer me, Lori."

"I already told you why, James," Lori said. "After you sent back those pictures of the house and all over the town, I couldn't think about coming back there to live, and —"

James put his hand on her shoulder, and she flinched. He pulled it back.

"Do you think I drove back to Noxapater from Kenner and came in at two in the morning that Friday for the fun of it? After what I'd seen that day?" he said.

"All right. I'll play along. Why did you, James?"

He might not actually hit me, but he looks like he wants to.

"Lori, I needed to find something—anything—that reminded me of my life before that storm came through. My daddy's place was part of that. But you were, too, and you weren't there, Lori. Not in any of it. You were at your mama's, where you still want to be."

"And where I lost my baby, and we can't seem to have another one. You seem to keep forgetting that."

She saw his face go white. "What can I do about that when I'm there and you're here—"

They heard the lobby door open, and Boyce was waiting behind it. "I think it would be best, Mr. and Mrs. King, for you both to take a copy of these documents and review them tonight and come back tomorrow morning at nine a.m."

James nodded. Lori scowled at Boyce.

He closed the door, and Lori looked up at James. "See if you can find something else to tick about in there tomorrow, James. Maybe we can keep this up all week."

She turned and started walking off. Halfway across the parking lot, Lori noticed that James was staying behind her on the way to her Honda instead of walking to his truck. She hit the remote on her key ring and started to open the car door.

James leaned against the passenger door. "Lori?"

"What?"

"We don't have to do this."

"Yes, we do, James," Lori said, staring at her car door handle.

"Why?"

In spite of herself, Lori choked up. She looked up at him. "James, I—"

"The only reason I moved up here was that I was tired of being alone at night," James said.

"But what was left down there for us? The house might have been fine, but so much of everything else down there was just—gone. Why couldn't you see that?"

"So I came up here like you wanted, and even after I did that for you, look where we are now."

Lori closed her eyes tightly. *I am not going to stand here and let him make me cry again.*

Before he could say anything else, she put her hands on her hips and stared up at him. "Listen to me very carefully, James King. I am only going to say this to you one more time. We're here because I found out that you loved Kenner more than you loved me. And when I finally called you on it—"

She stared at the concrete, took a deep breath, and looked back up. "Maybe it wouldn't have happened, James, if it weren't for you disappearing every weekend, or, or, or, or a hundred other things I could name."

Now it was James's turn to stare at his feet.

I can't take much more of this. She looked away, and then made herself turn back around to face him. "Moving there was a mistake, and now I'm beginning to think our whole marriage was one big mistake."

She saw his jaw muscles bunch up as he looked off towards the highway. "You might be right about that," he said.

Lori closed her eyes and gathered in her breath to scream at him. *What's the use?* she thought. Instead she said. "Be careful going back."

"You, too," he said.

Lori watched him walk across the parking lot and climb into the Ford. As he drove off, she climbed into her car and rested her head on the hot steering wheel. She closed her eyes and thought about how he'd cried over the phone after she'd served him with the papers. She popped her car door open, got out, slammed it shut, and started walking.

She knew, deep down in his heart, the only reason he'd agreed to come to Louisville wasn't for her. It was because of Jack.

His funeral had been awful. They went, and everyone in Jack's family—people James had known all his life, had eaten at table with and lived life with, to a person, refused to speak to him. Only Marla Swindoll accepted his condolences at the funeral home.

"I know you would never have wanted him to do what he did," she'd said, tears running down her face. "You'd have rather lost everything you had than lose Jack. I know that much."

James had a thousand-yard stare on his face as he'd walked back out to the truck to go in the funeral procession. She drove because as soon as he climbed in, he broke down crying. She had to, for knowing how his heart must have hurt.

But her hurt had been lost in his. He took down the nursery for her, so she was spared that. But he was the one who went back and forth trying to sell the place, and when it wouldn't move because people knew someone had been killed there by looters, he came back to Louisville a broken-down man. They bought a beautiful house by a lake because that had reminded him of home. He spent his nights watching sports—ESPN for college football, basketball, and baseball—rooting for LSU just the way him and Jack used to do. If there wasn't a current game on, he watched reruns on the classics channel. She would lie in bed, crying because she wanted to make love to him so badly to get their baby back, but he would stay up to all hours, using Mountain Dews and sometimes even No-Doz to stay awake for his job in the mornings.

After a couple of months, he started making weekend trips to see his family. She refused to go. At first they were day trips to see his parents. Then he renewed his friendship with Harvey Mason, another high school buddy—and Harvey became the new Jack Swindoll in James' life. Fishing trips, hunting trips, trips to see ball games—they became an every-weekend thing with him and Harvey.

Their final fight had been when he came in early one morning from being down in Kenner on a long weekend trip—school was closed Monday for a holiday, and he stayed down in Kenner until the wee hours of Tuesday morning.

"Where in the world have you been?!" she'd shouted at him.

"I'm sorry—we got tied up trying to get the boat back to the rental place because of some bad weather there. I drove as fast as I could," he'd said.

"I thought you'd been in a wreck somewhere. I thought you were dead. I was about to call the Highway Patrol in Mississippi and ask them to look for your license plate. You couldn't even call?" she said.

"Maybe I didn't want to get yelled at over the phone where everyone could hear you. I was having fun. You don't even know how to anymore. We can't even have sex without you making it a production about being the right time of the month," he'd said, using air quotes for "right time of the month."

And then she'd slapped him in the face.

"Oh, is that the way you want to play?" he said in a cold, flat voice he'd taken to using ever since they'd lost their baby for whenever he got angry.

He started toward her, hands out in front of him, and she knew she'd pushed him too far. She thought he was going to strangle her.

She snatched the other Glock he kept on the bedside table and pointed at him. "Don't move," she said.

"You don't have it in you to shoot me," he'd sneered. "You twitch every time a gun goes off on TV."

He dove at her to take her down, but she sidestepped him just quick enough, and he hit the floor. She straddled him and pointed the gun down at his chest as he rolled over to get back up.

She stared at him as he looked up at her, and deep down, she knew he was right. He held his hands up in the air in surrender.

But for the next bit to work, she had to be very convincing. "Listen to me very carefully, James King. I don't care where you spend the night tonight. It can be Kenner, it can be a hotel, it can be in hell. But if try you go to sleep here, you'll wake up dead. Do you understand me?"

He nodded.

She moved aside to let him up. He grabbed her leg, pulled her down beside him, and smacked her arm hard on the floor, knocking the gun loose. He snatched at it and threw it way out of reach of either of them. Then he grabbed both her arms and rolled her over on her back and held her wrists down with his hands and placed his knees on each side of her waist.

"Remember this, Lori," James said, his eyes empty, making her shiver. "You want to start something with me, you'd better be able to finish it. Next time I might not be so nice about it."

He climbed off of her and walked out, slamming the door behind him. She heard his tires screech on his way out of the garage and off down the road. She'd laid there crying until the early morning light came in the bay windows overlooking the lake.

Lori looked around for the first time outside and saw the double doors of the Baptist church. *At least it'll have air conditioning.*

She pushed open the door and walked in. She looked around and sat down in the corner of the last bench and thought about driving back in tomorrow to face it all again, and she put her forehead on the back of the bench in front of her and started crying.

"Do you need some help, young lady?"

She looked up, startled. A big guy in a suit and tie was standing in the middle of the aisle. She recognized him from his picture in the paper on his weekly church articles.

Lori stood up quickly. "No—I just came in to sit for a minute. I'm sorry if me coming in bothered you."

"You're not bothering anyone, hon. But something's obviously bothering you."

"I'll be okay."

He raised his eyebrows. Lori felt like a little girl again meeting the senior priest when she was twelve years old before going into the little room for her first confession. Before she thought, she said, "I just came from Boyce Watson's office, and I'm upset."

"You're getting a divorce," he said.

I guess that's all he does. She nodded.

"You don't want one?"

"Yes. I do. I filed for it. There was a problem, and we have to come back tomorrow." Lori sat back down. The preacher sat down in the bench in front of her and was silent. She looked down at the floor. "Actually, my lawyer tried to slip something by my husband, and he caught it."

"Your lawyer?"

"Well, me, too, because I didn't tell him to change it."

The preacher cocked his head as he looked at her.

She shrugged. "It looked like a good way for me to screw my husband over. So I took advantage of it." Then she remembered where she was, and her face burned.

He didn't react at all. "He must have hurt you very badly."

Lori looked up. He was looking at her with his head tilted to the side. His thick glasses made his watery blue eyes look bigger than they really were. "We lost a baby—and he didn't seem to care. All he cared about were his friends and his family. Whenever we tried to talk, he got so cold and distant—and scared me. He wasn't the man I married anymore. One night we had a fight about it and—" She felt her face burning, and she just started crying.

His brow furrowed. But he didn't ask any more questions.

She looked down. "I need to go," she said. "I've got to call my boss and tell him I have to come back tomorrow."

"Is there any chance you could forgive your husband?" he said.

She laughed, thinking he was joking.

He still looked at her, and she realized he was dead serious.

She cast her eyes down. "No. Not after our last fight." She took a deep breath. "And tomorrow it's going to be over, and I probably won't ever see him again."

"Do you mind if I pray for you and your husband?" he said.

"I'm not sure how much good it can do us now," she said.

"What's his name?"

"James."

"And yours?"

"Lori."

He bowed his head and closed his eyes, and Lori sat staring wide-eyed at the floor blurring at her feet. She heard a lot of words like forgiveness and reconciliation and peace and grace, but she wasn't really there anymore—she was back in the parking lot watching James drive off after asking her to take him back one more time.

Revelations

Ray and Wendy were getting settled in the labor suite when Rosie came in, breathless with excitement. She was so ready to see Wendy become a mom after so many years of trying and failing—the idea that it was going to happen for real made her feel so grateful to God for finally hearing their prayers. Wendy gritted her teeth as they hooked her up to an IV and wrapped the monitor around her belly. But she seemed to soften when she saw her come in. "Hey Rosie," she said. "Glad you were so close to come over and help us with this."

"I am, too! God has his hand on this, I know it," Rosie said. "How far apart are the contractions?"

Ray answered her. "I was clocking them at four minutes apart in the parking lot."

"Are they pretty strong?" the nurse asked.

"Yes, ma'am. At least I think so," Wendy said. "But I haven't ever done this before."

"You'll be fine. The doctor already called ahead and ordered you Stadol, so we'll hook you up and get you feeling better in no time."

After the nurse walked out, Rosie saw Wendy's eyes starting to unfocus and her head start nodding from the Stadol. "So your sorry brother-in-law came through with calling the medicine in ahead of time," Wendy said in Ray's general direction. "I might have to like him better from now on."

"Pays to have family in high places sometimes," Ray mumbled.

"I guess," Wendy said.

"You know he's the best we've got down here—especially if anything goes wrong," Ray said. "He gets on my nerves, too, you know."

Rosie knew Wendy didn't like Dr. Jack Rawson, who was married to Ray's sister, Reba. She'd confided in Rosie how creeped out she was whenever she was alone with him; he didn't think a thing about asking personal questions in the middle of dinner when the subject of her and Ray having kids came up—but she knew Wendy felt obligated to use him since he was family and one of the few OBGYN's taking new patients in Hattiesburg.

Wendy lay back to rest holding onto Ray's hand. "Stadol starting to work?" he said.

Wendy nodded with a little jerk at the end of it. *She's either really feeling that stuff or maybe she's not as far along as she thinks she is.*

Rosie moved to sit down in the chair next to the other side of the bed from Ray. "You'd better try and rest as much as you can now, Wendy," she advised, wiping sweat off of Wendy's forehead with her fingers. "Go on to sleep; it won't hurt anything."

Wendy's belly visibly tensed under another contraction. "Unh," Wendy grunted.

"Wendy? You need anything else?" Ray asked.

She shook her head and closed her eyes. Soon Rosie could hear her breaths even out as she seemed to relax with the medicine. "I'll be here in case she wakes up if you want to go get you a Coke or a snack," Rosie said.

Ray shook his head absently, not taking his eyes off of Wendy. "Not right now."

Rosie grinned. *He's just tickled pink to be here.* But she also knew he'd never been in a labor room before except for his firefighter training. *He's in for a rude awakening once this show gets on the road.*

"Don't see how she can sleep—they've moving right along three minutes apart," Ray said. "Must have been some powerful stuff they put in that drip."

Rosie leaned back in her chair. "A first baby usually takes its sweet time coming," she said. "You may as well stay sit down and get ready to wait."

She knew she was just talking—Ray Magnum never sat still. He started roving around the room, looking at the monitor from time to time. "Save some of that energy for later," she advised.

"I can't," Ray said. "Wendy scared me out of the recliner this morning screaming out from the pain. I don't think I'm going to settle down from hearing that for a while."

Rosie nodded. "I can understand that," she said.

Rosie knew Wendy knew what to expect—since their momma had died of emphysema while Rosie was pregnant with her first one, Wendy had gone into the labor room with Rosie for that birth, and each of the other two after that. Rosie remembered how itchy Wendy was to hold each of the babies as soon as she could.

She'd seen her sister, who so rarely smiled after their mother's lingering death, smile like each one was her own while she'd held them each in their turn. Wendy had been a good labor coach—much better than Lee, who'd passed out each and every single time right as his children had come into the world.

I hope Ray's tougher than that boy was. It was still a joke in the family, something Lee would never live down.

Rosie turned at the sound of the door opening a while later, expecting the nurse. Instead, Jack Rawson walked into the labor suite and grinned at Ray from behind his surgical mask, his grey eyes crinkling. Some of his blond hair was sticking straight up from where he'd pulled the mask on over his head, and Rosie could see his glasses stuck in his pocket. "Glad to finally see you in here. Ray. Beginning to think I never would."

"Long haul, Doc," Ray said, shaking his hand. "But I think she's more ready than either of us," Ray said and patted Wendy's hand.

Jack raised his voice. "Wake up, girl. I need to check your progress."

Ray shook her shoulder, and she woke up with a little jump. Wendy looked at Ray, then at Jack. Rosie saw her eyes go to slits. "What're you waking me up for?" she said.

Ray looked at Jack over her head. "Stadol put her to sleep."

Jack made a face. "Oh, well. Time to wake up." He went to the end of the bed and reached under the sheet.

Wendy turned her head toward Rosie, and Rosie didn't like the look in her eyes. "What time is it?"

"Late," Jack said before Rosie could open her mouth. "Very, very late."

"Don't think you can just talk about me any old kind of way, Jack Rawson," Wendy said, looking down at him.

"Come on, Wendy—got to get this show on the road and we can both go back to bed," Jack said.

"You're the one we've been waiting on," Wendy said.

"I'm not the one coming in here two days after the due date, Wendy," Jack said, grinning at Ray. "Do a better job of counting your days next time and maybe you won't have to wait so long."

If she could get up from this bed right now, I think she'd kill you where you stand.

Ray picked up Wendy's hand and touched her fingertips to his lips. "Not much longer, now, hon, and you'll be holding that baby."

"Feels like I've been pregnant forever as it is," Wendy said. Rosie saw Ray wince as Wendy tightened her grip on his hand. "Another one, right?" she said.

Ray looked over at the monitor. "You're right. Can she push yet, Jack?"

"No, I wouldn't advise it. Not quite there yet. I'd think you'd want that epidural in before you think about that."

Rosie looked at the door and saw the anesthesiologist came in. "How far along, Jack?" he asked.

"Seven centimeters," he said. "I'll step out and let you take it from here."

Jack strode out and let the door bang behind him.

Rosie saw Wendy grit her teeth.

"You've got to sit up for me, hon, and let me get to your back, and remember you can't move around while I'm doing this," the anesthesiologist said.

Wendy pulled up on the rail. "It's all I can do to be still as it is lying here."

He pointed at Ray. "Lean up on him. You hold up her arms and help her out."

She turned to Ray and closed her eyes as she leaned up on him. He put both hands on her shoulders and held on.

He's always taken such good care of her, Rosie thought. *I know he'll be a great daddy.*

Rosie saw Wendy clench her fists. "God—"

"I'm moving just as fast as I can. You're doing good. Just like that—don't move," the anesthesiologist said.

Ray smoothed her hair back. "It's almost over. You're going to be all right."

Wendy squeezed her eyes shut and sucked in her breath sharply between her teeth.

She doesn't look like she's going to be all right.

"Ray, I can't do this. I can't. I can't do this. Ray—I don't care if it hurts Reba's feelings. Next time I'm coming in here with some other doctor than Jack. I'm not putting up with him one second longer than I have to after this—"

"He's almost done, hon. Just hang on a minute; don't cry."

Suddenly Rosie saw Wendy's face relax. She looked up at Ray. "Is he done?"

"Yes ma'am, I am," the anesthesiologist said. "Now you lay back careful and take the last chance you're going to have for a while to get some rest. You're going to need it once that baby gets here."

"That helped you out, didn't it?" Ray said to Wendy.

Wendy nodded, closed her eyes, and rolled over in the bed. Ray put his hand on her shoulder and she batted it away. "Leave me alone. Don't."

Ray looked at Rosie with a hurt face.

"It's all right," Rosie said, taking Wendy's hand and patting it. "Everything's going to be all right." She looked at Ray. She hoped she sounded more convincing to him than she did to herself.

A bad feeling grew on her. It wasn't like Wendy to not want Ray talking to her when she was mad and not feeling good. All their lives—after their daddy died in the wreck, after their home had burned, after their momma had been buried—Ray had been there for their family, especially Wendy. And Wendy after wanting a baby for so long—acted like she didn't even want to be there.

She sat back down and let Wendy's hand drop when Wendy's grip weakened.

Rosie didn't realize she drifted off to sleep too in the chair until Jack came back in. "How's she doing, Ray?" he said.

"I don't know. She looked like she was fine once the medicine went in, but—the way she's been wallowing around in the bed makes me think that's over with."

Rosie watched Jack lean over the bed. "Hey, Wendy. How are you making it?"

Wendy opened her eyes and blinked. "I just want to go home. Just let me go home," she whispered.

Rosie's eyes widened. *Things moving pretty far along for Wendy to be talking like that.*

"Can't do that, Wendy. Just hang on a little while longer. Can you feel anything in your legs?" Jack said, with a new note of gentleness in his voice.

Wendy shook her head no. "Just let me go back to sleep, Jack."

"Okay, Wendy. We'll leave you alone for a bit," Jack said.

Rosie saw Ray shake his head. "We'll just hang in here as long as we can." *He looks worried, too.*

"How are you holding up?" Rosie asked after Jack left out again.

Ray tilted his hand back and forth. "So-so," he confessed. "Hard to believe we're so close now."

Rosie smiled. "Oh, I know you're going to be such a good daddy and Wendy a good mama, too," she said, trying to reassure him—and herself.

Wendy jerked in the bed and moaned. The nurse came quickly from her station by the door. "Wendy? You awake?" she said.

Rosie saw Wendy open her eyes—she looked scared to death. "I thought with the epidural you wouldn't feel anything," she whispered.

The nurse came closer. "Let's see."

Wendy looked confused. Ray leaned over. "Baby, sit up some so they can take a look at the epidural. They don't much like how you're twitching around."

Wendy leaned forward and rested her forehead on her knees.

Suddenly she sat straight up. "Ow. Ow. Ray—oh my God. Ray!" she cried. Rosie saw a wild look in her eyes. "I think this is it!"

The nurse leaned back towards the door. "We're about to have a baby in here—somebody go get Dr. Rawson!"

Ray was standing up next to the bed holding one hand, and Rosie reached for the other as Jack came at a trot through the labor room door. "Okay, Wendy—let's see what we can do."

"You want her to start pushing?" Ray said.

Jack did a quick check. "Ready whenever she is. Push on a ten-count, Wendy."

Wendy squeezed her eyes shut as Jack counted down. "Good job, Wendy. Give me another just like it."

Wendy took a deep breath. "You're doing good, hon. Keep going," Ray said.

And keep going they did—for another hour.

With every push, Rosie saw Wendy get more and more

desperate-looking. "Why is it taking so long, Jack?" she asked finally. "What am I doing wrong?"

"You're not doing anything wrong, Wendy," Jack said, that note of gentleness back. "We may be in a hurry, but that doesn't mean the baby is. She'll get here, though. Even if she does take her own sweet time."

"I'm so tired. I just want to go to sleep," Wendy said, that wild look still in her eyes. Rosie couldn't imagine what she seemed so afraid of.

"God's with you, Wendy," Rosie said.

"Please, Jack—"

"Time for that later, Wendy," Jack said. "Push for me again."

She took another deep breath and pushed. Her eyes were leaking tears and strands of hair were stuck to her face with sweat. "I want my baby, Ray. I want my baby," she said through clenched teeth.

Ray went stock-still and stared down at her. "I want my baby," she repeated.

"Hang on, you're going to be okay!" Rosie said.

Rosie watched Ray's face go white. "Ray? What's happening? What's wrong?" she said.

He let go of the Wendy's hand and stared at her like he thought she was fixing to turn into a snake and bite him.

Jack looked up. "Ray? What's wrong with you?"

Ray backed away. "If you're going to fall out on us, at least back up some more so you don't crack your head open on the bed," Jack said. "That's one more problem I just don't need right now."

Rosie looked down at Jack. *Who do you think you are?*

Ray backed up some more, then turned and headed for the door.

Jack raised his voice. "Somebody go check on him and make sure he doesn't pass out in the hall! I've got my hands full right now!"

"Jack, what's wrong? What'd he see? What's going on?" Wendy said.

"I don't know, Wendy. Someone's going out to check on him. I need your help right now. Push for me."

She leaned back and closed her eyes. "I don't want to, Jack. Just leave me alone."

"Wendy, I can't let you do that. The baby's got to come out. Come on. I swear, two more good ones and we're done. I wouldn't lie to you about it. Come on."

Rosie knew he *was* lying—her doctor had told her the same thing every fifteen minutes through her labor with her first baby, where she pushed for four hours.

"I can't. I can't do this." Wendy whimpered. "Not without Ray—"

"Wendy, help me out here," Jack said, his voice hardening.

Wendy didn't answer. Rosie tried to sound encouraging and calm. "Come on, Wendy. You—"

"Stop it, all of you!" Wendy cried. "I can't!"

"Fine. We'll do it the hard way. Forceps," he said to the nurse. "Over there."

Wendy somehow sat up again. "No. We agreed we weren't going to do that. Don't you dare, Jack Rawson."

"Then push for me before she runs out of oxygen, Wendy!"

Wendy clenched her teeth again and pushed. "You've got my number all right, haven't you. Jack? Being away from here didn't change you a bit. I'm still not yours to boss around."

Jack looked up at her. "And I'm not yours either. You're not going to tell me what I'm going to do in my labor room. When you're in my hospital, I'm the boss of you. Now push again."

"You're not getting the satisfaction of watching me cry in here," Wendy said. "You men. So tough and talking and telling me how I'm going to do. I'm the one doing all the work. I'm the one that's been watching out for every single thing to make sure we got this far. All you're doing is standing there. What are we paying you for?"

Jack's eyes twinkled at Rosie from above the mask. "Well." He turned to look at his labor nurse. "If I knew making a momma mad worked so well getting this done, I'd have started doing it a long time ago," Jack said.

He turned back to Wendy and it was all business again. "Push again all the way to ten this time—we've about got it over with. Come on—you can do this."

Jack counted off as Wendy pushed. Rosie looked down at Jack. She heard Jack muttering under his breath. Then silence. Then wailing.

Wendy sat straight up. "Where is she? I want to hold my baby! Give me my baby, Jack! I want my baby!"

"Take a good look here at your new baby girl, Wendy," Jack said.

Rosie could see he was smiling as he held the baby up for Wendy to see. "You can't have her yet, though—we've got to get her cleaned up and you taken care of."

Rosie saw a headful of black hair before the nurses took the baby over to the warming bed. "Oh, baby. I'm so glad you're finally here. I can't wait to hold you, Judy Ray," she heard Wendy say, voice shaking. "Oh, baby."

Rosie sat down in the chair beside the labor table, feeling spent. Wendy lay back in the bed and stared at the ceiling. "Jack?"

"What?" Jack said as he worked.

"Where's Ray at?"

"I think he's still outside, Wendy."

Wendy kept looking up at the ceiling.

"I warned him it's a little different when it's your wife lying there. I was there for Seth, but when they cut Reba to get Sadie out, it was all I could do to stand up straight holding onto the bed, and I got out of there when they were stitching her up."

"Wendy, are you ready to take her?" the nurse said, turning towards the bed.

Rosie looked over. The nurse was holding the baby all wrapped up the hospital blanket. The little pink cap on her head covered all but a few little strands of hair sticking out. She saw Wendy smile at the little fist trying to squirm its way out of the wrap. "Yes ma'am—please let me hold her," Wendy said.

The nurse placed her in Wendy's arms. Rosie heard Jack say, "You pet on her for a minute, and when we get you stitched up, I'll go find Ray and get him in here, okay?"

Wendy nodded at Jack but wasn't looking at him. "Hey Judy. Hey, Judy Ray. It's Mama. Can you look at Mama?" she said in a sing-song voice, the same one she had used for all of Rosie's babies.

Rosie's heart swelled with pride. "You did it, Wendy. You did it!" she whispered. "Praise God."

Rosie startled when she heard Wendy moan like she was dying. She looked up at her sister. The haunted look was all over her face now as she stared at Judy Ray. Jack looked up. "Wendy?" he said.

Wendy didn't answer. Rosie saw her chest start heaving. Tears started running down Wendy's cheeks, and Rosie noticed that her legs were shaking under the sheets.

"Wendy?" Jack was now standing over her at the foot of the bed. "Tell me how you feel."

Rosie saw her shake her head.

"Ma'am, I'm going to have to ask you to leave," Jack said, hand moving up the wall to press the emergency button instead of the ordinary call button. "I think she's going into shock. I don't know why, though."

Rosie heart sank. *Dear God, no. Not after all she's been through.*

Wendy closed her eyes, and Rosie saw her shoulders slump. Rosie reached out to grab the baby before Wendy dropped her in her lap or worse, on the cold hard floor. She had one hand on the baby until the nurse got in to take the baby off of Wendy and put her in the bassinet.

"Don't do that," Rosie heard Wendy say. "Don't."

"But Wendy, we've got to make sure you're okay. She'll be right here," Rosie heard the nurse say as Rosie backed away.

She felt her own hot tears coming as she turned to go out. She heard Judy Ray let out a long wail that didn't end from being taken away from her mama, even as Rosie went out the door and closed it.

She saw Ray sitting on the floor beside the door. "You okay?" she said, leaning down to look at him.

Ray looked up at her with a strange look—like he was scared of her.

"I'm sorry I left you in there," he said.

"That's okay," Rosie said. "Between me and Jack and Wendy, we got her here. She's beautiful, Ray—lots and lots of black hair."

She saw Ray start to smile. He stood up unsteadily. "Excuse me," he said absently, staring at the door of the labor suite. "Can I go in?"

Rosie's mouth went dry. "N-not yet."

Another nurse came to the door, then another.

Ray looked at Rosie. "What's going on?"

"I don't know—"

"What—"

"I don't know. Jack said she was acting like she was going into shock—what from I don't know," Rosie managed to say.

Ray's eyes widened. "You mean—"

"I don't know, Ray. But I know who does know, and I'm going to pray right now for Wendy." She grabbed Ray's hand and bowed her head.

She didn't pray out loud because she knew Ray nor Wendy believed in praying. Their losses early in life and the long struggle of trying for a baby had left them both hardened to the things of God, while the opposite had been the case with herself. Sometimes Wendy would indulge Rosie and pretend, but she knew Ray had no use for hearing any of that. So she prayed, and as always, the fear passed in Rosie's spirit, replaced with peace. *If I have to help Ray raise Judy Ray on his own, I will and be glad to do it, God,* she prayed. *But I ask you now even as I stand here a sinner saved by grace that you'll save Wendy's life and bring her to you in your own time and way.*

She opened her eyes, and she looked over at Ray. Ray was staring at the labor room door, and Rosie didn't care for the look in his eyes at all. It reminded her of the look he had in his eyes when she first saw him after the storm, when he had gotten up the next day to grab a quick slurp of coffee to go back out to the firehouse—angry and cold and dead inside. She shivered.

Finally, finally Jack came out, sweaty and white in the face but smiling.

Ray took one stride up to him and grabbed his arm. "What's going on?"

"She's fine—now," Jack said. "Both her and the baby are fine. She just had something make her blood pressure drop all of a sudden."

Rosie saw Ray's face relax. "But she's fine."

Jack nodded.

"Can I go in now?" Ray said.

"No one kicked you out the first time," Jack said.

The labor room door opened, and the nurse came out pushing Judy Ray in the bassinet to the baby room. She stopped beside Ray, and Ray craned his neck to look at her. "Oh, my goodness," Rosie heard him say. "She's so tiny."

Suddenly the bundle let out a little wail. Ray kept staring as they moved on down the hall. Suddenly he turned. "I'm going to go check on Wendy. How was she?"

Rosie's mouth went dry. "I think scared," she said. "She looked scared."

Ray shook his head. "Didn't sound easy," he said.

"I don't think it was," Rosie answered.

Ray turned and went in. Rosie decided to give them a little time to themselves and headed down to the vending machines to get herself a Coke and a Snickers bar.

After they got Wendy settled into her regular room, Rosie and Ray sat with her while Lee went back out to call and check on their kids. Soon they wheeled the baby back in, and Wendy sat up to look at her in the bassinet.

"Ray, she's such a beautiful baby," Rosie said.

"Guess we know who she takes after then—and it ain't me," Ray said.

"Oh hush," Rosie said. "All baby girls are beautiful. That's the way God makes them."

"You can't tell who they take after this early," Wendy said from the bed. "Her eyes still have to change color and all that."

"That headful of black hair is all yours," Ray said.

"That got my attention, too," Rosie said. "Mama always told us we were both bald as eggs when we were born. Took forever for our hair to come in."

"But remember Uncle Joe always talking about Daddy and how he came out with a mess of black hair," Wendy said. "Maybe that's where it's from."

"Maybe," Ray said.

Rosie thought about their daddy swinging an axe to cut firewood and singing, always tunes like "Sixteen Tons" or "Joshua Fit The Battle."

Wendy seemed to be thinking the same. "I wish Mama and Daddy was here to see her," Wendy said.

Ray looked over at Rosie. She shook her head and put a finger to her lips. "We all do, Wendy," Rosie said, leaning over to touch her hand.

A knock on the door and a nurse came in to talk to Wendy about nursing. Ray reached up to rub the back of his neck. "I'm going to go find Lee," he said. "You girls go right on."

About halfway through their talk, Rosie heard heavy steps coming to the door at a pretty good clip. The door banged open, and Jack came walking in. She shook her head and pointed back out. He saw the lactation nurse and swung around, going back out. Rosie saw his face was red. She heard a thump as he leaned back on the wall of the hallway.

The nurse finished and walked out. Rosie caught a glimpse of him still standing out in the hall. The door wasn't shut when he came barging back in. He walked up to the side of Wendy's bed. Rosie backed up against the wall, feeling invisible. She noticed his face was redder.

"Wendy, I just found out Ray's blood type. It's AB negative," Jack said.

Rosie could still see out the door as nurses walked by. "Okay. I'll have to write that down somewhere, I guess. Why were you telling me that?" Wendy said.

Jack lowered his voice to a whisper. "Don't act stupid with me, Wendy!"

Rosie turned to look at Wendy. Wendy put her hand on her hip. "Then try to talk sense," she said.

Rosie's mouth fell open.

Jack leaned closer to Wendy until he was within inches of her face. Wendy didn't look away, matching him stare for stare as she looked up at him. "That bracelet on that baby says Judy's type O positive, Wendy," Jack said quietly. "You can't get a type O baby from a type A mama and a type AB daddy. Theoretically, maybe. But in twenty years, I've never seen it. The genotypes don't work that way."

Wendy stared at Jack. "What are you getting at?"

Rosie watched Jack suck in his breath. "I'm only going to ask you this one time, Wendy. Is there anyone else her daddy could be?"

Rosie caught her breath. *What in the Hell—*

She stopped the thought. Then she stood up. "Wendy, maybe I should leave so you two can talk," she said.

Jack turned around and looked at her like he'd just realized she was there. She saw his face get redder the longer he looked at her.

Wendy turned to look at her. "I don't think so, Rosie. I think you and me will stay right here with my baby."

Wendy turned to look back at Jack. "You can leave whenever you're ready, Jack."

"Not without an answer."

Wendy sat without moving, just looking at him. The silence stretched with no sound except Judy Ray's breathing. Rosie watched Wendy's eyes get brighter the longer she stared at him without blinking. *She's not arguing with him.*

"You're just going to look at me, Wendy?" Jack said.

Wendy still didn't move.

Jack leaned down and put his hand under her jaw. "You little—"

Wendy slapped his hand away. Rosie saw him make a fist behind his back, then relax it.

Jack turned to walk out, and Wendy finally spoke. "If you're ever tempted to bring this up again outside this room, I would hope you'd think twice about it before you did."

Jack turned back around to stare at Wendy. "It's none of your business, Jack," she said.

Jack cocked his head at her and slowly paced back towards her. "None of my—"

Then he shook his head. "Have it your way, Wendy, and be sure to find yourself another doctor."

He banged out the door of the room, but not before Rosie heard him call Wendy a name under his breath. *Ray would have shot him graveyard dead if he'd heard that.*

She heard Wendy kick her sheets off. "Is he gone?" Wendy said.

Rosie turned and saw Wendy standing next to the foot of Judy's bed. Her face was drained white, and the gown hung off her right shoulder. Wendy grabbed up one of the pillows they'd left out and put it up to her face with her right hand and started crying into it.

Rosie saw her wrap her other hand around her arm, and dig in her nails before she turned to face the wall.

She walked over to Wendy and kept her hand on her shoulder until her muffled screaming eased off. Rosie knew better than to try and stop her—she'd seen what Wendy did to Ray one time when he'd tried to stop her from scratching her arms.

Wendy let the pillow fall to the floor and bent over double, taking deep breaths with her hands on her knees, still bent over facing the wall. Rosie saw blood running down her leg onto the floor. "I'm sorry, Rosie. It was all I could do not to claw his eyes out while he was in here."

Rosie looked up above Wendy's head. *Lord, I'm going to need your help,* she prayed. "What I don't understand is why you didn't tell him he didn't know what he was talking about."

Wendy stood up straight, turned around, and looked at her. "You mean why did I lie there and let him talk to me like that without answering him?"

Rosie didn't remember seeing Wendy look so angry ever. "That's exactly what I mean."

Wendy looked down. "Because he likely does know what he's talking about, Rosie."

Rosie stared at Wendy. "Wendy—you don't mean—"

Wendy turned away again and stared at the wall. "Look at her, Rosie. Where have you seen those eyes, those lashes, that nose before? Not in our family—or Ray's either."

Rosie looked down, but Judy Ray was still asleep. "How could you possibly—who?"

Wendy started rubbing her hands up and down where she'd scratched her arms.

Rose sat down and stared at the floor. *Hurricane baby.*

She looked up. "Wendy—that boy."

Wendy didn't answer.

Rosie got up, walked across the room, and put her hand on her arm. "Wendy?"

Wendy cut her eyes over to her without turning her head.

"That boy—the one that stayed over in the storm," Rosie said.

Wendy rolled her eyes up and looked at the ceiling. "He's just a year younger than you, Rosie."

Rosie sat down in the chair. She stole a look at Judy Ray sleeping, and then looked back up at Wendy. "What went on between you two?"

Wendy tossed her head. "Doesn't she answer that question?"

Rosie rolled her eyes and looked toward the door. "Wendy—"

Wendy sighed. "I know."

Rosie could hear nurses shuffling up and down the hall and patient beepers sounding in the rooms. She looked back up at Wendy. "Why?"

Wendy turned her back, but not before Rosie saw her close her eyes and put her fist up to her mouth. "Because he was there," she said.

"Wendy!" Rosie gasped.

Wendy turned back to face her, and Rosie saw the tears shining in her eyes. "Do you think I like how that sounds? Why do you think I let Jack Rawson stand there and call me a whore every way he could without using the word?"

When Wendy spoke again, it was barely above a whisper. "And even that's not the right answer, Rosie. It doesn't really say what I mean, but I'm not smart enough to come up with a better set of words for it."

She moved and sat down on the edge of the bed. "All I know is I went to pieces during the storm, Rosie, and he was trying to hold me together—and then he came apart at the seams, too. Then—I decided if I was going to die anyway in that storm it didn't much matter what happened to me beforehand."

I am not hearing my sister tell me this. Never in my worst nightmares.

Wendy leaned over and put her elbows on her knees and her face in her hands. "I never wanted anyone to know. I'm sorry Jack didn't have enough sense not to come in here like that, and I'm sorry you were here to hear it."

Then her voice broke. "I guess I can just thank God it was you in here and not Ray."

"Wendy—you have to tell Ray," Rosie said.

Wendy looked up. "No."

"Wendy—you've got to," Rosie said. "He deserves to know."

Wendy tilted her head, eyes shining. "Then we can watch Ray go hunt him down?" she asked, voice steady. "I don't think he'd go easy on him. Then Ray goes to the pen for the rest of his life? Then you can watch me shoot myself in the head?" She shook her head. "Then who'll raise Judy Ray? You and Lee? Or Jack and Reba? No ma'am. I don't have to tell Ray."

"You can't keep living a lie, Wendy."

"Rosie, I have thought and thought and thought on this. Believe me, I've had a long time to think about it. And it's not fair for what I've done to mess up everyone else's life. I did it, and I'll do the paying for it. Not Ray. Not Judy Ray. No one else. Just me."

Right now if I could shake some sense into her I would, God. "I am not talking about paying for it, Wendy—I'm talking about being forgiven. That's what you should be looking for," Rosie said. "From Ray and from God. I don't know what Ray might do. But God forgives. And believe me, honey, you need forgiveness for this."

Wendy sat still. "So that's the way it's going to be?" she finally said. "I thought you didn't believe in judging."

"I'm not judging," Rosie said. "I'm just stating facts."

"What are you going to do if I don't tell him?" Wendy asked. "Tell him yourself?"

Rosie opened her mouth to say *yes*, then closed it. *He wouldn't believe me if I did. And then if I say I found out from Jack Rawson, I think I know what Ray would do to him, too.*

She sat back in her chair. "Wendy—" She stopped.

Lord, I don't know what else to say.

Suddenly Rosie heard a knock on the door. Wendy looked up. "Who is it?"

Rosie heard Ray's rumble. "It's me."

Wendy eased back onto her bed before she said, "Come on in."

Ray came up into the room. Wendy didn't speak.

"Wendy wanted to make sure you got to hold the baby some before she went back to sleep," Rosie managed to say.

Ray sat down next to the bed, and Rosie lifted Judy Ray out of the bassinet and handed her to Ray. "Here's your—daddy, Judy Ray."

Ray rocked back and forth in his chair. He looked at Wendy.

"Lay back and rest, and I'll get the nurses in to get her in just a minute."

Wendy looked up at him. "What time is it, Ray?"

Ray looked at the wall clock. "About 7:30. We got here around one in the morning I guess after you woke up screaming."

Rosie saw Wendy flinch, then watched her suck in her breath. *She looks like she wants to scream again.*

"Ray, it was awful—I dreamed that I held her—and she had curly blond hair and brown eyes just like yours," Wendy said in a rush.

Rosie saw she was tearing up. "The nurse looked at me and said she looked just like you." Then the tears started coming down for real. "And when I looked back down in the crib, she was gone. Just like that."

Ray looked at Wendy, blinking his eyes. "Wow. Some dream, wasn't it?"

Then he smiled. "Well, I guess since the part about her looking like me didn't come true, the other part won't either, now, will it?"

Rosie felt herself go weak inside.

Wendy sat up in the bed and started heaving sobs. Ray looked down at the baby and then back at Wendy. "Baby, I didn't say that to make you cry."

"You don't understand, Ray. Listen to me. I'm trying to tell you something—"

Ray stood up and moved the baby to the crook of one arm. He clicked the button for the nurse and then put his free arm around Wendy's shoulders. "I'm here. She's right here, too. See? And you're here. It's all right. It was just a dream. Shhh. Nothing but a dream," he said.

"I know," Wendy said. "I know," as she continued to sob.

I have to get out of here. Rosie got up and headed for the door.

"Rosie?" she heard Wendy cry. "Rosie!"

Once she got outside the door, she walked down the hall blindly to find Lee, letting her own tears fall. *Not my sister,* she thought. *Not my sister. The only kin I have left.*

But she knew deep down that if she kept this secret for her sister, she would be complicit in her sin. And she couldn't bear that.

She found Lee outside the hospital in the early morning light, walking around on the concrete with his hands in his pockets. She collapsed in his arms and sobbed out the entire sordid story—what she had noticed that didn't make sense during the storm, what had happened between Jack and Wendy in the hospital room, and what had happened between her and Wendy.

"What should I do, Lee?" she finally heard herself repeating over and over. "What should I do? I can't—I can't tell Ray. Because Wendy's right about what would happen. What can I do?"

Lee held onto her until she was too exhausted to talk any more. Calmly, he said, "What does the Scripture say about your sins?"

"That—that they will find you out?" Rosie said.

Lee nodded his head. "You don't have to do anything. Let God do what only he can do—work in their lives and draw them to him. He can use this circumstance for his glory; you know that. Just trust that he will. Just trust in him."

"But how do I—what do I say to her, now that I know?" Rosie said.

"Our job is to love," Lee said. "You told her the truth. It's up to her to act on it. Not on you to beat her over the head. Sounds like she's doing a number on herself in that department already."

Rosie nodded. "Go back inside with me—please?"

Lee nodded. "But first we're going to pray for discernment and wisdom."

Rosie laid her head on his shoulder as he prayed aloud, but she didn't hear a word he said above the drumbeat in her own heart. *Not my sister,* she thought again. *Not my sister. Not now.*

The Day Before a Year After

Cindi heard tires crunching up the gravel in the driveway as she sat in the living room of the house that she and Tommy shared with Marilee. She looked at the clock on the oven—three a.m.

She'd spent the time between midnight and now finishing cooking for Tommy. She'd put up homemade seafood gumbo from last week's leftovers in the deep freezer, put red beans and rice she'd let simmer all day in storage containers for the refrigerator freezer, and had fixed up some spicy jambalaya the way she knew he liked it at eat on for the rest of the week. She was tired—but knew she still had a long day ahead of her.

She willed herself to sit quietly. It didn't sound like Tommy's truck, but he could have gotten someone to drive him home—at first when he went out, he'd been able to drive himself back. But the past few times he'd been out this late, someone always drove him home. *I guess it's good someone has that much sense not to let him drive.*

She listened to the kitchen screen door slam shut, then Tommy's footsteps—slow and deliberate. *The more he drinks, the slower he walks. Tonight sounds like a special case.* She got up and flicked on the lights in the room.

"Cindi? That you?" Tommy said.

"Yes," she said.

"Girl, what you doing up so late?" he said as he squinted against the light.

"Boy, what you doing out so late? Do you plan to go to work tomorrow?"

"I can sleep it off."

"Oh, sure you can."

"I've got to go to bed. I'll talk to you in the morning," Tommy said, moving past her toward their bedroom.

Cindi stood up. "Maybe I won't be here in the morning."

He turned his head, his eyes narrowed. "You say that every night I try to go out and relax. It's getting old."

"What else is it going to take for you to see what you're doing to yourself? To us?"

Tommy closed his eyes. "I don't need you preaching at me. I don't need you telling me what to do. I'm a man, and I'll handle my own problems myself. That's what I'm trying to do."

"Tommy, you're not even making any sense."

"I can't take any more of this. I'm going to bed," Tommy said, starting to walk slowly to the hallway.

"I'm not done talking to you," Cindi said.

"What do you want me to say, Cindi?"

"I don't want you say anything. I want you to listen to me very carefully."

Cindi reached behind the chair she'd been sitting in and pulled out a suitcase. "I am leaving this house before the sun comes up, and I'm taking Marilee with me, and I'm not coming back until you prove you can put down the booze."

Tommy stared at her.

She continued. "I've got to pack Marilee's things before I wake her up."

"Where do you think you're going?" Tommy said.

"Back to Baton Rouge. Maybe a little while without me and our baby around will be enough for you to come to your senses. I don't know what else to do."

She heard the desperation creeping into her voice. "I don't

want to leave. I want to work this out. But until you want to also, I don't have a choice. I've cooked you a lot of food to tide you over until I can come back. I hope it's enough."

"You knew who I was before we moved in together," Tommy said.

"You weren't like this. You may have been a rough case then, but I could see who was underneath all of that," Cindi said. "That man is gone. You replaced him with a sorry sad-sack drunk, and I don't want to live this way anymore."

"You're going to leave me, and your job, and your family, and the only place you know how to be—"

"Yes, I am," she said, cutting him off. "Go to bed now if that's what you want to do. I might wake you up so Marilee can say goodbye to you. Or I might not. I haven't decided."

She saw his face change. "So you're going to blackmail me with our baby."

"What else can I do?" Cindi said. "You won't listen to me anymore. Maybe hearing goodbye from her will snap you back to your senses."

He took an unsteady step towards her. "There's someone else, isn't there?"

Oh my God. How drunk is he? Cindi stared at him, shocked. "You know better than that."

"Maybe I don't," Tommy said, still slurring his words. "Maybe you've been planning this for a long time. Maybe you were spending your time with someone else during the hurricane while I was out trying to help people."

Cindi's mouth fell open. "I was spending my time during the hurricane trying to keep body and soul together for all of us—me, Marilee, and Grand'Mere. I was trying to get food, and gas, and ice. I didn't have any time to take up with someone else."

"I don't believe you," he said, coming at her.

She backed away, step for step from him. But he backed her into the wall. "Tell me who it is, Cindi. Tell me."

"There isn't anyone else," Cindi said, her voice rising. "I don't want anyone else. I want you, the way you used to be."

"You'll learn a lesson about lying tonight, that's for sure," he said, pulling his hand back.

Cindi knew then how drunk he really was. She ducked under his arm and ran to Marilee's room, locking the bedroom door behind her. She started throwing Marilee's clothes into the Cinderella suitcase she kept under Marilee's bed.

She heard his steps coming down the hall, still slow and deliberate. She stopped dead still, waiting for him to start banging on the door.

But the steps went on by, back into their bedroom. She heard the creak of the bedsprings as he collapsed into the bed.

The beer slowed his reflexes, she knew; she'd seen him in fights before where he put down men twice his size. *If he'd really meant to hurt me, I wouldn't have been able to duck away.* She couldn't handle the idea that it might have been the opposite.

She started pulling Marilee's toys out of their drawers, trying to decide what to take and what to leave. She'd called her Grand'Mere earlier that day and told her the plan, and her Grand'Mere understood. "You can't win a battle with the bottle—the bottle wins all the time unless they're ready to give it up, and it's worse than any flesh-and-blood fille is to give up," her Grand'Mere said.

As she packed, she remembered the day she'd told her parents she was moving in with Tommy. She knew the Church was against a woman living with a man she wasn't married to, but she liked the idea that if it didn't work out, it'd be better to just be able to leave instead of do all the legal stuff to get out of it.

Her daddy threw a fit. "Don't think you're coming back here after it blows up in your face!" he'd said, right before he went out the door, slamming it behind him.

Her mama helped her pack. "Don't mind him," she said. "He doesn't know times are different now."

Cindi batted at her eyes with her hand.

She stopped packing once the suitcase was full; she wasn't taking everything because she hoped that someday soon they'd be coming back home. She looked at her watch. Five a.m.

She went into the bedroom she shared with Tommy and saw him sprawled out on his stomach in the bed, snoring. She set to getting her own suitcase ready, picking out her favorite outfits and her old Bible—she knew living with her grandmother meant going back to church, and she didn't dread the thought—maybe God would answer the prayers she offered there instead of here in the house at night when Tommy was late coming home.

Once she finished getting her own things, she shook Tommy by the shoulder. He rolled over on his back and batted her hand away. "Stop it," he growled.

"I guess you don't want to say goodbye to your little girl, then?" Cindi asked.

He sat bolt upright. "What?"

Cindi felt her dander come up. "You don't remember anything about coming in, do you?'

He stared at her. "So that wasn't a dream."

She shook her head.

"Hon, you don't have to go—"

"Yes, I do. When you're so blackout drunk you don't remember trying to punch your woman who's leaving, she doesn't have a choice," Cindi said.

His eyes were desperate. "But—"

She started to turn away. "I'm going to get Marilee. I'm going to tell her we're going to visit Grand'Mere for a while and that you're not going because you have to work."

She heard him get up out of bed and felt his hand on her shoulder. She turned back just a little, and next thing she knew his arms were around her. He touched his forehead to hers, then moved in for a kiss.

She smelled the sour Budweiser on his breath and recoiled. "No—"

"Please?" Tommy asked. "Please?"

She knocked his arms away. "I said no!"

She saw his eyes go black, and she backed away.

Then he seemed to come to himself. "I guess you can go get Marilee then," he mumbled where she could barely hear him.

She nodded, not trusting her voice at that point.

She walked into Marilee's room and turned on the light. "Marilee? Come on. Wake up, baby."

Marilee rolled over under the sheets and sat up. "Hi Mama."

Her blond hair was tousled, and her bright eyes were heavy with sleep. She rubbed them with her long-fingered hands.

Cindi took a deep breath. "Come on and get up. We're going on a trip to Grand'Mere's and need to tell Daddy bye."

"Why he can't go?" Marilee said.

"Daddy has to work, sugar," Cindi said. "Come on. You can go back to sleep in the car, and when you wake up, we'll get breakfast at Grand'Mere's."

"Okay!" Marilee got up. "Am I wearing my jammies?"

"I guess you can today," Cindi said, wanting out of the house as soon as they could leave.

Marilee slipped out of the bed and ran to the living area. "Daddy!" she called. "Dada!"

Cindi stepped out of her daughter's room and saw Tommy sitting in his favorite leather chair in front of the TV with a can Coke. "Hey!" he said. "You going to Grand'Mere's?"

"Uh-huh. Mama said you have to work."

"Yes ma'am. I wish I could go."

Cindi imagined that she could hear his voice tremble.

Marilee ran up to him and gave him a hug. He put his arms around her and squeezed tight. "Be good for your mama, Marilee," he said.

"I will. Bye-bye!" Marilee said.

"Bye-bye, princess," Tommy said.

He let go, and Marilee ran back to her mama. "Talk to you tonight?" Tommy said.

"We'll see," Cindi said.

"At least let me know you got there safe," Tommy said, his eyes pleading.

Cindi nodded. "I'll text you."

"Okay," he said. "Bye, hon."

"Bye," Cindi said.

She turned and started walking to the front door. Marilee grabbed her hand and held it. They went out the front door and got into Cindi's silver 1981 Chevy Malibu Tommy bought her for her twenty-fifth birthday—the best car she'd ever driven.

Cindi backed slowly down the driveway, and when she turned back to look out of the front windshield, she saw Tommy standing in the door.

A feeling washed through her—she felt like she was closing the door on one life and going to live in another. She didn't mean for this to be it forever—she told herself surely she'd go back. But she couldn't let her feelings get to her, not with this.

She started down the road and got to the main highway out of Metairie going to Baton Rouge. She drove I-10 and was glad to see she was beating the traffic by a good bit leaving so early—it wouldn't take long to get there.

She got to Kenner with her stomach growling, but she looked back and saw Marilee was asleep in her seat. So she decided to just stop quickly for gas and wait to eat at Grand'Mere's just as she planned. She pulled into a gas station and opened her wallet to get out her credit card.

But before she could pull it out, she saw the last family picture they took when Marilee turned two. She stared at it—Tommy in his suit, herself in her favorite red dress, and Marilee in a fluffy pink tulle dress she loved because it made her feel like a princess every time she wore it.

Cindi leaned forward at rested her forehead on the steering wheel, staring at nothing but remembering Tommy's voice as he begged her to kiss him goodbye—"Please?"

She let the tears come down without a sound—she didn't want to wake Marilee.

She had to do this—living with him was bringing up too many memoires of living with her daddy, who could wrap his mind around going to Mass every morning hung over as blue blazes. She learned that the Church didn't care when she'd gone to her last confession, not long after she met Tommy.

After the customary greetings, she had crossed herself.

"What is your confession, young lady?"

She told the priest about hiding her father's bourbon and other hard liquors under her bed one night before he came in from work so he wouldn't get drunk that night and maybe be more like his old self, when she was younger. She had lied about it when he started asking questions, and that was what she wanted to confess to.

"Stealing and bearing false witness goes against the Ten Commandments, my dear," the priest said after a long pause.

"I know, Father. But—"

"And they also command us to honor and respect our mother and father. This is a matter your mother and father need to handle between themselves without interference from you. You understand?'

"Yes, Father," she had said, her face getting hot from the blood rushing into it.

"You are to recite five Our Fathers, praying for your father earnestly that he not fall into temptation for drunkenness again. And you need to return the bottles to your mother so she can put them away. Yes?"

"Yes," she echoed. She decided that was enough confession for today and forever. "Lord Jesus, Son of God, have mercy on me, a sinner," she forced herself to say.

The priest dismissed her, reciting the words to end the confession.

She had stumbled out of the confessional and ran down the hallway to where her mother waited. She never said the Our Fathers, preferring to pray to a God who understood her sadness at growing up in a drunken house to one who told her to honor her father no matter how he acted.

She shuddered. She had done as the priest asked, though—she'd given the bottles to her mother when they got back home. Then her mother told her father what Cindi had done when he got back home that night.

I need to tell Tommy this, she realized. *I never have. Maybe he'll see what I'm so scared of. Maybe he'll change.*

She picked up her cell phone and slowly dialed Tommy's cell number. It went straight to voicemail.

He must be at work. I'll tell him tonight.

She started the car and kept driving her way to Baton Rouge. She turned the words over and over in her head: how to tell Tommy how her daddy had made her bend over with her hands on her knees and whipped her with a belt across her back for what seemed like hours, her screaming for him to stop and hearing her mother sob in the master bedroom but not say a word against what he was doing to their only daughter.

How he'd finally stopped once her voice was so given out she could no longer cry out and said, "Have you learned your lesson about lying now, Cindi?'

"Yes," she whimpered.

Another lick. "What did you say? I can't hear you."

"Yes," she said a little louder.

Another lick. "Would it hurt your jaws to say 'yes sir'?"

Another lick. "Have you learned your lesson about lying?" he repeated.

"Yes sir," she whimpered again, hating herself for how she sounded—weak and powerless against her father's rage.

She and Marilee got to Baton Rouge, and Marilee woke up when Cindi picked her up out of the car. "Are we there yet, mama?"

"Yes, little ma'am, we are," Cindi said.

Grand'Mere had a meal ready for them, all of Marilee's favorites: pancakes with beignet sugar, scrambled eggs, and bacon. Cindi went back to the bedroom she usually slept in and sank down into the comforter and slept, fatigued from the ride and the memory she had buried for so long.

When she woke up, it was suppertime, so Cindi knew Tommy would be home finally—at least she hoped he was. No matter what, she had to talk to him before going out and eating or she'd miss her chance to catch him at home if he was planning on going out again that night.

So she dialed. After a few rings, Tommy picked up. "Cindi? Is that you?" sounding like himself again.

"Yes, it is. You asked me to let you know we made it."

"I'm glad," Tommy said. "How's Marilee?"

"She's happy—she's been playing with Grand'Mere all day."

"How are you doing?" he said, a gentle note in his voice.

"Okay," she said. "But there's something I need to tell you—to explain why I'm doing this."

"Okay," Tommy said.

"Promise me you'll listen all the way through," Cindi said.

"Whatever you need, hon," he answered.

She took a deep breath and told him everything about that day so long ago—the confessional, her obedience to the priest, the whipping, the screaming, how she'd been sent to her room without food and stayed there for days, with her mother applying poultices and salves to the marks her father had left to draw out the bruising, to ease the pain, and to minimize the scars. How she cried that she couldn't sleep from the pain, couldn't eat, and couldn't shake the fact that her father loved the bottle more than her.

After she finished, Tommy was quiet. "How drunk was he?" Tommy finally said.

"That's the miserable part about it, Tommy—he wasn't." Cindi said.

"He was cold sober when he did all that to you?" Tommy said in disbelief.

"Uh-huh," Cindi said.

Cindi listened to Marilee's laughter from outside the bedroom door as Tommy seemed to be taking his time to think about what she had said.

"Why didn't you ever tell me this before?" Tommy said.

"Because I have tried to forget it, and—I've never had reason to. But now I do. Do you see what I'm so afraid of now?"

'That—I might one day do the same thing?"

"Uh-huh," she said, tears threatening again.

She heard Tommy suck in his breath.

"Do you really think that's the kind of man that I am? That I'd beat my Marilee within an inch of her life? Do you really think that about me?" Tommy shouted in her ear.

"No, but—"

"But what, Cindi? Your daddy somehow could convince himself he was a good Catholic man while doing the things he did to you? And you think I'm like that? What in the world—"

"No, I don't think that—yet." she said.

"All I'm doing is going out and having fun with my friends for a while. I'm providing for you and Marilee. I'm good to you. I would never hurt you or Marilee like that! Never!"

Cindi said, "Tommy—you took a swing at me *last night*. Do you not remember that?"

"I don't believe you—"

"You did!" Cindi cried. "You were so drunk you didn't know what you were doing! But you did! If I hadn't ducked away, you'd have given me a black eye! You're on your way downhill just like—"

"If you say one more time that I'm just like him—"

"You're not! You can still stop! He never did!" Cindi interrupted.

"All I'm hearing is that you think I'm some kind of animal. I can stop whenever I want to."

"So stop! And when you do, I'll come home."

"I don't know if I want you here if you think that way about me!" Tommy said.

A new fear stabbed at her. "You don't mean that. Tommy—"

"Good bye, Cindi," he said.

She heard the phone click.

She dropped her phone and threw herself back on the bed, crying. "That's not what I meant! That's not what I meant!" she whispered.

Lucky

Mike was driving down to Gulfport from Petal to take on a lot-clearing job from FEMA. He got a good start early that morning and listened to an old Michael W. Smith CD of praise-and-worship songs until he got down around Saucier, when he turned on the radio to check traffic.

He was startled to hear Jim Cantore broadcasting from Biloxi Beach telling of the devastation in that town from Category 4 winds. He pulled over on the side of the road and stared at the radio incredulously. After a minute or so, he realized he was hearing a replay. He gave his watch a good look and realized it was August 29, 2006.

He swore under his breath and turned the radio off. They'd be playing that stuff all day, he knew, and he didn't want to hear it again. Once had been enough.

He was heading to a house on Beach Boulevard and looked at the new GPS that FEMA gave him. Only a few miles left to go, but he knew to turn left onto US 90 and drive down about a mile to get to the home place he was going to.

After a bit, Mike pulled up to a lot in Gulfport and stopped at the edge of the drive. He saw a guy climb out of a big fancy RV hitched to a black Lexus SUV. "Are you from FEMA?" he said.

"Yes, sir," Mike said.

"That's hard to believe. FEMA has never come this quickly when I've called before," he said. "You must be a private contractor."

"That's a little fancy a word for me," Mike said. "I lease some equipment from them and take whatever call they send along."

"Do you have your own crew?"

"No sir—it's just me."

The guy squinted at Mike over the top of his reading glasses. "You're a little long in the tooth for this kind of work, aren't you? Well, take a look around and name me your price, I suppose."

They paced around, and Mike counted ten oak trees on the ground, some snapped off halfway and others completely uprooted. That was when Mike realized the guy stopped following him.

He turned and saw the guy looking off at the foundation of his gone-for-good house. "I retired here in June from forty years practicing law in Jackson and bought my dream home—all 6,000 square feet of it. I closed on my mortgage four months before the hurricane. We did some remodeling before we moved in—granite counter tops, rain showers, new air-conditioning. My flood coverage would have kicked in August 31. I sent my wife back to our home in Jackson and decided I'd stay to try to protect my investment, and now it's all gone." He looked at Mike. "Where do you live?"

"Slidell, sir."

"Did you have any damage to your home?"

"Some. The roof, mostly," Mike said.

The guy looked at Mike and spat on the ground. "Lucky."

Mike usually kept his trap shut talking to people about storm damage. But something in the man's tone of voice—

"Easy for you to say," Mike muttered as he turned away.

"What did you say?" the old man demanded.

"Easy for you to say," Mike shot back.

The old man narrowed his eyes.

"You got a home to go back to, it sounds like," Mike said.

"I'm living in my mama's front yard in a pop-up camper with my wife and three kids and have been for a year. We've got another six months before we can move back in. Insurance isn't paying because they're arguing the trees were already dead before the hurricane uprooted them onto my house. Five big oaks. I'm starting to think maybe I didn't come out of it so well after all."

The old man made a face at him. "Making plenty of money cleaning up for people like me, though, aren't you?" he said.

"Yeah—on people like you who can afford it," Mike said. "But I've got at least twenty checks for work I've done that I can't cash because the insurance and the *lawyers* are holding up all the money that goes to little guys like me. So save your breath telling me how *lucky* I am."

"I didn't ask for your opinion," the old man said.

"And I didn't ask for yours, either," Mike retorted. "Do you want me to clean up as much as I can today or not?"

"As long as you're here and you deem me *worthy*," the old man said.

Mike opened his mouth to deliver another insult, this time on the old man's parentage, when that word "worthy" sank into his mind. He closed his eyes, took a deep breath, and mumbled, "I'm sorry."

"What?" the old man said.

Mike raised his voice. "I'm sorry," he said.

The old man simply nodded. "I'll leave you to it," he said. He tromped off to his RV and climbed in, slamming the door behind him.

Mike got to work, cutting down what was left of the trees first, then going back and chopping the branches from the trunks and the roots off the uprooted stumps. He tried to keep his mind as blank as he could, but the old man's last word "worthy" kept rolling around in his mind.

He worked all morning and went to take a break for lunch when he just couldn't take it anymore. Dinah packed him one of the kids' old lunchboxes—a metal Charlie Brown one with a rusty latch on the lid. He opened it and stared at what she'd packed—a peanut butter sandwich, a banana, Doritos chips, and a thermos.

He opened the thermos first and lifted it to take a swing—and it was bone-dry. No water.

How in God's name am I supposed to eat a peanut butter sandwich without water? He slammed the thermos back into the box and flipped the lid shut.

He took out his wallet and counted some change. *Not enough to even go get a water bottle from the gas station.* He sat in the truck, spent from the morning's work and angry at his wife. *I guess she wants me to die of heatstroke out here.*

He shook his head violently.

No help for it, he realized. He choked down the banana and left the rest.

He went back to work.

Within a couple of hours, he began licking the sweat from his upper lip as he cut trees up for firewood. The water helped his mouth from being dry, but the salt just made him thirstier. He thought about asking the old man for a cup of cold water but shook off the notion in a grim determination to not admit he needed anything to the old man.

Around three o'clock, he seriously started to think about knocking off for a half-hour to conserve his energy. He'd gotten there at seven in the morning, so the hours would line up okay. But he decided against it so as to not give the old man an excuse to accuse him of goldbricking on the job.

Around four-thirty, Mike was sweating more than ever, and the ground was starting to swim before his eyes. *I'm going to finish this job at five and go home and drink all the water I can hold.* The hope of being able to quit soon spurred him on to finish up the last few trees remaining on the ground. He kept checking his watch, feeling time slow down with every look at his wrist.

His watch registered five-o-five, and he let the saw die and put it on the ground. His tongue was thick and sticking to the roof of his mouth. He surveyed the place; all the broken trees were down, and just about all the wood on the ground was where someone could easily haul it off in a trailer. He decided to tell the old man he was leaving and would be back in the morning to do just that.

He knocked on the old man's RV door. "Yes?" he heard him growl.

"I'm winding up for the day," Mike said.

The door opened, and Mike felt a welcome rush of cool air from inside. The old man stood in the doorway.

"I need you to come take a look at everything and decide if you want me to come back tomorrow and haul everything away on my trailer or if you want someone else to handle that, maybe sell it for you as firewood for the winter," Mike said.

The old man glared at Mike. "I think you and I have had enough of each other today, don't you?"

Mike licked his dry lips and didn't answer.

"How many trees did you cut down?" the old man demanded.

"Ten," Mike said. "And I cut branches off what was already on the ground."

"What will you do with it if I let you haul it off?" the old man said.

"Probably save it for firewood for myself," Mike said. "We have wood heaters throughout our house."

"Tell you what," the old man said. "I can either pay you going rate for trees which would come out to $5,000 total, or I can let you have as much of it as you can load for yourself as firewood. But not both. I'm not paying you for the privilege of harvesting firewood off my place. For all I know, you're going to sell it yourself."

Mike felt the anger rise in him again. He'd made the same deal with everyone else he'd worked for—he'd cut it up and they let him keep it. The old folks had a word for what the old man was trying to do to him, but he knew too many good Jewish people to use it, even in his head.

"I don't need money or firewood that bad, mister," Mike said. "Good night."

"Now look. I'm not trying to do you out of a reasonable payment," the old man said. "I just—"

"Never mind that," Mike said. "I've got a long drive tonight and need to get back to my family. Good night."

Mike turned on his heel and walked away. He heard the old man muttering under his breath, but he sounded pleased with himself, so Mike let it go. He got into his truck and made sure to trench his way across what was left of the beach grass on his way out.

He floored the accelerator going back up Highway 49, going as fast as was safe on the twisty-turny road. Before the hurricane, it sported the most billboards per square foot of any road in the nation. Now you didn't even see Richard Schwartz's "One Call—That's All" slogans; the winds snapped them off the poles and blew them around like so many playing cards.

It was nine by the time he got home to Petal, and he knew the kids would probably be asleep. *But Dinah should still be up.* He skidded down the driveway and tossed the gear shift into park.

She was; she met him at the door. "Goodness, you came in fast," she said. "Are you all right?"

"Can you get me some water, please?" he asked.

"Sure," Dinah said.

She brought him a plastic cup of tap water from the sink. He sat down at the small camper table, opened the lunchbox he'd carried, and started eating.

"You didn't eat today?" Dinah asked.

"Or drink," Mike said. "My thermos was empty when I opened it."

"Oh! I'm sorry!" she answered. "You didn't even stop to get something on the way home?"

He turned out his pockets, spilling change all over the floor. "With what?"

"You got another check you couldn't cash yet, didn't you?" her voice rising.

"I didn't get anything. I told him I didn't need his money," Mike said.

"Why on earth would you say that?"

"Because it's true. God took care of me out there when you didn't bother. So I figure he'll take care of us one way or another—since no one else seems to give a damn about us right now," Mike said.

Dinah recoiled. "What happened to you today?"

"Forget I said anything. I'll pack my own lunch from now on."

"Mike, tell me what is going on!"

"Nothing! Except day after day I'm out here trying to do for people who don't appreciate it and don't give me one more thought after I leave their property," Mike said. "Between the old man I helped today and the insurance holding out on us, we might be here another year. I don't know. I just know I'm tired and hungry and thirsty, and talking to you is keeping me from eating and drinking and getting to bed. So lay off, will you?"

He saw Dinah's eyes widen, and she swallowed whatever else she was about to say. She turned, snapped off the front light, and headed for their larger bed toward the back of the trailer.

He heard her pull back the bedcovers and climb into bed, and she switched off the lamplight beside the bed, leaving Mike in darkness.

Mike finished his food and stumbled towards the back to the other side of the bed. He felt his hands shaking and realized he might be closer to dehydration than he'd thought. He went back to the kitchenette to get another glass of water and sat down, his feet feeling like lead on the ends of his legs. His hands were still shaking, and he wondered how he'd ever been fool enough to stay out there so long without water.

He imagined himself passed out in the floor for Dinah to find in the morning. She wouldn't know what to do for him except try to lug him to the hospital. She'd have to call an ambulance, but it just might be too late for him.

Just like that boy back in Slidell.

He stood up and got one more half-cup and drank it. Then he stumbled to the back of the trailer where the bed was. He didn't even take off his work clothes, just climbed into bed, covered in sawdust and sand and grass clippings. He lay his head on his pillow with his eyes wide open.

He heard Dinah sniffling. He couldn't tell if she was crying or if her allergies were bothering her, and right that second, he didn't even wonder. He shifted in the bed to be closer to her, only for her to shift further toward the edge of the bed away from him. He caught a whiff of his own sweat and made a face. But it was too late for him to go over to his mama's and take a shower. So he just lay there in the dark, wide awake with anger surging in his blood.

God, if you're listening—I don't know what's wrong. Either I'm doing something wrong or I'm not listening to you or something. I need you to tell me I'm on the right track here. That I'm doing something that matters. That's all.

He heard Bracey sit up from his pallet. "Daddy?"

He sat up in the bed. "What do you need, son?"

"C'mere, please," Bracey said.

So Mike got up out of the bed and knelt down beside Bracey. "What?"

"When do we go home?"

"I don't know when we'll go home. First we have to fix the house, though."

He heard Bracey sniffling. "I want to sleep in a bed again."

"Here," Mike said. "You sleep here with your mama. I'll take a turn on the floor, okay?"

"Okay!" Bracey said. "Good night!"

"Good night," Mike echoed.

He heard Bracey roll over, and Dinah rolled over and sat up in the bed. "Now you be still and go back to sleep," she whispered.

"Okay, Mama."

Mike heard Dinah get up and settle herself on the floor on the opposite side of the bed.

The trailer went quiet again. Mike laid down on the flat pallet pillow.

God—Mike thought. But he fell asleep before he could even finish the thought.

Harvey Mason's Wedding

James looked around at everyone laughing and talking and wondered what he was doing there. *Why in God's name I told Harvey I'd do this is beyond me.*

He knew why he'd been asked—him and Harvey Mason grew up together in Kenner like brothers and walking up each other's heels ever since: pledging the same fraternity at LSU, winding up in the same major, and after some more twists and turns, James landing the high school counselor's job in Kenner just when Harvey moved out of it to Ridgeland, Mississippi.

But the last place he could think of wanting to be right now was at a Baptist church in Baton Rouge getting ready to be a groomsman for a wedding between his one of his best childhood friends and one of his own ex-girlfriends.

Can't decide if I'd rather get blasted or slit my wrists after I get away from here. Maybe a little of both.

The wedding director tugged at James's arm. James turned to look at her. "Yes, ma'am?"

"This is Leilani Tyler, Moira's younger sister. You'll be escorting her in just before the maid of honor comes to the altar. Leilani, this is James King. If you would both stand over here until I can get everyone else arranged," she said.

She walked off, leaving James staring at the cutest blond

curly-headed girl he'd seen in a long time. Her eyes were grey and were set wide above her elfin nose. "So you're the famous James King," she said, smiling at him.

"I guess—why famous?" he said.

"I've heard a lot about you."

"Hopefully what you heard was good."

"Most of it," she said as her smile grew even wider.

James found himself grinning in response. "Which parts do you believe?"

"Most of it," she said again. "Let's see—you and Harvey have been friends forever, you live in Kenner, you like to hunt and fish, you're a good cook, you drive a maroon Ford F-350, and you're thirty-three years old."

James looked at her. "Doesn't seem like there's much you don't know about me."

"Yes, there is," Leilani said. "Why aren't you married?"

Because I'm divorced? "I've been told I have a little too much don't-give-a-damn in me to suit most women," he said.

She didn't even blink. "What don't you give a care about?"

"What other people think about me, mostly."

"Independent."

"If you say so."

She shrugged. "Okay." She smiled again. "Now what can you tell me about me?"

Uh-oh. "Let's see, you're the baby of the family—it's Regina, Jon Mark, Moira, then you." He looked at her. "Right so far?"

She nodded.

"There's six years between you and Moira?" he said.

She nodded again.

"And you work in the arts somewhere in New Orleans."

"Close. I'm a buyer for an art gallery on Chartres Street."

"And I'm afraid that's all I know about you," James said.

"So I'll have lots to talk about to you?" she said.

"I guess so."

"Good. I like to talk. But I like to listen, too," she said.

"So can I ask you a question?" he said.

She nodded.

"How did you get your name?"

She grinned. "My parents went on a vacation to Hawai'i, and—I was born the next year," she said.

James took a second to put that together, and then felt his face get hot. "Ah," he managed to say through his embarrassment. *Say something else. Anything.* "So why aren't you married?" he blurted out.

She took his awkwardness in stride. "Because God hasn't sent the right one along," she said. "But that's okay. I can wait."

Moira walked up to them. "Nice to see you two getting acquainted," she said.

Leilani turned to her. "And that is quite enough from you tonight, Sis."

James looked at Moira. She tossed her jet-black hair over her shoulder with her hand. "James, don't mind Leilani—you'll get used to hearing her say exactly what's on her mind over the weekend, and don't bother getting mad about anything she says, either. She's too cute for you to stay that way."

She gave James a grin. *Sucker. You've been set up, James King.*

He looked at Leilani as Moira left. "So was that a hint to me or to your sister?" he said.

"To her," she said. "Ever since she got engaged, she's made it her next mission in life to get me married off."

She smiled again. "But don't let her scare you—I'm not the clinging-vine type and won't be hanging on to you all weekend."

I'm not sure I'd mind if you did. "What did she mean by you're too cute to stay mad at?"

She shrugged. "That was something Daddy always said about me."

Baby of the family. Likely spoiled rotten, too.

"I don't try to make people mad," she went on. "I just say what I really think instead of playing silly games with people." She blinked her grey eyes at him. "Why are you really not married, James?"

"Because my wife left me after the hurricane. She didn't want to live down in Louisiana anymore, and—she said I didn't seem to want to leave."

Her expression turned serious. "You didn't love her enough to follow her?"

"I tried it—and it didn't work out. By that point, I don't think I was much of a husband to her, anyway. We got divorced a year ago."

"I'm sorry," Leilani said. "That must have been hard."

He shrugged. "If all I lost was a woman who didn't want to stay with me, then I came out of the hurricane better than most other people did."

"Is that all you lost?"

James felt his face turn scarlet. He looked away toward the altar at the front of the church.

"I don't mean to get too personal. Moira says I must have some kind of emotional radar for people because I can read their expressions so well. You just look like you've gone through a lot of sadness in your life, and that's not something I was prepared to see the way Jon Mark and Moira talked about you. So it made me wonder."

"What did you expect to see?"

"Someone who didn't give a care about anything."

She smiled again. "So tell me something about you and Harvey and Jon Mark in college—something I can embarrass them with at a family get-together."

So James told her about what became known at the Fiji house as "the goalposts incident", leaving out the parts about Jon Mark and the cheerleader and why exactly he himself wound up being locked out of the place all night.

Leilani shook her head and laughed. "Bad, bad, bad boys, all of you." She gave him a long look. "I think talking to you might be more interesting than I expected."

James shook his head. "What?" she said.

"You are something else entire," James said.

She blinked. "What do you mean by that?"

"I think I know why you're not married."

"Why?"

"Because most men aren't used to women who talk like you do right off the bat. I imagine you've scared quite a few off."

"Do I scare you?" she queried.

"I don't scare very easy."

The wedding director was clapping her hands for everyone's attention. She pointed for the bridesmaids to move to their positions in the back of the church. Leilani turned and made a "bye-bye" motion to James with her hand before following the other girls off.

James walked back towards the other groomsmen wondering about Leilani Tyler. Jon Mark turned to him as he walked up. "I see you met my little sister."

James nodded.

"You'd better watch out, or you'll wind up sitting in her lap telling her your life story before the night's out," Jon Mark said. "She's never met a stranger."

"I can imagine worse places to spend my time than that," James said.

Jon Mark narrowed his eyes. "I don't think she's really your type, James."

"Why do you say that?"

"She's not a party girl like Moira was."

"It's been a while since I've done that kind of thing myself," James said. "I don't think you have much to worry about, Jon Mark."

Jon Mark laughed. "I've known you too long, James. Any brother of a pretty girl knows they have to worry about a guy like you. But Leilani can take care of herself—I've seen her do it. Just keep one thing in mind."

He leaned forward. "Leilani plays for keeps, or she doesn't play at all. Think about how ready you are to get involved again before you make any moves on her."

"I'll be sure to," James said, feeling his face turn red again.

The wedding director started clapping and pointing fingers again to get everyone where they needed to be. James stood and watched Moira, her mother, and the wedding director go back and forth about where everyone should stand.

After the bachelor party the night before, they'd gone bar hopping, and the alcohol kept him buzzing enough that nothing there got to him too much.

But Harvey's dad asked him to make a toast at the rehearsal dinner, and he'd just told him flat out he'd drive a long way back home the next day and wouldn't be staying for it. He knew it'd make people talk, but it'd also bug Moira that he wasn't there, and that was a trade-off he could live with.

The pianist started playing, and the ushers went to light the candles. Then two other couples paired up at the back of the church and walked up the aisle to where they'd stand.

James looked over at Leilani across the way. She winked an eye at him and said, "Smile!"

He looked down at his feet.

The wedding director gave him a gentle push towards Leilani, and he met her as she walked across from her side. He took her arm and looked down at her.

"I want you to know I'm going to be praying for you through all this tonight," she whispered as they started walking up to the center of the altar.

"I appreciate it," he whispered back.

She squeezed his arm with her hand before they separated to go to opposite sides.

James idly watched the rest of the proceedings while occasionally looking over at Leilani. All the girls whispered back and forth as Moira and her mother both tried to talk to the wedding director at the same time.

Harvey Sr. turned to look at James. "Heard you and Lori called it quits back last year."

"Yes sir," James said.

"Hate to hear that. You two looked good together." He grinned at James. "Looking to check out a replacement this weekend?"

James shook his head. "Too many of these girls know me too well already. They know better."

Harvey Sr. rolled his eyes. "You got that right. I never did get to say thank you for helping us clean up around the place when Harvey couldn't come after the storm. That was a big help."

"Don't mention it, Mr. Harvey. Glad I could give you a hand. How's business going?"

Harvey Sr. looked at the floor. "Slow. Don't know as we'll ever get back to where we were." He looked up. "Still going back to the hotel after this?"

"Yes sir."

Harvey Sr. nodded. "Get you some rest, then. Maybe you can convince that blonde looking at you to join you," he said with a grin.

James turned and caught Leilani's eye as she quickly turned back to the front. Harvey Sr. smothered a laugh. "You still got it, son. Never have quite figured out what it is, but you've got it."

James stared off looking above everyone's heads at the windows. *Slit my wrists. That sounds good. If I get blasted, I still wake up tomorrow.*

He ducked out in all the confusion at the end and drove back to the hotel in one bad mood and ready to sack out. *Thanks for nothing, Harvey Mason. Some kind of a friend you are.*

He got back to the hotel, shucked his suit coat and pants, and left them in the floor while he went to bed in his shirtsleeves.

Rolling over on top of Lori in the hotel bed. Don't know how she got there and don't care either. Heard her giggling like she always did when she was enjoying herself.

"Admit it, James. Don't you miss this at least a little bit?" she teased.

"A sight more than that," he said back as he buried his face in her neck and started to kiss his way down.

Screaming on the other side of the wall nearly made him jump out of his skin. "What was that?" Coming from behind the door in the wall. "Stay put," he told Lori.

Turned on the bedside light and climbed out of bed. Walked over and opened the door. Pitch black outside except for a flashlight. Marla standing there screaming over Jack's body on the ground. "Why did you have to die? Why? Why? Why?"

Lights out. Wind howling mixing with the screaming. Hear the roof start to give way as he crossed his arms over his head and hit the floor—

James woke up on his hands and knees in the floor sucking in air and staring at the dark. He'd dragged the covers half off the bed and was soaking wet with sweat.

"Jesus God," he whispered. "Please don't let me do that again."

He climbed up and sat on the edge of the bed, staring at the clock. One a.m. He shook his head and reached for the TV remote.

He felt himself drifting off to sleep and dropped the remote on the floor—

Walking up the aisle with Leilani again with the piano in the background. "Why aren't you married?" she said.

"Because God hasn't sent the right one along," he said.

He pulled off his wedding ring and put it in the palm of her hand. "Will you keep this for me until I need it again?"

"Sure," she said and smiled up at him.

He opened his eyes hearing the phone ringing for his wake-up call. The TV was tuned to The Today Show.

He sat up and winced. His neck was stiff from propping up to see the TV. *I'm not supposed to feel this bad and have been cold sober.*

He met up with the other guys outside the church, and they went to find Harvey and his dad. On their way, they met the bridesmaids going into the sanctuary for pictures.

All James saw of Leilani was her smile and the goosebumps on her tanned shoulders from the March wind blowing at the strapless dresses Moira put the girls in. But that was all it took.

He felt his face get hot. He hadn't let a girl make him so hot under the collar in a long time—and it scared him.

Moira was coming out of the reception hall when James saw her. She stopped and spoke to everyone until she got to James. "We missed you last night," she said.

"I headed back to the hotel," he said. "I didn't feel up to staying."

"You haven't been yourself this weekend, James. You're not upset about me marrying Harvey, are you?"

James looked at her in disbelief. "If I remember correctly, I'm the one who kicked you to the curb when I found out about you and Mike Johnson. I don't care *what* you do."

Moira's blue eyes narrowed. "That's a really sweet thing to say to me today, James King."

"I'm not the one who brought you and me up, Moira."

Moira stayed staring at him.

"To answer you, I'm glad for you and glad for Harvey. You two look happy together," James said.

She smiled a little. "And you actually mean it, too, don't you?"

He nodded. "You'd better get going," he said.

She tilted her head. "Leilani was looking for you last night. Be careful with her, James."

"I will, Moira," he heard himself say. She patted his cheek and walked off.

He stared at the ground as he walked along to catch up.

Like most weddings he'd been involved in, there was a lot of hurry-up-and-wait going on. After their pictures, James found the room where Harvey was waiting, looking out the window and twisting a pencil in his fingers.

"What's all this about, James?" he said suddenly.

"All what?"

"This," he said, tossing his right hand in the air. "Getting married. What's the point?"

James shrugged. "The girls care a lot about it."

"You and Lori went what—six years and then she left you?"

James nodded.

"Because of the hurricane, of all things," Harvey said. He looked at James. "You still love her?"

James looked at his feet. "No," he said. "But sometimes I sure do miss her."

Harvey snapped the pencil in half. "You're a lot of help," he said, staring back out the window.

"All right, then—here's my advice, Harvey. Believe me or don't—whatever. If you want out, now's the time to do it—not after. Been there. Done that. Trust me."

Harvey looked over at him and shook his head. "Can't give her up like that, James."

"Then stop asking questions and love her. That's not hard, is it?"

Harvey grinned. "You're right. Thanks, buddy."

James went weak in the knees. But he kept upright and reached out his hard to Harvey. They shook hands and heard the wedding director asking the groomsmen to go to their places. James punched Harvey lightly on the arm. "Last call."

"I'm in," Harvey said.

As usual, the wedding itself went quick. James walked up with Leilani on his arm and looked down at her before he let go. She winked at him and smiled.

After the ceremony, James found himself standing in the foyer of the church with Leilani still on his arm.

She looked up at him. "Are you staying for the reception?" she asked.

"For a little while," he said. "But then I'm heading out."

He was very aware of how close she was still standing to him. He made sure he kept his eyes on hers when he looked down at her. She smiled. "Would you like to walk me back that way and see if we can get first dibs on the strawberries?"

"Sure."

They made their way through the crowd and went to the dining hall. The Tylers put on some kind of spread, and people were already digging in.

Leilani headed for the tray of white chocolate strawberries and popped one in her mouth. "Mmmm," she said. "Just right." She looked up at him. "How about we just get a plate of these to start off with?"

James went and picked up a glass plate, and she filled it up with the fattest ones from both trays and headed to a back corner. "I know what's coming next—I'll be stuck in the receiving line with Mom and Dad and they'll all be gone by the time we're done."

James picked up one of the dark chocolate ones and held it up to her mouth. She bit off half, and he finished it up. "As well as you know Moira, you'll appreciate this," she said. "The biggest reason she wanted to get married in March was that the Hammond strawberries would be in season."

James laughed out loud. "That sounds about like her. Hope she's put at least that much thought into actually staying married to Harvey."

Leilani looked up at him. "You think she hasn't?"

"I'm not saying that," James said. "I just know now that my wife and I didn't talk enough about what being married was going to be all about—that's all." He fed her another strawberry before she could ask what he meant.

He looked off out the church doors and saw the reception line beginning to form. *Now or never.* "I would like to see you again soon—if that's all right with you?"

She smiled. "I wouldn't mind at all. If I gave you my cell number, do you think you can remember it until you get to where you can write it down?"

"I'll do my best," James said.

Her smile faded as she looked up at him. "I want to tell you something first," she said. "Jon Mark didn't think it was a very good idea to introduce us."

"Big brothers are like that, I hear." *Wonder what all he said.*

Suddenly she gave him a big grin. "Just so you know—I can't eat Mexican food. Everything else is okay."

"I'll keep that in mind."

She squeezed his hand. "I'm glad I met you this weekend."

"So am I," James said. "Call you soon."

She stepped back and waved bye-bye before she moved off into the crowd.

James walked out to his truck, wrote her number down on the back of one of his business cards, and stared at it for a long time before he cranked the truck and headed home.

Telling the Truth

Ray came in slowly from the front porch one April afternoon to see Wendy at the sink washing dishes. She turned to him. "So did you get Hal off all right?' she said.

"Yeah. We stood and talked for a minute before he went out to repair the deer stand."

"Good," Wendy said.

Ray sat down and stretched his leg out on the kitchen chair. "Wendy—he brought up something else we need to talk about."

"What?" she said.

"Getting him to draw up a will."

Ray saw Wendy's face go white. She dropped the plate she was holding, and it busted on the floor. *She was not ready to hear that.*

"You know he's right," Ray said. "Got to keep things from getting out of hand."

Wendy bent over and started picking up the pieces. "What does he want to do?"

"Just make sure you get everything less taxes and bills, Wendy. But we need to have you do one, too, so in case anything happens to both of us, Judy Ray'll be okay."

She tossed the broken plate away. "Okay. I guess we can get that together whenever he wants us to do it."

Ray sat back up straight. He didn't like being still, not when he could be up and around working. But his stroke a few months back had changed all that for him. He could still move, but not without pain—he used to try hiding it, but he knew Wendy could see it by the way her mouth would draw up with worry whenever he would get to pacing around the house.

But today he had something on his mind and didn't feel like sitting still. He needed to think on it for a while before telling Wendy, so he got up and headed for the kitchen door.

"What are you getting up to?" Wendy said.

The right answer came to him just in time. "I'm going outside and shoot for a little while," Ray said. "Want to come along?"

"I might after I finish up some work I've let slide in here," Wendy said. "What are you taking out?"

"The .44 Mag."

"I may just watch from the porch when I get through in here—that's more your play-pretty than it is mine."

Ray got up and walked back to the bedroom to get the weapon out of the dresser drawer and his targets and safety equipment out of the closet. He went outside through the kitchen backdoor and stepped slowly out a ways back of the house and tacked the target to the biggest tree the storm left in their backyard. He fitted his eye goggles and ear protection on his head as he paced off 30 yards back towards the house.

He turned and sighted in to the target, cocking his head since he was taught to shoot with his right hand but found out in the Guard that he was left-eye dominant. *Steady, breathe, fire.*

Scotty Reynolds from Red Zone?

Two shots in the chest.

He wouldn't dare. He knows Wendy'd laugh him out of the room.

Tommy Cade?

One shot in the midsection.

His wife'd race me to tear him limb from limb—and he knows it.

Jack?

Shot to the head.

He stripped off the goggles and walked over to look. The head shot ranged a little high this time.

He's not that stupid.

He tacked up a new target and paced back 15 yards.

Maxey?

Shot to the head again.

Just got divorced before the storm. Except that McKay dropped him a load of generators just like he did me. Too busy.

Smitty?

Two shots—left shoulder, right shoulder.

Not hardly. Wendy'd break him in half if he looked at her cross-eyed.

Judd McKay?

He walked back out to the target. Perfect shots at that range. Time to back it back up thirty five yards. New target.

Reloading.

"Don't know what to think," he whispered.

Shot to the heart again.

I've seen his wife—he's got his hands full already.

That stock guy we let go right after the storm—what was his name? Jimmy Wells.

Two to the stomach.

No. He went back to Kiln where he came from.

Roger Timms?

One in the neck.

His heart wouldn't hold out for that.

One of the Sims boys?

One to the right hip.

Wendy wouldn't go for that even if I was out of the picture.

Someone in the church group she's in?

One to left hip.

But she didn't go there until after Judy Ray was born.

Who was that guy that kept following her around back when she was in school? Robin Farrell?

One in the gut again.

Where'd he wind up anyway?

Reloading.

Lee?

He lowered the barrel. "God help you, Ray, you've lost your mind," he whispered.

He yanked off his earpiece and threw it at the tree. *If I keep thinking like this, I'll shoot myself in the head before I'm done.*

Ray looked down at the gun in his hands. *Don't know as I'd want him to die that quick anyway. Plus he'd never know who did it or why. Might be better to let him keep on going as a warning to keep his britches on next time.*

He turned the gun over in his hands and looked down the barrel. *Or maybe shoot my way up—knees, stomach, chest, and then between the eyes.*

He shook his head. *Have to use something other than this, or I'd blow his leg off before we could get started good. Maybe a nine-millimeter.*

He held the gun up and pointed at the target without firing—left, right, midsection, chest, between the eyes—

He stopped. *Got to either go ahead and shoot or convince him you will if he so much as looks sideways at her again.*

He remembered what his daddy always told the hunters that he ran off from the woods out back of their place every year. Someone would always say, "Well, if you shoot and kill me, you'll go to jail for it."

And his daddy would tell them, "Yeah, and you'll still be dead, too."

Ray squinted down the barrel and pointed back at the target. *Can't put a face on it. If I can't do that, what am I doing even wondering?*

"What are you thinking on so hard?"

He turned and just barely remembered to point the barrel to the sky as he saw Wendy walking up. "I saw you throw the earpiece and figured you missed a shot you should have made. Trying to figure out what you did wrong?" Wendy said.

"All I did was blink," Ray said. "Just did it at the wrong moment."

"How's it going?"

"A head shot went high at thirty yards. Everything else was on the money."

"I've about got dinner done if you're ready to come in."

He nodded. "Be in there in a minute."

He started to walk out to pull down the targets and clean up around the yard.

He finally let the thoughts in the back of his head come on out into the light. He knew there was another way things could have played out, but he couldn't for the life of him think about how *that* would have happened without someone winding up dead—either the one that did it if Wendy picked up a gun or Wendy herself for fighting back and getting her throat cut for her trouble.

Maybe she couldn't fight back.

He stopped walking and looked up toward the targets. He couldn't get the thought out of his head—someone coming up on her while everyone else was gone and she was alone outside—grabbing her from behind with a knife to her throat and forcing her to go inside to their bed and—

He lifted the gun again, firing shots to the crotch area over and over without stopping until the gun was clicking in his hand and he was covered in sweat.

If that's what happened that's what I'll do to whoever it was. I'll just shoot until I run out of bullets.

He looked out to the shredded target. *Take a long time to die that way. Maybe that's the best way.*

Suddenly he shook his head. *That doesn't make any sense, though. No way would she not tell me that.*

He went and stripped down what was left of the target. *Felt good to blow some holes in something at least.*

He remembered a guy in Saudi who'd decided he didn't care how he got home, so he'd aimed his sidearm at his foot and fired. Trouble was, the bullet ricocheted off some ordnance on the ground, and he got in it the head instead. Ray found him between the tanks before anyone else did.

He stood up and pulled off his safety glasses and slung them back towards the house.

"Never figured you for a coward, Ray Magnum, but that's what you are," he whispered. "A coward."

He pulled out his cell phone and dialed his sister Reba's number. "Reba. Ray. Can you do me a favor?"

He made arrangements for her to pick up Judy Ray from daycare.

He went back inside. "Wendy? I know I gave you a shock earlier. I'm sorry for springing the idea on you like that."

"I'm not mad. I'm okay," Wendy said. "You just startled me."

"Can you sit down for a minute?"

Wendy turned. "Okay. I'll go get Judy Ray from daycare, and we'll eat dinner later."

"I asked Reba to pick her up for you this afternoon."

"You didn't tell me that."

"I did it just now on my way back in from shooting."

He took a deep breath. "You and me need to talk, Wendy."

"About—what Hal said?"

"Sort of." He looked at her. "We need to talk about Judy Ray."

She sat down in the chair in front of him. "I thought we'd already worked out what we would do with the money for her," she said.

"That's not what I'm talking about, Wendy."

"Then tell me."

He looked down at the floor. "I may not be the sharpest tool in the shed, Wendy. But I'm not stupid, and neither are you. I shouldn't have to ask you this. But I do."

He looked up. No matter how hard he tried, he couldn't get his breath after seeing the look in her eyes. "What is it, Ray?" she said.

"Judy Ray isn't mine, is she, Wendy?"

Her face went white again. She didn't say anything in reply.

"The question's not supposed to be that hard to answer, Wendy," he said.

"If I get my hands on Jack Rawson, they'll have to give me the chair," she said.

"What does that mean?" he said.

She ignored him. "Why are you asking me this, Ray?"

"Because I'm tired of trying to deny what's staring me in the face every time I look at her, Wendy," Ray said. "You forget I was old enough to remember your daddy before he died. That's not who she looks like."

Wendy kept staring at the floor. "I wasn't positive until we were in the hospital with her when she was born," she said.

He felt all the blood drain out of his face and saw her image swim before his eyes. "What does that mean?" he said again.

"When they typed her blood, Ray. That's when I knew for sure."

"When they said we couldn't give her blood if she ever needed it."

Wendy nodded. Ray closed his eyes. *So now I know.*

"Who?' Ray said.

She put her face in her hands. "None of it matters except that you're the only daddy she's ever known. You've been good to her and good to me. Why do you want to get into all this now?"

"Because I've done something bad wrong somewhere down the line—"

"It was nothing you did, Ray!"

"Then what was it? Who was it?"

She dug her nails into the palms of her hands and didn't answer.

Ray pulled himself up out of the chair and leaned over to her. He put his hand under her chin and lifted up her face. "What do you want me to do, Wendy—start picking names out of the air?"

She knocked his hand away and ran back to the bedroom. She slammed the door behind her, and he heard her start tossing through the dresser for his .38. She'd chambered the first round by the time he got back to her from the kitchen. He opened the door, and Wendy stared at his reflection in the mirror. "Put the gun down, Wendy. You'll blow a hole in the wall if you drop it after you turn off the safety," he said.

"You're going to have to come make me," she said.

"Then you'll have to shoot me first."

She closed her eyes. "Judy needs one of us alive, Ray!"

"Then she needs you more than me! You're her mama!"

She started screaming then. "She needs a daddy, too! You're here! I'm here! I'm not anywhere else!"

"You mean wherever he is."

"I don't *know* where he is! I haven't seen him since—"

She stopped.

"Since when, Wendy?" Ray said.

"Since after Katrina," Wendy said.

"What?"

"You're going to make me say it out loud, aren't you?" Wendy said.

"It'd help," Ray said.

She looked down at the gun. "Judd McKay."

She looked back up to the mirror at him staring at her. "You're the one that thought it was so cute to call her a hurricane baby, Ray. You just didn't know how true it was."

She flicked the barrel of the gun towards the door. "Now, if you'll go back out there, I'll shoot myself in peace. If it'll make you feel any better, I'll walk out to the back instead."

He didn't move. "Fine, then," she said, putting the barrel of the .38 under her chin and closing her eyes.

He moved quicker than he thought he ever could and knocked the gun out of her hand. "You think I'm going to stand here and let you do that, Wendy?" he growled as he bent over to pick it up. As soon as he let go of her arm, she went after it again. He caught her by the shoulders, then wrapped his arms over hers and clamped them down as she wrestled to get away.

"You don't understand—let *go* of me, Ray! Let go!"

He lost his grip on her right arm and almost fell over onto her. "I hate to say it, Wendy," he said in her ear. "But you can't keep fighting me like this. Stop it."

"Why did I take so long to load the gun?" she whispered. She went limp and started crying.

He kicked the gun underneath the bed and sat down on the covers, holding onto her still.

He didn't know how long they sat there, but he didn't ease up on his grip until she stopped fighting for breath. "Wendy—I've got to ask you one more thing," he said.

"What?"

"Did he force you?"

She sucked in her breath. "You *want* me to lie, don't you?" she said. "No, he didn't, and you knew better than that before you asked it—it's not in him to do that." She took a deep breath. "You got anything else you want to ask me?"

His arms tightened around her. "I wondered out there what I'd do if I knew who it was," Ray said. "About as far as I'd let myself get in my mind was hunting him down, until today. Trouble was, I couldn't come up with anyone who fit the part."

He heard Wendy grinding her teeth. "I guess I deserve to hear that," she said.

"Not many men I know around here with the balls to take you on like that. Honest to God, when I thought about it that way, the only name I could come up with was Jack Rawson."

"Just go ahead and shoot me yourself if you're going to keep talking like that!" Wendy said as she tried to twist loose from him.

He held onto her as she fought his grip again. "Wendy, listen to me. Settle down and listen to me."

She stopped fighting. "Knowing it was McKay makes a lot of things make more sense," Ray said.

"Like what?"

"When he was out helping us after the storm, a lot of folks

wondered about him," Ray said. "He knew what do with that saw, but he scared Jason Sims when we were working in the woods. Sims said he didn't seem to care if he lived or died—and he was so careless that Sims flat refused to work next to him and told him to pull himself together before he killed somebody. McKay walked off cussing himself for about fifteen minutes, then settled down."

Ray shifted on the bed. "And how crazy he was to get out of here when I came back. I asked him how you were doing and he said okay. I asked him if you'd been crying and he said some." He stopped. "Was that when—"

"No," Wendy said. "Earlier."

He heard rain starting to spatter down on the roof as they sat.

"And I couldn't figure you wanting to work in the back, either," Ray said. "You did a good job for me and helped us out. But out of all the things I said you could do, you picked the books, and I knew you hated doing that. You didn't want to run into him again, did you?"

She shook her head.

"He scared you showing up on a Monday instead of a Friday the last time he was here, didn't he?"

"If this isn't hell on earth, I don't want to know what is," Wendy said. "Ray, I don't want to talk about this anymore."

"Why not?"

"Because I have spent a lot of time trying not to think about it anymore," she said. "I want to take a knife and cut the storm out of my mind. I get sick thinking about how scared I was. Every time they told on the radio how she was tracking up Highway 49, I got a little more scared, and when they found all those people dead in Harrison County before they even knew where all to look— "

"And when the storm came in I wasn't here—he was," Ray said.

She wrapped her fingers around her wrists and dug in deep.

Ray let go of her right arm and smoothed her hair back

behind her ear. "So when you would talk to me about quitting the firehouse because of Judy Ray, you really meant because of yourself. Why couldn't you say it that way, Wendy?"

"I don't know, Ray."

She started rocking back and forth, and he tightened his arms again. "Stop it. Please."

She went still.

"He had chances at you again after that, didn't he?" Ray said. "He still came through here every couple of weeks."

"I guess so, Ray—all I know is he seemed to bring orders in about twice a month on Fridays."

"And I sent you over there to where he was staying when he was here for his last run. I saw where he'd gotten over halfway through a bottle of bourbon before he'd gone to sleep. He told me he'd never done that before."

Wendy nodded her head.

"I was sitting there trying to get him to tell me what happened to him. No wonder he wouldn't look me in the eye."

He remembered how white the boy's face had been.

"You told him about Judy Ray then?" Ray said.

Wendy bent her head down. "I told him she was yours."

"But you didn't know that for sure."

"It didn't matter that I didn't know for sure, Ray."

"What'd he say?"

"He said if I wanted her to be yours, then she was. But if I wanted her to be his—she could be."

Ray finally unwrapped his arms from around her and put his hands on her shoulders instead. "And you came home and stayed with me."

"Yes, I did."

"Why?"

"Because I wanted to. Because I'd loved you for half my life, and I still did, and I still do now and God knows, Ray, I wish—"

She stopped.

"What?" Ray said as he rubbed her shoulders.

"I started to say I wish it'd never happened. But I guess if it didn't—we wouldn't have Judy Ray."

She looked up at his reflection. "So as much as I want to say that to you, Ray, I can't."

She put her hands up to her face as he kept working his hands on her shoulders.

"What do you want me to do, Ray?" she said. "Do you want me to leave?"

"No," he said. "I feel like maybe I finally just got you back."

Wendy groaned. "I tried, Ray. I've tried to treat you right. I thought I acted better than that."

He pulled her hair back and tangled his fingers up in it. "Rosie and Jack tried to tell me that how you were was just how girls get after first babies. But it went on too long for that, and now it's gone. You sound more like yourself, and you feel more like yourself." He moved his hands back to her shoulders. "You used to skitter like a colt whenever I laid a hand on you. I got used to it. But you're not doing it now."

He took a deep breath. "Did you ever get up with him about Judy Ray after that?"

"No." Wendy closed her eyes tight. "Ray, he told me the best thing for me to do was try to forget him, and he was right. What would I say to him if I did? No sense in that."

Rain started coming down harder outside.

"I don't know what else to say to you, Ray," Wendy said.

"If you don't want to tell me anything else, you don't have to. If you do, I'll listen."

He waited.

"Do you remember how I let you know she was on the way?" Wendy finally said.

"You wrapped up a bib with 'I Love My Daddy' on it and gave it to me on my birthday."

"Do you remember what you said to me?"

Ray stared off, trying to think. "That I'd been waiting for this my whole life." He looked down at her. "And I had."

Wendy looked down at her hands in her lap. "Every time I tried to get the nerve to tell you about her, I thought of that look on your face when you were so excited to find out."

She wrapped her arms around herself. "I couldn't take that away from you. If you decide tonight or tomorrow you hate me I'll understand. But please don't do that to her. It's not her fault. It's mine, and I'm sorry for that. I've been sorry for it for a long time."

She looked up at the mirror again. "Do you hate me?"

Ray felt his bad arm tingle like it was losing circulation at her words—this was worse than hearing the name. "Hate you?" Ray said. "Wendy, I love you. If I hated you for it, I wouldn't have gotten back here before you could shoot yourself. You think I didn't know what you were up to? I'd've taken my time."

He squeezed her shoulders. "Turn around and look at me."

She shut her eyes. "I can't."

"Please, Wendy."

She turned and sat cross-legged on the bed, still looking down. He put the tip of his finger under her chin and lifted it up. She let him but still kept her eyes closed.

"You said it wasn't anything I'd done."

She nodded.

"Did you mean that?"

She squeezed her eyes tight. "Ray, when those winds hit us, I started screaming, and Judd was just trying to get me to stop—"

She started rocking back and forth again. Ray took her by the shoulders and held on. "Wendy. Be still and listen to me." He took a deep breath and let it out.

"Before I could ask you about Judy Ray, I decided how I was going to deal with whatever answer you gave me. I knew whatever went on then wasn't going on now, and you've stayed with me through everything when it would have been easy to leave if that was what you wanted to do, and I decided that I didn't have the energy—or time— to worry anymore about it as long as I finally knew the truth."

She opened her eyes and stared up at him then. "Don't talk like that. Stop it. Stop talking. Don't say anything else," she said as she reached for him. He pulled her to him and held her as she cried one more time.

The Happiest Day

Tommy sat and stared out at the darkness of the den on what used to be one of the happiest days of his life—April 30, Marilee's birthday.

His eyes flicked across the desk drawer he'd put his pistol in when he'd last taken it out of the truck. *What am I going to do?* he thought. He rested his elbows on his knees and put his face in his hands.

Riiiing.

Who's calling here for me?

Riiiing.

He couldn't think of anyone he wanted to talk to right then.

He remembered staring at the empty bottle of bourbon as he drained his glass and let his phone ring without answering when he'd gone on his last binge at the bar a week ago—the first time he'd seriously resorted to the hard stuff.

Riiiing.

He thought about reaching for Cindi as she walked by. "C'mere, baby," he would say, and she would fold into his arms like she did for all their life together.

Riiiing.

He felt like a ray of ice was stabbing him in the gut. *I'll never be able to forget that. Never ever.*

Riiiing.

He reached for the desk drawer, pulled out his .38, and unloaded all but one of the bullets, tossing them onto the top of the desk.

Riiiing.

He saw Cindi's shoulders trembling after she turned her back on him as she walked out the door, holding Marilee's hand. He knew she was crying, but he couldn't make himself go to her to comfort her.

Riiiing.

He'd heard her tires screech as her little car fishtailed on its way out of the driveway the last time he saw her and Marilee.

Riiiing.

God, help me. I'm going to leave it in your hands.

He spun the cylinder and clicked it in. He put the barrel between his teeth, cocked it, and pulled the trigger.

Click.

Riiiing.

He remembered driving his boat in Metairie on his way to the Thompson place and seeing nothing dry on the whole street but a treehouse high up in an oak with a tricycle wedged in the branches. *Some little kid got that for Christmas some year. And now it's the only thing left.*

Riiiing.

He thought about watching the firetruck speedometer climbing faster than he could count as the driver sped on his way to the hospital with the Thompson baby.

Riiiing.

He heard Cindi's voice echoing in his head. "What else can I do!"

Cindi, I didn't know. Forgive me someday, please.

Riiiing.

Again he spun the cylinder, clicked it in, and bit down on the barrel with his eyes closed.

Click.

Riiiing.

He remembered how happy they'd been in their little trailer when they first started living together. He knew he'd never find another girl as sweet as she was. He teared up.

Riiiing.

He remembered driving through Metairie at three a.m. trying to get back to the house from his binge last August, gunning his truck to beat the red lights on his way back home, hoping she wouldn't be awake waiting for him to smell the stench of alcohol on him. But she was.

Riiiing.

He remembered reaching for her and her slapping his arms away. "Don't you dare touch me!"

Riiiing.

He saw Marilee's face when Cindi let him hug her good-bye before she left him.

Riiiing.

I can't go on like this, God.

Riiiing.

He squeezed his eyes shut. Again.

Click.

Wonder when my luck's going to run out.

Riiiing.

Whoever it is, they're not giving up. He reached for the phone on the desk. "Hello?"

He heard a sound like a little girl's tears. "Marilee?" he said.

"Hey Daddy. I told Mama I wanted to you tell good night. She dialed the number for me," she said in her weak little voice.

"Are you having a good time at Grand'Mere's?" Tommy managed to say.

"Yes sir. But I wish you would come to my birthday party," she said.

Guilt stabbed at him. "I know, honey. But I'll see you when your visit is over and you come back. Okay?"

"You promise?" Marilee said.

"I promise," Tommy said, swallowing the tears that threatened to break loose. "You sleep tight, you hear?"

"I will. I hope you sleep good, too, Daddy," Marilee said.

"I will, baby," Tommy said. "Is your mama where I can talk to her?"

"She's on the front porch with Grand'Mere. They talking."

"Well. I'll just let them talk then," Tommy said, his stomach sinking down. "I love you, princess."

"Love you, too. Good night."

"Good night." Tommy heard the phone thunk on the floor on her end. "Grand'Mere! I'm done!"

He hung up himself before she could say anything else. He stared at the receiver. Suddenly he thought of the guy he'd helped clear his place in Slidell who talked about God so confidently.

Tommy looked back down at the pistol in his hand. *Nobody around to clean up the mess I could make with this.* He laid it on the desk with the barrel pointing away from him. He sat back in the chair and looked up at the ceiling, listening to the sound of the house settling. *I'm going to sit here and drive myself crazy.*

He stared at the pistol for a long minute before he pulled his own cell phone off his belt and punched in the information line.

Ring.

He put the phone between his ear and shoulder and picked up his .38.

Ring.

He snapped the cylinder open and reloaded it.

Ring.

He got up and walked out to the truck and listened to it ring twice more as he locked the gun in his glove compartment. He waited through the menu of options and said he wanted Rich Nelson in Slidell, Louisiana.

He kept the number in his head long enough to dial it and waited. Three rings and Nelson answered the phone. "Hello?"

"Rich Nelson?'

"Yeah."

"This is Tommy Hebert. Roscoe Jackson's friend?'

He waited for Nelson to make the connection.

"Oh, yeah. I remember you. It's been a minute."

"Yes sir. Am I calling at a bad time?" Tommy said.

"Well, I just put all my little ones to bed. so I guess you could say you're just in time to talk before I go to bed myself. What's on your mind?"

Tommy closed his eyes. "Have you ever thought about killing yourself?"

Nelson let out a long breath. "No, I don't suppose I have. What's got you so bad?"

Tommy told him the whole story—the continued bouts with alcohol. The screaming matches. The morning Cindi walked out of his life and took Marilee with her. The fact that tonight was Marilee's birthday, and he hadn't even spoken to Cindi in forever. The fact that his little girl called him to tell him good night was the only reason he wasn't dead already.

"I don't have anything to live for but her and her mama," Tommy said. "But I don't know what to do. I feel like no matter what I do, it's going to blow up in my face, just like everything else in my life always has."

Nelson was silent.

"I just need someone to tell me what to do," Tommy said. "You're the only person that's ever talked sense to me since the hurricane—that made me feel like maybe there was a way out. I didn't listen very well before. But I'm listening now."

"Well, if you called me, I think you already know one thing you can do for your daughter and her mother even if you never see them again—and that's pray."

"I don't have the faith—"

"It doesn't take much faith," Nelson said. "How about you try right now? I'll stay on the phone with you as long as you need."

Tommy leaned over again and closed his eyes. His tongue felt thick. "I don't remember any prayers, Rich," he said. "It's been so long since I said them."

"Doesn't have to be fancy. Just talk like you're talking to your daddy," Nelson said.

Tommy stared at the floor, his eyes wide open. *What do I have to lose?*

"God, please be with Marilee. Help her to be good and go to sleep not worrying about me and her mom. Just let her rest," he whispered.

He felt himself choking up.

He stopped. He felt strange doing something like this. But he felt a pull to keep going, even if he didn't remember any of the prayers.

"Let her know I love her. Somehow, God, let her know that no matter where she goes in the world that there's someone who loves her and is praying for her." He took a deep breath.

"Keep her safe, God. Help her grow and be healthy. Protect her from all the germs kids get and keep her from sickness—"

Her lying in the isolette at the hospital when she'd been born flashed through his mind. He put his fists up by his head. "Thank you for letting her live," he said. "I don't know what you have in store for her in her life or mine or Cindi's. I don't know whether I can ever see her or not again. I'm leaving that in your hands."

He stopped. *I don't know what else to say.*

"Thank you for leading me to call Rich like this tonight, God," he whispered.

He paused again.

"Amen," Nelson said.

Suddenly Tommy felt his face burning, and hot tears started falling. He sobbed into the phone. "I'm sorry. I shouldn't have called and burdened you with my problems. I'm going to let you go."

"Okay," Nelson said. "Just hang in there, man. I'll pray for you."

Tommy clicked the phone off, and it was all he could do not to throw it in the woods.

He took a deep breath and stared out the windshield.

I wonder if I could—

He shook his head. *I don't need to do that. No use going over there and getting into a screaming match with Cindi.*

After he got back inside, he tossed the cell phone on his desk and walked towards the back. *May as well get to bed.*

When he got to the bedroom door, he stopped in the doorway with a hand on each side of the doorjamb, staring into the dark. He'd finally stopped sleeping the bedroom because it brought on dreams of Cindi walking out on in him, of Marilee dying in a hospital room from her asthma and him getting there too late to say good-bye, of the drunken brawls he'd started getting into at bars. But tonight his mind felt clear for the first time in a while, and he was exhausted. He walked over to the bed and slipped under the quilt Cindi's Grand'Mere had made for her when she was a child.

Tommy opened his eyes in the morning to see the sun streaming in the bedroom window. He checked his watch. Seven a.m. *At least I don't have anywhere to be today.*

After he showered and dressed, he walked out and sat on the front porch steps and stared out at the horizon.

He looked down at his feet. *I guess turkey season's just about over. Seems like I remember them saying it closed earlier this year.*

Tommy stood back up suddenly and walked out into the yard.

He spent the rest of the morning running the mower, trimmer, and edger wherever the yard needed it—the lawn in the front, the hedges out back, and the flowerbeds with spots of grass poking out here and there from under the layers of pine straw and bark. He kept his mind on what he was doing, making a mental list of what he would get to later, knowing that he was working to keep something tamped down inside.

He was pulling his saw down off the wall when he let out his breath. *I know I'm working out here to keep from walking back in there.*

He pulled the saw down and started back out the door. He noticed he didn't have the shakes he usually got from handling the saw. Maybe he was getting better?

He stopped in the doorway and looked out on the backyard. *God—are you trying to tell me something? Or am I just talking to myself again?*

Tommy remembered walking out of Marilee's hospital room

after her last asthma attack and trying to stay calm until he got to the small waiting room on the kids' floor. Cindi's mother was there waiting to hear from him how it went, and he couldn't get a single word out before he broke down completely.

Mrs. Delafosse told him later he kept telling her he was sorry—he was sorry she was sick and sorry that he couldn't help her and he didn't have the faith to even pray over her for healing.

He didn't remember actually saying any of that, but Mrs. Delafosse said one thing that stuck with him throughout the rest of the night— "God will forever hold you in his hands if you hold Jesus in your heart."

Tommy put down the saw and walked inside the house. He slowly walked back to the bedroom and got the Bible his mother gave him at his first Communion out of a box stuck way back in the closet. His mama put a bookmark in it when he left home after his daddy kicked him out.

His hands shook as he turned to the 139th Psalm. "If I say surely darkness will hide me, and the light be dark around me, not even dark is dark to you. Night will shine like the day," he whispered. "Where can I go from your spirit? Where can I go from your presence? If I ascend to heaven, you are there. If I sleep in hell, thou art there also. If I rise on the wings of the dawn, if I settle on the sea, even there your hand will guide me; your right hand will hold me fast."

He closed the Bible and lay back on the bed. "God, I'd love to believe you meant what you said right there," he said out loud, staring up at the ceiling. "Help me."

No answer.

He rolled over, picked up a pillow, and threw it across the room. "I knew it," he growled. "I'm too far gone even for you."

Tommy got up from the bed and started to walk back up front. He jumped as the phone rang. He picked it up before it rang again. "Hello?"

"Tommy! Glad I caught up with you!" Tony Showalter said. "We're over here at Daddy's and me and Mark were wondering if you'd like to come over and check out some DVD's. We've got *Terminator, Predator, Ocean's 11, Spiderman III*, all that kind of stuff. What do you think?"

Tommy started to say no but stopped.

"I know," Tony said, as if reading his mind. "But getting out and getting your mind off it some might help. No booze, either, just us hanging out and being friends together again, and you can cut out whenever you want and no hard feelings."

Tommy stared at the wall at a picture of him, Cindi, and Marilee around Marilee's second birthday.

"Last call," Tony said.

"I guess I'm in," Tommy said. "Be there after I get cleaned up. See you then. Thanks, Tony."

"Don't mention it. See you in a bit," Tony said and hung up.

No booze, huh.

The thirst was gone.

A Homecoming

Dinah looked back at all the kids in the van. "Everybody strapped in?"

"Yes, ma'am," they said all together.

"Everybody gone to the bathroom?"

"Yes, ma'am."

"All right. You all read your books."

"Yes, ma'am," Candi and Jamie said.

Bracey rubbed his eyes. *He'll be passed out before we hit the highway.* She looked over at the camper. Her brother Randy was supposed to come get it that afternoon after he came back from helping them in Slidell. Dinah hoped she'd gotten it as cleaned up as it was when she got in it so they wouldn't have to do it. *Lord, thank you again for family like these,* she prayed. *We couldn't have made it without them.*

She cranked the van and slowly pulled out of Mrs. Seabrook's driveway. The camper kept them from having to live with Mike's mama the past two years. Dinah liked Mrs. Seabrook, but she was glad she didn't live right under her feet while they worked on the house in Slidell.

Dinah punched up one of the praise CD's the kids picked out for the trip. She hummed along to "Awesome God" as she drove through Petal with the last of everything they'd needed to move back home.

As they got closer to Hattiesburg, Dinah looked back and saw Candi staring out the window. "Candi, what do you look forward to the most about moving back home?" Dinah said.

"Seeing everybody back at school," Candi said. "I've really missed my Girl Scout friends."

"Well, now, you know some of the kids in your school might be like us and moved off and are still gone," Dinah said.

"I know, Mama. I may can make some new friends I like just as much."

"Well, that sounds like a good idea," Dinah said. "Jamie, what are you looking forward to the most about moving back home?"

"Being back in our old room with the new paint and carpet and everything," Jamie said. "We'll have enough room to spread out all of our stuff and play and go up there where Bracey can't bother us."

Dinah smiled. The camper blessed them, but they did spend a lot of time trying to stay out of each other's way. At least the girls walked across the yard to go visit Mrs. Seabrook when cabin fever got the best of all of them.

"Mama, what do you look forward to about moving home?" Candi said.

"Cooking in my own kitchen with my own pots and pans and being able to cook whatever we want," Dinah said. "What do you all want to eat this week? I'll try to buy it at the grocery store if I can."

"Chocolate cake!" Jamie said.

"Mashed potatoes with gravy!" Candi said.

"Chicken and rice," Jamie added.

"And a real breakfast of pancakes and sausage and scrambled eggs tomorrow morning. Please, Mama?" Candi said.

"All that does sound good," Dinah said. "Bracey, what do you think you would like?"

"Turnip greens and cornbread!" he said, his voice cracking at the end.

"So that's what all I'll try to cook for supper tomorrow night," Dinah said.

"And Mama—please, please, please no macaroni and cheese for a long time," Candi said. "I'm wore out on that."

"And no peanut butter either," Jamie added.

Dinah shook her head. "I don't think you have to worry about any of that for a while. Mama got just as tired of it as y'all did."

Dinah made the run back and forth from Petal to Slidell so much over the past year she could just about do it in her sleep. It felt weird to know she wasn't going to have to come back on Sunday night this time. *But it sure does feel good.*

She turned off on the Slidell exit off I-59 and wound around to get to their neighborhood. Most of the houses stayed in the same families for a generation or so, and it really got to Dinah to see that some didn't look like they were going to be rebuilt.

At least we could go before it hit.

She'd argued with Mike about going—she didn't feel right moving back in on Mrs. Seabrook so soon after they'd cleared out for Dennis, who'd fizzled out to nothing before he hit land.

"Dinah, I am only going to say this one more time," Mike said. "I'm going to be at the hospital and not here to help you out. I want you and the kids someplace other than here. Drive on up to Jackson if you want—but you're not staying."

"All we're going to get is a bunch of rain and wind, just like we did with Andrew."

Mike shook his head. "We didn't have kids when we rode that one out here. I don't mind taking chances with my own life, but I'm not going to with Candi, and Jamie and Bracey. Besides, you and Mom always have a good visit when you go over—and she'll get a kick out of getting to love on them all."

"If it's so bad that we lose power and all, I'm not sure Petal's going to be much better," Dinah said back.

And we were both right. She looked back at the kids—Bracey passed out in his seat belt, Jamie drawing in her art book, and Candi reading one of her Laura Ingalls books.

Dinah smiled. The book Candi brought with her when they first went to Mrs. Seabrook's was *The Long Winter*—the one where Pa and Ma and Laura and her sisters lived through blizzards for seven months in Minnesota and almost starved to death. There wasn't anything that went wrong during the storm that didn't remind Candi of something in that book—whether it was eating peanut butter sandwiches for lunch and ham sandwiches for supper every day, to Dinah's brother, Randy, and Mike going out and spending the better part of a Saturday scrounging for gas in the generator.

"They're just like Cap Garland and Almanzo going after the wheat," Dinah heard Candi tell Jamie. "They rode horses to hunt and hunt to find it and paid extra for it because they had to have it or the whole town would starve. That's what Daddy and Uncle Randy are doing."

Except we weren't going to starve, just burn up from the heat. She had the dickens getting Bracey back used to wearing clothes again—he'd spent two weeks wearing nothing but his shorts so he'd be cool enough.

Dinah pulled into the driveway and was startled to see another five or six cars scattered around the yard. She pulled up into the garage next to Mike's new-to-him Nissan and got out to start unloading.

Mike met her at the back of the van with a big smile and a hug. "How was the trip?"

"Real good," Dinah said. "Who all's over here?"

Mike shook his head. "Dinah, you won't believe this. All our old Sunday School class got together and came out to help us unpack—and brought enough food to feed an army."

Dinah's mouth fell open. "You're kidding."

"No, I'm not," Mike said. "There's five women putting up things in your kitchen by that list you gave me, and me and Randy and the guys have all the furniture for the kids' rooms put together."

Candi popped out of the van. "You mean we're going to sleep in real beds tonight instead of the air mattresses?"

"Yes ma'am, I think you are," Mike said, smiling down at her.

"All right!" Candi yelled.

Dinah went to the kitchen only to be greeted with hugs and helloes from all her friends. "You folks sure have put yourselves out for us," Dinah said.

"Were you surprised?" Renee said with a grin.

"Surprised isn't the word—more like shocked."

"Well, since you weren't able to come for a while, we took plenty of time to plan," Janet said from the sink where she was washing glasses.

Dinah looked at the food spread out on the counter. "We're not going to be able to eat all this for lunch today," she said.

Mitzi batted her eyelashes at Dinah. "Oh, we brought more than just lunch for today, honey. Sara, show her what's in those other bags."

Sara grabbed Dinah's arm and pulled her over to the table. "We got you flour, and rice, and sugar, and tea—all that stuff you need to get started cooking again."

Dinah swallowed against the lump in her throat. "You folks shouldn't have spent all this money."

"Oh, we took up a collection from everybody and then me and Sara went to Sam's," Sandra said. "It wasn't a lick of trouble at all."

Thank you, God, for Christian friends, Dinah prayed as she sat down and stared at the food. "Me and Mike and the kids just thank you all so much," she said as she started crying. "I don't know what we'd have done without all y'all have done for us."

"And we were glad to do it," Janet said as she came over and hugged Dinah. "Now, I know how particular I am about where stuff goes, so we haven't put any of it up—we were waiting on you. So if we all get going, we'll soon be done."

"Let me grab the kids, and they can help, too," Dinah said.

By the time they finished, the men were coming in ready for lunch. Randy and Mike both looked about done in, but everyone was talking and laughing and having a good time.

Dinah helped Sandra unpack the paper plates and plastic silverware, and Ed and David lugged in a cooler of can Cokes from the garage. Mike stood at the door to the den, and Dinah knew he was wondering how to settle everyone down. She put two fingers to her mouth and whistled.

Everyone stopped talking and looked at her. She pointed to Mike. "I think he's ready to say the blessing."

Mike nodded and took a deep breath. "I want to thank you all for coming out and helping us today. We've gotten so much help from so many people I'm scared to start naming them because I'll leave someone out."

He grinned. "We even got help from people we'd never heard of—they heard about a need and put their time in to help our family with no thought of payback or anything like that."

He looked down, and Dinah saw him bite his lower lip. He looked back up with tears in his eyes. "I just want to say thank you to all my brothers and sisters—not just those kin by our blood but those we have by the blood of Jesus, wherever they are and whether we know their names or not. Let's pray."

Everyone bowed their heads.

"Lord, we thank you today for your grace and provision for us," Mike said. "And we ask—" He stopped.

Dinah glanced up at him and saw tears running down his face. "Thank you for loving us and providing these people who show your love—" He stopped again.

Then Robert began singing the old song about being glad to be part of the family of God.

Everyone joined in and sang until the end.

Dinah could feel everybody holding their breath in the quiet.

"Amen," Mike whispered.

The line began forming at the end of the table, and people joined in whenever they got ready. Mike was walking around shaking everyone's hand, and the kids were hugging everyone in sight. Randy walked over to Dinah. "Randy, I want to thank you for coming out to help us today," she said.

"No sweat," Randy said. "Needed to pay y'all back for helping us clean up and work on our place."

"Well, that was to pay you back for letting us stay there those three weeks we wound up spending with y'all," Dinah said.

"Oh, come on. We're family. It's always even when it's family. Isn't it, Mike?" Randy said.

"Yes sir, it is," Mike said.

Dinah watched him as he grinned and leaned over and caught Randy in a bear hug.

She went to collect up the kids and help them get their plates.

She settled them all into chairs with their food when Randy came over with his plate. "I'll sit with them—you go get you something to eat," Randy said.

Dinah did. She came back to the kids in time to hear Candi tell Randy about their new rooms. "Well, I'm glad you all have gotten back home and back settled in. It took a while, but everything looks so good even where you just cleaned instead of redid," Randy said.

"We just praise God that we have a house again, nice or not," Dinah said. "A lot of people we know are still arguing with the insurance people before they rebuild."

"How'd you get them to pay y'all?" Randy said.

"They haven't—not all of it," Dinah said. "We're still dickering over about $25,000."

"I thought it was all settled," Randy said. "How did you get all this done?"

"God provides, Randy," Dinah said. "Donation work, free materials, stuff provided at cost by members of our church—we've seen a lot of miracles happen to be where we are."

People were finishing up and starting to clean up the tables. Dinah and the women finished setting up the kitchen stuff and outfitting the bathrooms with everything they'd need.

They heard a whoop from upstairs, and Candi and Jamie came racing down the steps. "Hush up! What's got you all so excited?" Dinah said.

"We opened our closet doors and found new uniforms for school, Mama!" Candi said. "We've each got three to go with the ones we were able to clean up!"

Dinah looked over at Mitzi. "This was yours and Ed's doing, wasn't it?"

Mitzi smiled. "Well, we thought about a couple of ways to make getting them ready for school easier on you all, and Ed just said, well, I'm the headmaster and if I want to give them uniforms, I can give them uniforms. So he did." She turned serious. "They're not new—they're put together from the swap we held last fall, and I want them to try them on before I leave to make sure they do fit."

Dinah just threw up her hands and sat down in a chair. "I don't know what to say to you all. Thank you is just not enough anymore."

"Yes, it is," Sandra said, hugging her. "We've seen how Mike has done and done and done for people all up and down the Coast, taking pay when FEMA told him to and doing for free on his own time when he wanted to. Y'all got the worse end of the hurricane than any of us, and we've been determined to help."

Dinah saw Mike standing over in the corner of the room, his lip trembling. She saw Ed come up to him and put his hand on his shoulder.

Next thing she knew Mike turned to Ed and started sobbing—an outpouring of tears that startled Dinah and everyone else in the room. Dinah could count on one hand the number of times she'd seen Mike cry like this—once when his daddy died and again after each of their children were born. She ran across the room and put her arm across his shoulder and walked him towards their bedroom. She heard a concerned murmur run through the crowd as the ladies started moving and packing up what food was left and the men filed outside to bring in the last few boxes.

She pulled the bedroom door shut behind them and turned

and put both arms around Mike as he continued crying. "It's okay," she said. "Whatever it is, it's okay."

"How can we ever pay this back, Dinah?" he said hoarsely. "The food, the work, even the kids' clothes—they did so much for us. We'll never make it square—"

"We don't have to," Dinah said. "Just take it as a blessing, Mike. A blessing from the Lord."

"But these people— "

"Shhh. It's okay. They saw what a blessing you've been to others and wanted to help us out, too."

"But I don't—I can't—" and then Mike lost the words again in the sobs.

"You just stay back here until you can pull yourself together, okay? It's all right. Everyone understands," Dinah said.

"But Dinah—"

"Shhh. No more talk. I'll come back and check on you in a bit. It's been a long day and a long couple of years," Dinah said.

He sat down on the bed with his face in his hands. She eased the door open and shut it behind her quickly.

Everyone mumbled goodbyes on their way out the doors—the ladies all hugged Dinah's neck, and Dinah promised everyone that they'd be in church the next Sunday. Mike emerged just before Robert and Janet left, and Robert went up to him and shook his hand, clasping both his hands around Mike's, then patting him on the arm before moving outside, misty-eyed himself.

The girls were still bubbling over at how happy they were to be sleeping in their beds instead of the bunks they'd been on for months on end. Bracey just sat in the den, looking around with a big grin on his face. "It's good to be home," he said before heading back into the kitchen to get more to eat.

After the kids finally settled down that night, Dinah came back out to the den to see Mike sitting up in his recliner with a haunted look on his face.

"Dinah," he said, then stopped.

"What's going on with you, Mike? You're not yourself."

"I've got to tell you something," Mike said. "And ask you to forgive me."

"For what, Mike?"

"For living a lie. In front of you, and everyone else, apparently."

Dinah shook her head. "I don't understand. What have you lied about?"

"The real reason I started working for FEMA," Mike said. "It wasn't near as pretty as I made it out to be."

"What do you mean, Mike?"

She listened as he talked haltingly—about the guy who'd died in his ER. His talk with JD and his anger at Hatchett that made him say he was going to work for FEMA. "It wasn't what I made it out to be, Dinah. I just said it for something to say to him when he asked me where I thought I was going. It just—popped out. I didn't think about it; I didn't pray about it; I just—said it. Then I thought it might be a good idea—where I could help more people."

Dinah caught her breath at the harshness in his voice.

"I was mad at God. For letting that boy die in my care. For letting everything happen the way it did. Where so many people lost so much, and I started feeling sorry for myself the longer the fight with the insurance dragged on. I kept sinking deeper into deeper into being mad and feeling like God forgot all of us during the storm—everyone I ran into had a something to cry about. I would try to talk to them about moving on—but I didn't believe half of what I said anymore myself."

He started cracking his knuckles—something told her he wanted to smash his fist into one of the brand-new walls. "And hearing Sandra talk about me like I was some kind of saint—like I did all I did because I loved God so much—and seeing how people who *really* loved God treated us—now I don't know what to do. I want to go and beg them all for forgiveness. But I feel dirty for even thinking they would—"

"Mike," Dinah said.

He stared at the floor. "If I were half the man they thought I was—"

"*Mike,*" she said again.

He looked up. "What?"

"Stop talking and listen to me for a second," Dinah said.

"What can you say, Dinah? How can I—"

"*Stop* it, I said," Dinah repeated.

Mike swallowed whatever he planned to say next and was quiet.

Lord, let me get this right, Dinah prayed. "You're forgetting something."

"What?"

"All this talk about paying back and being square with people—you can't. There's nothing you can say and nothing you can do to be square with anyone. You just have to weather the trials and enjoy the blessings."

"But I—"

"But nothing. I'm just sorry you've been carrying all this all alone. Why didn't you just explain it to me earlier?"

Mike hung his head. "I didn't want anyone to know."

"Well, now I do," Dinah said. "And I'm not going to tell you that you can't tell anyone else. But I think you have more work to do on yourself before you'll be peaceful about this."

Mike nodded slowly. "Can you pray with me, Dinah?"

She nodded. "But I can't say the words for you."

"I know," Mike said.

He bowed his head, and tears began to run down his face again as he begged God to forgive his lies and his pride.

After he was finished, he stood up and gave her a small smile. He embraced her again, gently this time. "I think I'm ready to go to sleep."

"I'll be there in a bit," she said back.

Dinah walked around the house just looking at everything. *Thank you, Lord for friends and family and people we didn't even know and won't ever see again,* she prayed. *It was all your doing, and I bless you and thank you for it. Thank you for giving me my husband back after all he's been through. Help him to heal—and to experience your love tonight in a way he hasn't before. Amen.*

A Beginning

Leilani was just pulling the cornbread out of the oven in early September when James came in from fishing with Harvey all afternoon. "Mmmm, cheri," he said. "Something in here smells good."

Leilani smiled. "I'll bet it does. Go ahead and have a seat at the table; I'll bring you a plate out."

James went into the dining room, and Leilani heard him whistle. "Wedding crystal! What is this?"

"Well, you just wait," Leilani called out from the kitchen. She opened the oven just long enough to check on the bread pudding to see if it was browning nicely. It looked done, so she cut off the oven and pulled it out with a potholder in each hand. She set it on the counter and poured the creamy sweet sauce over it to sit and cool down.

She spooned a generous helping of white rice and crawfish etouffee on his plate and cut a triangle of cornbread out of the pan, then walked into the dining room, a plate in each hand. She placed James' plate in front of him on the table and poured him a non-alcoholic Pimm's Cup from a pitcher she'd kept in the refrigerator all day. His eyes widened. "My God, Leilani. What are you buttering me up for?"

She smothered a giggle at the look on his face. "Let's go ahead and eat while it's hot," she said.

"You don't have to tell me twice. Thanks be to God," he said, his version of a meal blessing.

Leilani fixed herself a smaller plate, but James still finished before she did. He refilled his glass and sat back in the chair. "Whoa," he said.

She got up from the table. "Hold on," she said. "We still have dessert!"

She went into the kitchen and scooped the bread pudding into dessert glasses and poured more sauce over it. She then carried the warm confection back to James and handed it to him with a spoon. "Oh, boy," James said. "If I'd known this was coming, I wouldn't've finished off that plate. You know how much I love this stuff."

"I sure do. Oh. Wait, I almost forgot. Something came in the mail for you today."

James looked like he hadn't even heard her. So she went out and got the envelope she made up and brought it to him. "Oh, God," he said. "Is this the electric bill or something? Is it bad?"

Leilani just smiled. James gave her a sidelong look. "You'd better not ever play poker for money," he said. "You have no game face."

She giggled as he opened it and pulled out the sonogram picture. He let the envelope fall to the floor. "Honey. Is this you?" he said, staring at the grainy black-and-white image.

She nodded, too overcome at his shock to speak.

"We're going to have a baby?" he said.

She nodded again.

James jumped up from his chair, leaving his dessert half-eaten. He grabbed her up in a full-body hug and lifted her a few inches off the floor and spun around with her in his arms. "Oh, cheri. I love you, and the baby, and this house and the world and everyone in it. How far along are you?"

"They say twelve weeks," she said. "You know I've never been on-the-nose regular so it took me a while to realize I was skipping periods. I went to the doctor yesterday."

James closed his eyes. "I must be dreaming this. I thought I'd never be a daddy. Lori said—"

He shut his mouth. Leilani saw the tears in his eyes.

"I'm not dreaming. This is happening, and I'm going to enjoy every minute of it with you from now to eternity."

He put his hand on Leilani's belly. "Welcome to the world, Baby King. I can't wait to hold you," he said, looking down.

Leilani put her hand over his.

Then she pulled it back and said, "I guess I need to go clean up the kitchen some and put everything away."

"No, cheri. Let me do that. You go and put your feet up in the den," James said.

She looked at him. He said, "You think I didn't notice you didn't eat much? Is your stomach already bothering you?"

"A little," she said.

"Well, if you're on those vitamins, they'll probably mess you up for a bit, I hear," he said, ushering her into the den. She sat back into the couch.

"Thank you," she said. "I have been on my feet a lot stirring and such this afternoon."

"Right," he said. "You relax."

She closed her eyes. "Okay."

She listened with her eyes closed to him clearing off the table, then putting leftovers in the fridge. She even heard him handwashing the good china and crystal instead of putting it in the dishwasher. She smiled to herself. *I really got him this time. He was so surprised.*

She heard him putting away the dishes, then she heard him sigh a very heavy sigh. After a long moment, he stuck his head in the den with a hand on the doorjamb. "I think I'm going to go out and walk off some of this bread pudding," he said, his voice unsteady.

She opened her eyes and sat up. He looked like he was ready to cry. "It's already dark out," she said.

"I know," he said. "I'll take a flashlight. Just want to walk outside for a while. I won't take long."

"Okay," she said. "See you in a bit."

James crossed the den and grabbed the small flashlight they kept by the table lamp for blackouts. He walked out without saying another word.

As soon as she heard the door shut, she stood up to make sure the kitchen was clean. She felt her stomach lurch, and she bolted for the door of the half-bath and vomited up her dinner.

Leilani leaned over the sink with both hands on the counter. *What is wrong with him all of a sudden?* she thought. She was envisioning a quiet night of talking about the nursery and when to call her parents and tell them about the baby. Looking forward to going to bed early and snuggling into James' chest and going to sleep with his arms around her.

She glanced at her watch, his wedding present to her back a year-and-a half-ago. It was already seven-thirty—they usually watched movies on TV together at night, whatever they could find on cable. "What happened?" she whispered to herself.

She went back into the den—she was scared to wash her mouth out or brush her teeth because she didn't want to kick off the nausea again. She hated throwing up; she wanted to go to bed and lie there not moving so she wouldn't get sick again. But she wanted to stay up until he came home or, God forbid, something happened and he needed her to be by the phone.

She walked back into the den and spotted his cell phone, which was lying right where he always put it, next to where the flashlight usually rested. *He must have forgotten it,* knowing that he'd never do any such thing.

She sat down and wrapped her arms around herself. He acted happy about the news, but maybe once he thought about it, he regretted having agreed to start trying for a baby. He started to say something about his ex-wife but stopped. *What was he going to say? Why would he be thinking about her anyway?*

They never talked much about Lori—she knew James didn't even try to stay in touch with her or her family, and she seemed to return the favor. All she knew about their divorce was that he gave up Kenner for her, and since she spent all her spare time at her mother's house since it was close, he stayed gone more than he should have. She didn't think she'd ever even seen a picture of her—unless one hid in his wallet?

The longer she sat and thought, the more worried she got. When she checked her watch again, it was eight o'clock. There wasn't that much of a neighborhood to walk around in—it's not like they lived in a subdivision, anyway; Kenner wasn't that neatly planned out where they lived. Besides the new neighbor and his wife, not many people were around the small lake they lived on.

By eight-thirty, she was pacing the floor—mapping out a pattern through the den, kitchen, master bedroom, and back again across her own tracks.

At eight forty-five, she went out the front door and looked over at the neighbor's house. She saw a light in the garage and felt the anger rise up in her. *If he's been sitting over there talking to that guy all this time, I'm going to be mad.* The couple seemed okay, but she hoped for a night talking of the future with her husband, not one where she was worried sick about him with him not twenty feet away shooting the bull someone he barely knew.

At nine, she walked over to the light. The guy was tinkering around with an old Camaro; he was covered in grease and smut wearing overalls and a t-shirt. "Hey Miz King," he said.

"Have you seen James?" she said, hating herself for how needy she sounded, like a child.

"No, ma'am. I haven't."

She searched his face for any sign that he might be lying—shifty eyes, tongue licking his lips. He looked concerned, but not overly so— "What's got you looking for him?" he said.

"He left before seven-thirty saying he was going out for a walk," she said. "He left his phone, so I can't call him and see where he is. I hope nothing's happened to him."

He must have noticed the edge of worry in her voice. "He's probably just down at the lake at the end of the road. It's real pretty out there at night."

"Okay. I'm going out there to find him," she said, standing up straight and looking the guy in the eye.

He blinked. "Do you want me to walk with you out there?" he said.

"*No.* I'll go back and get the flashlight and go by myself," she said firmly.

He shrugged. "Have it your way," he said, turning back to his car.

She turned and crossed her arms against the chill in the air. She walked back to the house, went in the front door, and went to their bedroom to get the flashlight out of the bedside table. She went back out the front and turned right, walking away from their house with the flashlight beam bobbing in front of her.

She wanted to get away from the house before she started screaming his name. The hysteria was mounting, and she didn't know how to stop it. *Why would he be out so long? Why wouldn't he have his phone?* He should know she would worry. *Where could he be if he wasn't at the lake? Is he at the Lyles' house on the other side of it? Hit by a car? Or waylaid by somebody? Where could he be?*

She felt herself wanting to throw up again. She spat out some nasty saliva and kept walking, concentrating on the light in front of her and the contours of the asphalt road. When it turned to gravel, she knew she was close to the lake. She stopped and shone the light around, looking to see what she could see. She didn't want to wade into the marshy grass surrounding the patch of water out there. It wasn't much of a lake by Louisiana standards; you didn't even need an airboat to go across it. She and James sometime went out in a rowboat that he kept tied up to a tree. She cast the light around looking for the tree it should be at.

She was willing herself not to scream. She didn't want to wake anyone up at the Lyles', especially not the big black Doberman they called Midnight. She turned around in a circle and made out a figure at the edge of the lake. She shivered—not totally from the night air. She forced herself to call out his name in a low voice. "Is that you?" she said.

"Yes, ma'am," he said. "What are you doing out here?"

"Looking for you," she said, again willing her voice to remain steady.

"Didn't think I was coming back?" he said in a strange voice she'd never heard from him.

"I was scared you'd been bit by a car. You know how they drive out here. You didn't have your phone for me to call," she said. "It's after nine o'clock."

She saw him pop on his flashlight to look at his watch, and he swore under his breath.

He moved and came over to where she stood and grabbed onto her arm with a tight grip. They started walking back with him leading her along holding tight to her arm. She felt the tears coming, both from her worries and the pain from her arm. He was walking fast, and she struggled to keep up.

Then he stepped over a tree root she didn't see, and she tripped and fell to one knee. He turned and helped her up, then started walking again without a word. Then she started crying in earnest, sobbing as they walked along. The thoughts spun in her mind. *What is wrong with him? What did I do? I've never seen him like this before. Is he mad at me? For getting pregnant? For coming out and looking for him? For not telling him for three months that I wasn't having my period?*

But his silence made her keep her questions to herself.

They got inside the house, and she looked up at him and saw a grim determination in his eyes. He let go of her arm, and she ran to their bedroom, sobbing and crashing into furniture. She got to the door, shut it behind her, and locked it from the inside. Then she did run to the bathroom again, but nothing else would come up out of her twisted stomach.

She heard James rattling the doorknob, trying to open the door. "Let me come in there, Leilani," he said calmly. "I can explain—"

"Then explain!" she shouted at the door. "But you'll explain it through the door because I'm not coming out until you do!"

"But—"

"But nothing!" she shouted. "You've been gone for hours and made me come out and find you! It's late, and you didn't say a word to me the entire way home! What am I supposed to think?"

"I know," he said. "And if you'll come to the door where you don't have to scream for me to hear, I'll tell you what happened."

She got closer to the door. She heard his body thud against the door and heard him slide down to sit on the floor. She did the same, resting her head on her knees and willing her stomach to stop churning.

"I want you to know you made me a very happy man tonight, cheri. I thought this day would never come—that I might one day be a dad."

"Well, you've got a funny way of showing it," she said back.

"I know. I'm not myself right now. When I got away from you, a terrible feeling came over me. Like something horrible was waiting to happen. A premonition, and now I need to tell you what really happened to me during the hurricane."

"Oh my God," Leilani said. "On this night of all nights, you've spent it thinking about the hurricane? How is that supposed to make me feel, James?"

She heard him sigh. "I guess it's good we've got a closed door between us. Because I can't bear to think about this and watch you while I tell it."

"What?" she said.

He told her about Jack, the looting, and the miscarriage. The fights, the leaving, the recriminations, how he wasn't there for her in losing the baby and how she thought he cared more about his friends and family in Kenner than he did for her. How he left with her to get away from the memory of Jack but then pulled away from her too because she was a reminder of how much hope he'd lost.

She heard his body shift again next to the door.

"James?" she said.

He didn't answer.

"*James?*"

James sighed again. "I know it's crazy. But I couldn't shake the feeling that something awful was going to happen to us, too, and it drove me outside into the dark to walk it off. Meeting you was the first good thing that happened to me since the hurricane came through—and then you made me so happy tonight with telling me about the baby. But too happy. I tried to hold life lightly since Jack was shot, not to care too much about anyone or anything. But—you, I care. I care so much, Leilani. And I got the feeling I was just setting myself up for something else terrible to happen."

The fear and pain in his voice and her heart together was too much for her. Leilani started crying.

He heard him stand up and rattle the doorknob again. "Please let me in. I can hear you crying."

She got up, unlocked the door, and flung it open. "I wanted tonight to be special for me. For you. For us, and now—God!"

She stared at him and saw his face twist. "Leilani, I swear—"

"Don't swear," she said.

He closed his mouth.

"I'm going to bed. I'm going to pray for you and your fear and your heart. Do you understand me?" Leilani said.

James nodded. He moved towards her.

"Don't come a step closer," she said.

He backed up, eyes going cold again. "Don't take that tone with me—"

"Why not?" she said. "After how you've acted tonight—"

"You sound just like Lori," he said, his eyes narrowing. "I sat here and poured my heart out to you. I've told you everything. And you're going to push me away like this? Why should I even stay—"

She knew she had to be a fright to look at—she could see it on his face. But that wasn't important now—getting through his coldness was. "I don't hold life lightly. I want to live. I want us to face life together. What you just told me says you don't know how to do that."

His eyes stayed empty. "Everything I've ever cared about before is gone now—my folks, Jack, Lori, her baby, what Kenner used to be—it's all gone. Who wants to hold on when everything just slips through your fingers?" he said.

As much as that emptiness scared her, she willed herself to walk up to him and put her hands on his chest. "I haven't slipped through your fingers, James. I'm here. Where I'm supposed to be. Begging you to step into the happiness I know. The happiness we have together. That this baby will bring us. No matter what happens. Even if what you fear happens, we'll need something to hold on to tight. Don't you see that?"

He closed his eyes. "I want to believe you—I really do, Leilani."

"Then hear me out," she said. "Tonight I'm going to cry for you and for me and for your friend and for this baby. I'm going to pray that you really can be the kind of father you wanted to be for Lori for this baby, conceived in love and joy and innocence, and be the husband I know you can be. You're not him tonight."

He stared up at the ceiling, and Leilani saw tears leaking out of the corners of his eyes. "I know. But I don't know how—not anymore."

"Well, you're going to have to figure it out, then. And I'll help you. It starts with talking about what we fear. Then letting go of the fear and living life anyway. I don't deal in half-measures or meet people halfway. I play for keeps," Leilani said.

James looked at her with a small smile. "I know. Jon Mark told me that the day I met you."

"Come on," she said. "Let's go find a movie to watch."

James shook his head. "Not tonight. Let's talk. About you and me. And the baby. And the nursery. Help me think of the future instead of the past."

"I'd like that," she said, looking at his eyes, searching for something—anything to tell her who this man was now. But the emptiness was still there. She shivered. *Dear God, help us,* she prayed.

Requiem

The air was still as Judd drove up to Ray and Wendy's house with both his windows down trying to catch a little breeze in late September. Trees still surrounded the house—one on the corner next to the garage was full of dead leaves looking like it was ready to fall over. The porch was swept clean with a bright pink-and-blue plastic playhouse set up beside the front door on the left. They'd never replaced the porch swing that the hurricane sent into the living room, but several sturdy rockers sat lined up on the right.

Judd saw a guy in hospital scrubs standing in front of the porch smoking a cigarette as he stopped in the driveway. He looked up from the ground as Judd got out of the truck and came closer. "I'm looking for Ray Magnum," Judd said.

The guy dropped the cigarette and ground it out with his foot. "I'm Jack Rawson. I could ask who you are, but I don't think I have to."

Judd stared. "And I could say it's none of your business, but I won't. My name's Judd McKay, and I'm here because Ray asked me to come see him."

"Likely story," Rawson said.

Judd stepped closer. "I don't remember the last time I beat the fire out of somebody, but maybe it's time for me to take it up again."

"Then come on."

Let's try this again. "Can I please talk to Ray Magnum?"

"Only if you plan on going to the cemetery."

What? Judd closed his eyes. *God, you've got to help me out.* "When did he die?"

"A week ago today," he said. "I guess guys like you like to move fast, huh?"

Judd cocked his head. "I don't get you. I'm not here to cause trouble."

"Then what are you here for?"

"I already answered that. If he's dead, what are *you* here for?"

"Because I've been married to his sister for going on eighteen years. She's in there with Wendy now." He stepped closer to Judd. "And because I'm Dr. Jack Rawson, and I delivered Judy Ray Magnum into this world with no help from the likes of you, and if I were you, I'd get out of Dodge before anyone else sees you."

Judd took a deep breath. "I need to see Wendy."

"Yeah. I'll bet you do."

Judd tightened his hands into fists, then relaxed his fingers. "Okay. I'll put my cards on the table. I'm here because Ray wrote me a letter three weeks ago asking me to come."

Rawson's eyes narrowed. "Let's see it."

Judd started to say no but thought better of it. He pulled it out of his shirt pocket and handed it to the guy. Rawson started reading aloud, whispering to himself. "I don't know how much longer I have to be Judy Ray's daddy. I'm having clots moving in different places in my body and they've left me about half crippled. Now I have a big one in my head that they say could blow any day."

Judd felt the words read aloud like body bows to his stomach. Rawson kept reading. "All this to say that about five months ago I finally sat Wendy down and sorted things out with her. I'm not going to get into details with you, but she finally told me that she thought that Judy Ray was your baby girl. She said you were the only other one it could be, and that when Judy Ray was born she found out for sure she couldn't be mine," he whispered.

Rawson looked up. "I think I've seen enough." He tossed the letter at Judd.

Judd let it fall to the ground, then leaned down, picking it up without taking his eyes of Rawson.

They both startled a bit when the screen door to the house opened. "Jack? What's going on?" Wendy said.

Rawson turned. "You need to get back in the house, Wendy."

She stepped out onto the porch. "Nobody died and made you God, Jack Rawson. I—"

She saw Judd and froze.

Judd moved past Rawson to the steps. "How are you, Wendy?"

He could see her breathing hard. Out of the corner of his eye, he saw the doctor move behind him.

"It's okay, Jack," Wendy said. "If he's here now, he must have a reason."

"And I'll tell it to you, if you'll let me," Judd said.

He held the letter out in front of him. "Ray wrote me this, and I got it in the mail yesterday afternoon. I drove down from Tupelo this morning. I didn't know he was already gone."

He moved slowly to the front porch. Wendy was sucking air in through her teeth, and her face was red, from what, he didn't know. He laid it on the bottom step. "I want you to go inside and read it. If you come back out and want to talk to me, we can. If you don't want to talk to me, don't come out." He backed up. "Okay, Wendy?"

She nodded. "I'll be out in the truck," Judd said.

He watched her come down the steps and pick the letter up by the corner. She was close enough for him to reach out and touch her arm. But he didn't.

She looked at it, then him. "It's dated three weeks ago," Wendy said.

"He used an old address. It took that long to find its way back to me," Judd said.

She nodded, then turned and went back in the house.

Judd turned and walked back towards his truck. Rawson let him walk by.

He got in the truck. Rawson walked back towards him. Judd opened his glove compartment and glanced at his .38. *I don't know what his problem is.*

He stopped a few feet back. "Judd, huh? What kind of a name is that?" Rawson said.

"My daddy's."

"Uh-huh." The wind moved through the trees as Judd kept one eye on Rawson and the other on the screen door. "So Ray wrote you a letter."

Judd stared out the windshield.

"I figured Wendy would break down and tell him eventually," Rawson said. "He tell you to come up here and take your whipping like a man?"

Judd looked away. He knew the letter by heart—he'd spent the entire night reading it over and over, shaking in the dark. *I've made out a will and have peace of mind about that. What I'm not easy about is that Wendy's soon going to be alone in the world with a little girl to raise with me long gone. That's where you come in. I want you to come up here and we can talk man to man about what kind of help Wendy's going to need raising Judy Ray.*

He heard Rawson snort like a bull pawing the ground. "Got here as soon as you could, did you? Maybe I'll give the whipping to you for him," Rawson said.

That's enough. He popped the truck door open, got out, and slammed it. "I don't know where you got your ideas about me, and I don't care. Ten minutes ago, I'd never heard of you, and I'll probably forget you fifteen minutes after I leave. But I don't have to sit here and listen to you talk like you know something when you don't," Judd growled. "Understand?"

"So tell me what I don't know," Rawson said back.

"I don't have to tell you anything."

"So don't. Get your butt back in the truck and wait, then."

Judd didn't move.

Rawson lit a new cigarette and looked back up at Judd. "So how long you known about that little girl?"

"Since the January before she came."

"Real concerned about her, weren't you?"

Judd leaned back against his truck. "What has Wendy said that gives you such a hard-on about me?"

"Nothing," Rawson said. "All I knew before you drove up is that a man with Ray Magnum's blood type couldn't have a baby with Judy Ray's. That's all."

Judd looked at the ground.

Rawson was still staring at him. "So I'm standing out here wondering what Wendy's going to do raising that baby alone when here you drive up. So I put two and two together."

"And come up with something other than four."

Rawson shrugged. "You're not telling me anything to change my mind."

"You tell me why I should."

"Maybe your conscience can answer that."

"I settled that question a long time ago when I told Wendy if she wanted that baby to be mine, it could be mine," Judd said. "And she told me as far as she was concerned, she was Ray's."

He saw Rawson's eyes narrow as he looked at him. "That so?"

"Just because you don't believe me doesn't mean it's not true," Judd said.

"I didn't say I didn't," Rawson said. "In fact, it sounds so much like her I'd just about have to believe it."

Judd looked up at the trees that still surrounded the place. "What's she like?"

"Who? Wendy?"

"Judy Ray," Judd said. "What's she like?"

Rawson grinned for the first time. "She's a little sweetheart," he said. "She went through a phase a while back of biting anything that moved in the church nursery, but that's about the only trouble they've ever got out of her."

"They say I went through a spell of that, too—only I was five years old starting kindergarten and old enough to know better."

"I think every kid goes through that phase at some point." Rawson dropped his spent cigarette and ground it out with his sneaker heel. "You got any other kids?"

Judd looked at the ground. "No."

"You sure about that?"

Judd gritted his teeth. "Yes."

"And now you're here," Rawson said.

Judd nodded.

He heard the screen door open. Rawson turned. "Over here, Reba."

Judd stared at the ground as Rawson moved off towards his wife. He heard whispering and then Rawson. "I don't like this at all."

God, I don't know what you've got in mind here. Just help me with it.

He heard Rawson moving back towards him. "Reba tells me it's time for us to go. But I want you to know one thing. If you do anything to hurt that woman in there, I'll come up to Tupelo and kill you myself. Understand?"

Judd looked up. "How about this—if I do anything to hurt that woman in there, I'll let you. Deal?"

Rawson's smile stopped at his eyes. "Deal."

Judd stayed by his truck as they drove off. He heard the screen door slam again. He looked up. Wendy was standing at the top of the porch steps. "Judd?" she said.

"Yes, ma'am?"

"I'd like for you to come in so we can talk—if you still want to."

He moved to walk up the steps. She turned and walked back into the house. He followed her back to the kitchen. He saw kids' toys laying around in the hallway and clean casserole dishes stacked up on the kitchen countertops. Wendy stood by the refrigerator. "You want something to eat after your trip?"

"I'm fine, Wendy."

She nodded, staring at the floor. She moved to the kitchen table and sat down. Judd sat down across from her. "You're going to have to wait for me to get my thoughts together, Judd."

"I understand that."

She looked up. "Do you?"

"I had to get my thoughts together after reading that letter, too," Judd said.

He watched Wendy's face as she bit her lip. "What—did your wife say about you coming down here?"

Judd took a deep breath. "Laine and I are through," he said, lacing his fingers together as he put his hands on the kitchen table.

"Because of me?" Wendy asked.

"Wendy—after I left here back the last time I saw you, I—couldn't get Judy Ray off my mind," Judd said. "I started dreaming about seeing her. Every time I heard a little girl say 'daddy' anywhere—Wal-Mart or a movie theatre, everywhere—I turned to see if she was talking to me. I couldn't tell Laine; I couldn't talk to anybody about it. I thought about changing jobs, moving back, anything so I would have an excuse to come to the shop and maybe see her."

He stared up at the ceiling so he could take his eyes off of her stricken face. "I finally told Laine I wanted a baby—period. No ifs, ands, or buts. Either she got pregnant or we adopted. But I wasn't going to wait on her anymore."

He let out his breath and willed himself to be calm. "And she moved out and filed for divorce. I didn't fight it. It's been final for about nine months."

Wendy put her face in her hands. "God. Judd, I'm sorry—"

"It's not your fault," Judd said. "She wasn't going to change her mind no matter what I did or said—or what happened or didn't happen between us—or any reason. It was going to happen sooner or later, Judy Ray or no Judy Ray."

She moved her hands away from her face and started

rubbing her upper arms with her hands. Judd saw the fresh scratches on her arms and winced. *Please God, don't let her start that again.*

She looked away and took a deep breath, then let it out in a rush. "I can't believe I'm sitting here talking to you. I'm more scared of what's happening right now than I was waiting for the hurricane to land on us. I didn't think that was possible."

"I didn't come here to bring back bad memories, Wendy."

"I can't believe Ray wrote you to come here at all. I read the letter myself. I still don't." She looked up at him again. "What did you think when you got it?"

Judd rubbed his eyes. "I read it several times, and the only reason I didn't come last night was that I needed to have some time to think about if I was ready to face him or not, and I decided that I was, and I get here and find out he's—"

He broke off. "He said in there that him and you talked about Judy Ray about five months ago."

She looked above Judd's head. "I almost told him when she was born. I almost told him on her second birthday." She crossed her arms. "But I didn't. I waited for him to ask me outright. But at least we spent some time together without it between us. I suppose that was more than I deserved."

Judd leaned forward. "Wendy, can I tell you something?"

She looked back at him, and the hurt in her eyes almost did him in. "You did all you did because you loved him. I know that, and reading that letter, I can tell he knew that, too, and he didn't love you any less for that, and he's forgiven us both."

Wendy sat up straight. "Can't you see that almost makes it worse?"

He nodded. "But you have to accept forgiveness for it to work, Wendy."

Wendy stood up and walked towards the back door. "That's what I've got trouble with, Judd. But there's no use in hanging onto that anymore, is there? He's gone, and he's not coming back this time."

Judd got up and put his hands on her shoulders. "You're right. He's not."

She broke down then. Without thinking, he turned her around and put his arms around her as she reached for him. He felt all the tension drain out of her shoulders as she cried.

He lost track of time standing there with her in his arms. He felt his mind whirling back to the storm—the fear, the guilt, the desperation for something—anything—to hold onto. He wouldn't—he couldn't—not again.

Is this what I thought I was coming here for? Stop it, you stupid, stupid son of a bitch—

And that's when her sobs started to ease down. Judd touched her hair. "Feel better?"

He felt her head move as she nodded. He rested his cheek on her temple. "I've got to let go of you right now, Wendy," he whispered.

She pulled back and looked up at him. "It's time to talk about Judy, isn't it?"

He nodded. "I'm going to get a picture of her, and you can see for yourself what made Ray wonder about her," she said.

She brushed past him and walked out into the house. Judd sat back down, feeling drained. *Who do you think you are? Ray's not even cold in the ground.*

After a minute, she came back in with a picture frame. "This was last year, at daycare."

Judd took the photo and looked down. He saw his own blue eyes staring back at him out of a very serious little face, surrounded with straight black hair. He looked up at Wendy and saw the same angle to her jaw as he did in Judy's photo. "She's so pretty, Wendy," he said. His eyes blurred, and he looked back down at the picture. "I couldn't walk far enough away from her to deny it, could I?"

Wendy sat back down in her chair. "Even up until the day she was born, I wouldn't admit to myself that she might not be Ray's child. But when she opened her eyes for the first time after Jack handed her to me, I knew," She laced her fingers together in front of her on the table.

Judd looked up at her. "No matter what else we say to each other today, I'd like to keep this picture if I could."

Wendy nodded. Judd heard Rawson's truck finally pull out onto the blacktop. "This is where it gets hard, Judd," Wendy said.

"Why?"

Wendy looked at him. "I don't know you, Judd. I have a child with you, but I don't know you. Doesn't that sound crazy to you?"

"No," he said. "Because you're right."

"What am I going to tell her, Judd?" Wendy said. "She's three years old. How can I explain this?"

"I don't know, Wendy."

"And—God, help me say this—Judd, what can we be to each other at this point?"

Judd realized that something must have flashed across his face when she said it because she stopped cold. "That came out wrong, Judd. I'm sorry."

Her face crumpled again. "Ray's going, I was a little bit prepared for. You being here today—I wasn't. I don't know what I'm thinking."

He looked at the picture in his hands. *God, I don't want to lose her again.* His eyes blurred up again, and he squeezed them shut.

He heard her get up from her chair and come around the table, then felt her squeeze his shoulder with her hand. "I want you to know her, Judd. It's too hard for a little girl to grow up without a daddy. I know that much. But with everything else that's gone on—"

She stopped. He took her hand and kissed her fingertips. "Sit down, Wendy."

She hooked her foot on the chair leg and pulled it closer and sat down. He let go of her hand, and she put them both on her knees. "Whatever happens between us from now on needs to be right," Judd said. "Judy Ray's proof of how far being scared can take you and me."

She nodded.

"And we're there again now—except it's a little bit worse," Judd said.

She looked away. "I never thought it could be, but you're right—it is." She looked back at him. "That's what you were thinking about when I was crying while ago, wasn't it?"

Judd nodded. *Was it that obvious?*

Wendy looked down again. "You don't know how hard it was not to want to kiss you then," she whispered. Judd saw her squeeze her eyes shut. "It was hard not to."

Judd let out a deep sigh. "It was all I could do to let go of you. But I also knew it wouldn't stop there."

She stared up at him with a strange look in her eyes—almost black all the way through and wide open as a scared rabbit's. "I knew that when I was thinking it. I just wasn't sure knowing that mattered very much. You know. Like, who cares what happens now?" She looked down. "Of course, I would have probably shot myself in the head afterwards, I don't know."

Judd felt the bottom drop out of his stomach. "No more talk like that. We know it, we've said it, now it's time to talk about something else."

When she spoke again, it was a whisper. "I know Ray asked you up here to talk about taking care of Judy Ray. What do you want to do about this, Judd? Do you—want me to get her tested?"

He shook his head. "I don't need that to know." He took a deep breath. "First I want to see her."

Wendy nodded, still not looking at him.

"And after that—maybe me just come here for the day on Saturdays and get to know her—and you."

She stared off toward the back door. "I might not be what you expect me to be, Judd."

"I'm not the same person I was when I walked in here that weekend, either, Wendy."

He could see her trembling. "Judd, if you think about it—we need to find out if fear is all that made us reach out to each other." She looked back at him. "Do you understand what I'm trying to say?"

"I think so," Judd said. "But I think if we concentrate on what's best for Judy, we'll find out more about each other than we might otherwise." A thought struck him, and he reached for her hand. "Wendy, what are you going to do about the shop?"

"Ray sold it all to Tommy Cade in January when he saw how sick he was getting. So we have something from that to—take care of things. When Judy starts pre-K next month, I'll start as an assistant with the school, too."

"Let me know what it'll take to get her started out, and I'll help you with it."

"Thank you," Wendy said. "Who do you work for now, Judd?"

"Bubba Husky," Judd said.

Wendy rolled her eyes. "I'm almost glad Ray didn't live long enough to hear that."

"You should have seen my boss when he found out." He was glad to see Wendy smile a little at that thought.

They were quiet for a while after that. He saw her glance at her watch.

"If I need to go, Wendy, say so."

She shook her head. "No. That's not it." She stared at the floor. "Judd, we've said some things to each other we can't unsay."

"You're right," Judd said.

"Let's see if we can somehow start over. So that if we say them again, they'll mean something. You said something while ago about trying to do things—the right way." She looked back up at him. "That's what I want."

"Whatever it turns out that means?" Judd said.

She nodded.

He heard a car drive up. "Let me go on out, Wendy. You've got company."

She smiled—the first real smile he'd seen on her all day. "You do, too. When I went to get that picture, I called Rosie and told her to bring my baby back home."

Judd's heart came up in his throat. "Are you sure about this, Wendy?"

"If you are."

He nodded. "You come in the den, and I'll go meet them outside," Wendy said.

Here goes. "Do they know about me?" Judd said.

"Rosie does. I don't know what she's told Lee."

He sat down on the couch as she walked out. He saw Judy's baby pictures on the wall and her baby dolls scattered on the floor. He remembered all the dreams he'd had of this moment—how he'd never been able to speak when he met her in his mind. *If this is a dream, God, don't let me wake up. Not yet.*

He heard her before he saw her—talking ninety to nothing about riding in Aunt Rosie's van. She bounced in the door and stopped and stared at him. "Hey!" she said.

His heart almost stopped. She was wearing a pink short set and a cute little pair of pink sandals. Her black hair was down to her shoulders, and those big blue eyes seemed to swallow him up.

"Hey, Miss Judy Ray. How are you?" he said, fighting for breath, just like in his dreams.

"Fine. How are you?" she said with a smile.

"Pretty good for a Thursday," Judd said.

Wendy came in behind her. "Judy, this is Mr. Judd McKay. He's a friend of Mama's and Daddy's."

"Your name's like mine!" Judy said.

"Almost but not quite," he said.

"I'm Judy Ray after Daddy." Her face teared up. "But Daddy died."

"I know, sweetie, and I'm sorry."

The corners of her mouth turned down. "You look like you need a hug, Miss Judy. Can you come here and let me give you one?" Judd said.

She trotted up to him and held out her arms. Judd picked her up and hugged her. *I've waited years for this, God. Thank you.*

He looked up over at Wendy and saw her blinking and

batting her hand at her eyes. He gave Judy an extra squeeze. "Can you run go play for a second and let me speak to your mama? It was good to meet you."

"Okay! Bye!" And she ran back outside.

He walked over to Wendy. "Coming here for that was the right thing, Wendy—even if nothing else from here on out is. Thank you."

Wendy nodded, looking up at him. "Lee and the other kids are here, too. I'd like for you to stay for dinner before you go back. How does that suit you?"

"Sounds like a plan," Judd said. "As long as you don't mind another mouth to feed, Mrs. Wendy."

"No trouble at all," she said.

Judd looked out the window as the sun was starting to go down. *I've got to say it.* "It's not going to be easy, Wendy."

He heard her step closer to him. "Nothing ever is," she whispered. "Never ever."

The End

Tommy went out to his truck to get ready to leave. He looked back at the little trailer house Cindi had set up in Flora, Mississippi that they had spent all day moving her into. Tommy's job had been unloading the furniture that she had requested to keep, mostly the pieces that she brought into their shared home from her childhood bedroom. They had drawn slips of paper to split the appliances. He didn't know what to do with all the other stuff that Cindi hadn't wanted. Tommy had half a mind to throw away or pawn the lot of it so he wouldn't have to look at any of it anymore.

Seven years together going up in smoke, and he had been tongue-tied the whole time—until it was time for him to say goodbye to Marilee.

He squatted down so his eyes could meet hers. "Daddy's got to go now, honey."

"We can't go with you?" she asked.

He shook his head. "Not this time, baby."

She tilted her head. He didn't know what notions Cindi had put into her head about why they were so far away from home, but Cindi had told him she'd slept all the way up on this trip, so maybe she didn't even realize how far away he'd be from now on.

"You just be my perfect princess for your mama, okay, Marilee?" he said. "Just like always."

"Why aren't you staying?" she said, her lower lip starting to quiver.

He looked up at Cindi helplessly, not knowing what to say. Cindi didn't help any either—she kept her mouth shut, her lips a thin line in her face. "I'll see you when I can, princess. Sometime soon, I promise."

"You have to work?" Marilee said.

"Yeah, sweetie. I do," Tommy said, knowing that was something she could understand. She was getting old enough to sort all of this out, but he didn't want to mar their goodbye with the ugly truth of what had happened between him and Cindi.

She reached out to hug him. "Bye, Daddy." Her small arms hugged him tight. Even at eight years old, she still didn't have full strength for a kid her age. He swallowed hard and buried his face in her long hair.

"Bye, princess. I love you," he said.

"Love you, too," she said.

He stood up awkwardly; his left leg had gotten numb from squatting so long.

He nodded at Cindi, and she nodded back. He searched for any emotion in her eyes—hurt, regret, sadness, anything that matched how he felt. But her eyes were of no help to him; he might as well have been a fly on the wall she was about to swat.

He turned and walked out to the door. He heard her move behind him, and he left the door open as he went out, scared of how he might slam it off its hinges.

Cindi surprised him by following him out the front door. He couldn't imagine what she wanted to say by now—they'd talked about only the mechanisms of getting her set up to move out since about ten months ago, when she had blown out of his life for good.

Cindi and Marilee had come over to Metairie for a weekend visit, the third they'd made since Tommy had told Cindi he sobered up. He cleaned out the fridge of the beers long ago, giving them to Mark, and tossed the few liquor bottles he'd accumulated in one trip to the dump. He knew she was going to be watching him like a hawk, but this time she seemed to be easier in her mind. They had even made love after Marilee had gone to bed, and they fell asleep in each other's arms in their old bed for the first time in forever.

But the news had predicted rain that night, and Tommy woke up to a humdinger of a thunderstorm. Lightning crashing, rain splattering on the tin roof, and thunder rolling through the night sent him out of the bed at one in the morning to sit up front in the recliner.

He was holding it together. Proud of himself for doing so, too.

Then a nearby lightning strike lit up the living room like daylight, and a transformer up the road blew up with a boom, shutting down the hallway light they kept on since Marilee was still scared of the dark.

Marilee woke up. "Mama!" she cried. "I scared!"

Tommy got up and started for her bedroom—and met Cindi in the hallway. "What are you doing up already?" Cindi said.

Something in her voice raised Tommy's hackles. "I can't sleep through a storm such as this anymore," he said.

It seemed to satisfy her in the moment. "You go on back to bed. I'll check on her," she said.

He did—he lay on his back and waited for Cindi to come back.

When she did, she was carrying Marilee. "I told her she could sleep with us just this once," Cindi said, apology in her voice.

Tommy rolled over to the other side of the bed. "It's okay, hon. Come on."

He heard Cindi start whisper-singing "Fais Do-Do" to Marilee after they climbed into the bed. Marilee was between them and seemed to be asleep after a few repeats of the song.

Suddenly Tommy felt water coming in from the roof. He looked up and saw a huge hole open up, flooding the bed with water. He saw

Marilee floating away from him on the water. He started trying to swim to her, but she aways stayed just out of reach of his desperate arms.

Then he saw her slowly roll over and start sinking. He tried to shout to her to wake up, but his voice was soundless. He tried grabbing at her nightgown to pull her to him, but it slipped out of his hands, and she sank out of sight—

He woke up with a jerk, sitting up in the bed. He looked over and saw Marilee was still lying peacefully next to him, as was Cindi.

But the thirst was back.

He got up, slipped on his shoes, and headed for the front door to drive down to the convenience store for some Bud. Then he remembered—he might still have some in the shed where he kept the boat.

He went out in the weather that had finally slowed down to just a drizzle and found a lone six-pack in his shop fridge. He chugged them one after the other, standing in the shed and throwing the empty cans into the trash can before finally carrying the last one outside, where he sat on the wet ground under a tree the storm had left standing in their backyard and finished it off.

When he woke up with the blinding sun in his eyes Saturday morning, he rolled over on the damp ground and looked at his watch. Six-thirty a.m.

He cursed himself all the way back into the house, where he found a note on the kitchen table. It had one word written on it.

"Liar."

And Cindi and Marilee were gone.

But when Cindi came outside to walk him to his truck, he hoped it meant he would have some gentle word from her, so they could part on good terms.

Instead she crossed her arms on her porch and stared at him. "Tommy, I've got one more thing to ask of you."

"What is it?" he said.

She took a deep breath, held it, and let it out. "Don't come see me or Marilee ever again."

Tommy stared at her. "You're taking her away from me?"

Cindi nodded.

"Why? Why can't I see her?" Tommy said, trying to keep the desperation from creeping into his voice.

Cindi looked down. "It's over between us, Tommy, and there's nothing tying us together except her, and we're both young and can start over, and so is she. She'll forget about you if you don't come around, and that's what I want for her to do—to forget."

Tommy started to walk to the porch. "You can't do that to me."

"Yes, I can," Cindi said. "We've never been married, you never signed birth papers for her in Louisiana, and in Mississippi, the mother gets full custody if this happens. I already talked to a lawyer who said there's not a judge in this state that'll rule different."

"But Cindi—please, if you ever cared for me, let me see her at Christmas, at least."

Cindi shook her head. "We've drawn this out long enough. Good-bye, Tommy."

And Cindi turned and walked back into the trailer and shut the door.

He ran up the porch steps and banged on the door with his fist. "Cindi! Don't do this to me! Cindi? *Cindi!*"

He heard her whispering to Marilee but couldn't hear what she said to her. He kept hitting the door with both fists, willing himself to break through it.

But the cheap door didn't budge or even crack the particle board, no matter how hard he smacked it.

Tommy then turned and stumbled to his truck, climbed up through the door, and sat in the driveway. He imagined all sorts of ways to see Marilee—find out where she went to school and pick her up one day. Drive up and hope to catch them at home. He looked at the glove compartment that carried his .38. He could go kick the door in, grab Marilee, and run for his life.

But that's no life for a kid.

He slowly backed out of the driveway and drove down without seeing the woods surrounding the country place Cindi had picked out. As he drove, it started to rain buckets on him, almost to where he couldn't see the road. He knew the rain wasn't the only thing that made the road swim before his eyes.

He got on I-55 South and drove down. Suddenly he thought to look at his gas tank and swore. He needed to fill up, all right. He pulled into the gas station at the intersection at Highway 463 and I-55.

After he finished, Tommy wheeled out of the gas station and pulled onto Highway 463. He sat in the truck and tapped his fingers on the steering wheel as Van Halen blasted through his speakers and he waited for the light to change. He'd just dropped $100 for his gas tank. He'd stopped at the fanciest gas station he'd ever seen, built with Madison's trademark red-and-beige bricks and sporting a mural inside of a child's railroad train going along the top of the wall. Penn's Catfish built a stand inside, selling fried catfish and chicken-on-a-stick. A group of tables held men drinking coffee and scarfing down the fillets as quickly as they could eat.

Tommy looked at his receipt resting on the seat beside him. A*nd I paid for the fancy in there, too. God almighty.*

Now he was about to hit Jackson school traffic pulling a trailer through the Waterworks Curve and the Stack.

If you were a stranger just driving down 1-55, you wouldn't know a hurricane even went over Jackson, unless you knew where to look. The VA Medical Center sign was still down on the side of the road just before you got to the Waterworks Curve.

The lights were flashing on the speed limit signs, warning everyone to slow to fifty miles an hour while negotiating the S-shaped bridge that curved around Jackson's oldest water treatment plant below. Tommy slowed down, trying to keep his trailer under control as he turned the wheel left and right. One car went by him blowing its horn as it shot out of the chute and sped up on the straightaway. *He's lucky he didn't go sailing through the guardrail.*

He got to the Stack, called that because the bridges ran over and under each other like strands in a braid. I-20 West ran under the bridge to I-55 North, with I-20 East flying over them both with an exit leading to Highway 49 off to the right. Tommy went under I-20 East, looking out and down on the bingo halls that lined Highway 80, which ran along the ground at the bottom of the pile.

The rain got heavier as he exited onto I-20 West/I-55 South. He slowed down as he moved with the traffic through the orange barrels on the main highway. *If they finish this blasted road before I die, it won't be because they worked at it.*

It was already getting darker with the storm as he drove along, and he hoped the kick from the Mountain Dew he'd picked up in Madison lasted him until he got to where he'd fill up next.

From the I-20W/I-55S split as he moved south, he could still see where stands of pine trees were snapped off from the winds. All the cell towers he'd seen down before got rebuilt pretty quickly. Here and there you still saw billboards that blew loose hanging from their poles. He swapped out CDs and started tapping his fingers on the wheel to a Def Leppard album Cindi always hated as he drove along. He let his mind wander, trying to come up with something happy to think about. But all his memories were black and dark—loading people into his boat and getting them to shelter until late, late in the night. Laying on his back in their house as the heat raged before they'd gotten power back. Amy Thompson screaming. "Don't take my baby away!"

He remembered the resolve he'd seen in Cindi's face that morning as she shut him out of Marilee's life for good.

He sped up, looking for an exit. He wheeled over to the first one he saw and drove up to the convenience store. He walked through the florescent lights above the gas pumps into the brightly-lit store, making a beeline for the drinks section. He first grabbed up another bottle of Mountain Dew.

He glanced furtively over at the six-packs of cold beer in the next cooler. Both the tallboys and the pony-sized cans in whatever brand you could think of. He looked back towards the clerk, an older lady who was wiping down the counter with a wet rag, her brown hair piled high on her head, wearing a uniform shirt and black pants.

What am I doing?

Instead he just bought the Mountain Dew. She rang him up and then handed him the receipt. "You have a good day," she said.

"You, too," he said back.

He carried the bottle in both hands as he walked back out to the truck.

When he got back in the truck, he picked up another CD without giving it a good look and popped it in—then hit eject when Steve Perry started singing "Open Arms." He rolled down the window and threw the CD out into the parking lot.

Tommy pulled back out on the highway.

Marilee's probably in bed for her nap by now.

He drove further down until he came to the next exit. He pulled over into a hotel parking lot and stopped. He wanted a beer so bad.

He closed his eyes and laid his head back on the seat. *What am I going to do without Marilee? Without Cindi? Sit at home and drink all I want to, I guess.*

Tommy looked up and saw his reflection in the windshield. His face was pasty white, his hair was a matted mess, and he was still dripping from being out in the rain. *God, I look like death.* He felt his hands start shaking.

"I'll see you when I can, princess. Sometime soon."

"You have to work?"

"Yeah, sweetie. I do."

He remembered how good that first taste of Bud had felt to him, back in the late-afternoon heat in his house at Metairie waiting on Mark to come over and cut up the trees in his backyard. How good one would taste now in the hot night with the windows down as he drove back to his empty house.

Cindi's right. I'm a drunk. I'll always be a drunk. If I can't put it down after a day like today, when will I put it down?

He cranked the truck and almost lost his trailer as he skidded back out onto the highway. He turned up the radio with ZZ Top blaring loud enough to break glass. *God, I don't care,* he thought as he watched the speedometer climb as he hit I-55 heading south. *I don't care if I flip it over. I don't care if I wrap it around a tree. Just don't let me take anyone else with me if I do.*

After he'd passed a few cars while flying along he heard sirens behind him—they sounded really far away. He needed to find a dirt road something bad.

He thought he saw one up ahead and wrenched the wheel around to the right to take it. But he didn't make the turn. His back tire hit a wet patch, and he went spinning, bouncing off trees, hearing the ripping sound of metal with every hit. He let go of the steering wheel and covered his head with his arms as the truck rolled over.

When he finally stopped moving, it felt like the whole weight of the truck was resting on his chest.

When he finally opened his eyes, he saw twilight coming in the floorboard of the vehicle.

He tried to move and couldn't.

God, I wish I'd told Cindi I loved her. Let me live long enough to do that. Maybe—

Then as the light began shrinking down to a dot, he thought he heard Amy Thompson scream again in his ears—but then recognized the voice as his own, wordless and unending—

A Soul Restored

Mike sat up in his chair when he heard a commotion outside in the Lakeshore Regional Medical parking lot—a woman was screaming at someone but Mike couldn't hear what she was saying. He looked over at the half-asleep security guard. "You hear that?" he said.

The security guard shrugged his shoulders. "I can go check on it if you want."

"I'll go with you in case she's hurt."

"Okay," the guard said.

They both walked out the entrance to the emergency room, and Mike stiffened. A blond-haired woman was holding a handgun pointed at a scrawny guy four feet away from her, and she was screaming. "Don't you come any closer!"

The security guard looked at Mike and nodded his head back towards the door. "I can handle it," he said.

Mike nodded and backed away but stayed close to the door—he didn't know what the girl had in mind, but they only had one guard on duty in emergency, and he wanted to keep an eye on him. Mike himself had only been working six months after he got his certification back and was in a lot more laid-back position than before, and he was determined not to let the work get to him like he had before.

He heard the guard call out. "Lady, put the gun down and kick it in my direction. You don't need to be threatening someone with it like that. You can get in trouble."

"She's not threatening me," the guy said in a shaky voice. "She wants to kill herself, and I got her as far as the hospital in my car, but she got her hands on my Colt."

"Just go home!" she cried. "Take care of my baby and just go home!"

"Where's your baby, lady?" the guard said.

"In the car," the guy said. "She had him a week ago, and she's been going downhill ever since."

Mike nodded to himself. Postpartum psychosis. He had a specialty in psych training with his nurse practitioner license so he knew what to do—if they could just get her to put the gun down.

The guard had been inching closer to her as they all talked, and suddenly she noticed how close he was. She shifted the barrel of the gun to him. "Don't you get any closer either. I don't want to hurt you. I don't want to hurt anybody. I just want to kill myself in peace, if you'll let me."

Mike decided it was time for him to step in too, if at least to only give her more targets to attend to—surely one of them could draw her fire and the other two tackle her if it came to that. He didn't say anything, just casually started walking up to her.

When she flicked her eyes over his way, he stopped moving. "Hey. My name's Mike. What's yours?" he said in a conversational tone.

She looked at him but kept the gun pointed at the security guard. "Gina. Gina Trahan."

"Hey Gina. What's your baby's name?"

"Christian. Chris for short," she said, seeming to calm down some.

"And what about him?" Mike said, inclining his head toward the scrawny guy.

"My name's Christian Trahan, too," the guy said. "She's my wife."

"Okay," Mike said. "What's going on, Gina?"

"I just don't want to go on anymore. I can't do it. I can't do the feeding and the changing and everything else. He's got to work, and I only have a few weeks off before I have to go back to work," she said, her voice rising. "I can't be a mom. I can't be a wife. I can't help support my family. There's no reason for me to live. If I do it now the baby won't ever remember me and Christian can find someone who'll be better to him!"

The whole while Gina had been talking, the security guard had been ambling along, looking like he was pacing in circles but slowly getting closer and closer to her. Suddenly she turned away from Mike and fired the pistol—the bullet sailed over the guard's head, and before she could get another shot off, he grabbed her gun arm and Mike had moved in to grab her other arm. The guard brought up his knee and slammed it into the girl's wrist, knocking the gun loose. He kicked it away, and her husband scrambled for it as it skidded across the asphalt. He picked it up and ejected the magazine with a practiced hand.

The girl still had a lot of fight in her—she screamed and bucked and kicked the security guard in the knee, making him let go of her arm. Mike wrapped both of his arms around her midsection and lifted her off of her feet, with her dog-cussing him with words he didn't know women even knew.

He continued holding on to her and said, "You're safe now. You're safe now. You don't have to worry anymore. You're safe. We'll take you into the hospital and get you calmed down and talk to a doctor and see what they can do with you. But you don't have to fight anymore. You're safe."

She started to calm down in his arms as he moved slowly towards the entrance to the hospital doors. She started trying to twist away again, saying, "I don't want to be locked up; I don't want you shooting me up full of drugs. My mama had trouble like this, and that's what happened to her. She's still not right from some of the medication they gave her. I don't want it."

Mike said in a soothing voice. "Now look. No one's going

to hurt you. You fired a shot at a security guard, and they may want to hold you for that. But they'll let you stay in a hospital instead of a jail if you tell us your story and what is going on that's got you wanting to shoot yourself. It's going to be all right. I wouldn't lie to you about it. We're going to take care of you as long as you behave."

As he spoke, she fought less and less. By the time they got into the emergency room, she relaxed and started acting like she had some sense about her. The security guard and the husband filed into the hospital behind them, the husband having gone and gotten the baby carrier out of the car during the melee.

Mike led Gina to an ER room. "Now, I need you to put on this blue hospital top and pants."

"Why?"

"Regulations," Mike said, still talking in a soothing voice.

She reached out for the hospital clothes, and he saw old scars all up and down her arms. "So you cut yourself?" he said.

"I used to. I don't anymore," Gina said, sounding tired. Her gaze was wandering around the room.

"Have you taken any drugs prior to coming into here?" Mike said, making notes on a clipboard one of the nurse aides gave him.

"No," she said.

"Okay." Mike said. "I'm going to leave you with Katie here, and she'll help you dress. I'm going out to talk to Christian, your husband. Okay?"

"Whatever," Gina said, looking at her shoes and starting to untie them.

"Make sure you give Katie your shoes."

"Yes sir."

Mike went back out and saw the scrawny boy talking to someone from intake. The boy saw Mike and came up to him. "What's going to happen now?" Christian said.

"She needs to be seen by a doctor, and they'll probably hold her for three days because of the suicide threat and the shooting off the weapon. She'll go to the nearest mental ward that has a bed, and they'll treat her as best as they can and as much as she'll let them."

The boy shook his head, suddenly looking very young and very scared. "So I just need to go back to the house and take care of the baby, and when she's supposed to be let out someone will call me?"

Mike nodded. The boy's shoulders slumped in defeat. "Well, I guess I'll get the rest of this paperwork done and head home."

"Don't blame yourself. Okay? You were trying to get her help, and now she's going to get it. You just take care of that little man there, now."

The boy nodded his head and turned back to the lady at the desk.

Suddenly Mike heard yelling from the room Gina was in. "I'm not going to; I'm not. You're not going to stick me with an IV. I'll pull it out if you do."

Mike went back and found Gina lying in the bed covering up her arm and hand. "Gina. You need fluids because you're a young mom and you're likely dehydrated if you've been nursing. Calm down."

She looked up at him, then kicked the covers off and tried to sit up.

Mike heard a cough behind him. He turned and saw the attending physician for the night, Dr. Ross. "Hello. Mrs. Trahan, is it? I'm Dr. Ross, and I'm going to take you through a quick evaluation and see what we need to do for you, okay?"

Mike groaned inwardly. Ross was as competent as they come, but he was also cold as a bag of frozen frog legs. If Gina showed out on him, he'd have her sedated before the night was out. It was all he could do not to say "Be good" to her on his way out the door.

She seemed to sense that she needed to quiet down, and he didn't hear any more out of her—until towards the end of Mike's shift. He heard her sobbing loudly in the room and went in to check on her. She'd been on suicide watch ever since Ross had ordered her some Vistaril. But this wasn't just sniffling—it was full-out bawling.

Mike checked the clock and decided to walk in himself. "Gina? You need to tone it down—people are trying to sleep," he said.

The loudest sobs subsided, but the tears continued. "I've ruined my life. The state's going to take my baby away. My husband's going to leave me. I just know it," she sobbed.

Her words got so hysterical that Mike couldn't understand them. He checked her chart, and the doctor had ordered that if she stayed agitated or got worse. She was to get a shot of Ativan in her drip. So Mike measured the maximum dose out carefully that the doctor had directed. Almost immediately, her sobs subsided, and he saw her face smooth into peace.

After he gave the medication, he walked out and started writing up all of his notes to get ready to go home. The security guard that had helped calm her down was about to leave too; when Mike was done, they walked out together.

The guard laughed under his breath. Mike looked at him. "What?"

"Ain't no drunk like a crying drunk." he said, shaking his head.

"What are you talking about?" Mike said.

"That girl," the guard said. "Her husband said she'd put away the better part of a fifth of Jim Beam before he could coax her into the car to go to the hospital."

Mike's blood iced in his veins. "That wasn't in her charts—are you sure?"

"That's what the boy told me. I don't guess he told you, huh?"

Mike wanted to sink into the ground. The girl hadn't smelled drunk when she came in, but he hadn't asked either, and he'd just given her a massive benzo dose on top of all that alcohol.

Mike went back the way he came and found the boy in the lobby trying to feed the baby a bottle the nurse had given him. The boy confirmed what he'd said to the guard, but on further questioning, he said he wasn't sure how much had been in the bottle before she started drinking, just that she had finished it off.

Mike walked back into the nurses' station with a sinking feeling. He put the notes in the chart and noted the time he had been told by the husband. Then he went to find Ross.

Ross sighed exasperatedly at Mike. "Well, we'll just have to see how she comes out of it," he said.

Mike had an idea. "There's always Romazicon."

The doctor shook his head. "Too risky with the alcohol with the possibility for breakthrough seizures. We'll just have to watch her."

Mike said, "It was my mistake—I'd like to stay and watch her."

Ross shook his head. "We can't approve the overtime. I'll assign someone fresh from the new shift. You'll need to brief them before you leave."

So Mike did and left the hospital feeling lower than he had ever since he'd come back to nursing. If that girl died because of what he'd done—

Mike wished the thought away.

But they can't stop me from praying for her.

Once he got home, he knew he wouldn't be able to sleep—the girl was too heavy on his mind. He sat up downstairs in his recliner and prayed every scripture he could remember over Gina Trahan and her boy and her husband, prayed for her sanity, prayed for her health, prayed for her to live, to live with no side effects of what he'd done.

He dozed off a few times in the night, only to jerk awake because of a sound in the house and take up his prayers again. Finally he awoke to the sun rising up though the front room window. His bones felt every bit as sore as if he'd run a marathon in the night, and he reckoned he could call what he'd done a spiritual marathon. He prayed again with Dinah and took strength from her final words: "And God, if the worst has happened and she's gone, remind Mike that you are still who you are yesterday, today, and forever."

He came into the hospital at a trot, making a beeline for Gina Trahan's room. He looked around and no one was there—leading him to believe the worst. "Gina?" he called out quietly.

Then she came into the room from outside. She smiled a little when she saw him. "Hello. They say they're waiting on an ambulance to take me to a mental health center for a few days."

"I'm so glad to hear that," Mike said. "You take care of yourself."

"I'm going to try," she said, a full smile brightening her face. "Thanks for taking such good care of me."

Mike nodded—too overcome with emotion.

He walked out of the room with his feet on the floor, but his spirit was on shouting ground. *Thank you God, and thank you, Jesus. Thank you.*

Ave Maria

Lori King eased into the back of the hospital chapel. Her eyes adjusted to the dim light as she looked around. It took her a minute to place the music—"Ave Maria." She resisted the impulse to cross herself.

She saw James sitting on the front row with his back to her. He was sitting with his elbows propped on his knees and his forehead on his fists. She walked up as quietly as she could and sat down a space from him on the soft pew without speaking. *Better not startle him.*

After a minute, he looked over in her direction. "James, it's me," she said.

He blinked in surprise. "Lori?"

She nodded. "Moira called me to make sure I knew—"

"About Leilani," he said.

She nodded again. "I called the number she gave me and got your mother-in-law—Mrs. Tyler. She said you'd be over here. So I came by, and the NICU nurse sent me down here."

James was still staring at her. She reached out and touched his knee. "How are you holding up?"

He tipped his hand sideways and back. "We got Jimmy to take a little more formula today than he has been. They seem to think that's a good sign."

"I'm glad to hear that," Lori said. "But what about you?"

James took her hand and squeezed it hard.

The silence stretched out. Lori didn't know what else to say to him. She'd lost track of him after she'd sold the house in Louisville and moved in with her mama—that stopped his alimony payments. She'd spent most of the afternoon tracking him down.

She'd been surprised when the NICU people sent her here, but she guessed that losing a wife like this could shake even a man like James. She noticed he looked tousled, like he'd slept in his suit at some point. "Have you been back to your house today?" she said.

He shook his head. "Lila—Mrs. Tyler—brought me here yesterday after the funeral."

He stopped and sucked in his breath. "And I've been either here or in the NICU ever since."

"When do you need to be back to see him?" Lori said.

He looked down at his watch. "In another couple of hours."

"Mrs. Tyler told me she was getting ready to leave," Lori said. "How about I take you home and you get some sleep—or something to eat, at least? Then you can come back here whenever you need to."

James sat without moving. Lori didn't think she'd ever seen him so beaten down—not even after telling her Jack had been shot.

"Lori," he said, and then stopped. He tried again. "Lori, I haven't been back since she died. I don't know if I can take it."

"Well, I know how that feels," she said.

She saw him wince. "I know," he said.

She pulled her hand away and touched his shoulder. "That's why you don't need to go alone. Please let me help you if I can."

He stood up and looked down at her. "I appreciate it, Lori."

She got up and moved in front of him. "Do you need to go back up to get anything?"

He shook his head no. They started walking out with Lori in front to get to her car.

He gave her directions once she got away from the hospital parking lot. They led to one of the prettier neighborhoods in Baton Rouge, and Lori pulled up in the driveway he pointed her to.

She turned the car off and waited for him to decide when he was ready.

He stared out the windshield as the minutes ticked by. "We're renting this place. We moved here to be closer to her doctors," he said. "They wanted to check on her once a week whether she needed it or not."

Lori's heart sank. *How on earth can he do this?* she thought.

"Looks kind of out of place in the neighborhood," he said. "For the time of year, I mean."

She looked around at all the houses that seemed to have gone all in on the Christmas decorations on the street. "Well, at least you have the wreath on the door. That helps," Lori said.

James exhaled. "I ran out and bought it and put it there before I went to get Leilani from the hospital when they let her come home for the day on Thanksgiving."

Lori saw children playing outside a few doors down. She winced.

"It's not going to get any easier just sitting here, is it?" James said.

"Take whatever time you need."

He popped open the car door and stepped out. He fished in his pocket for his keys as Lori got out and locked up her car.

He walked up to the door and unlocked it without hesitating and opened it up. He held the door open and looked back at her. "After you."

She stepped in, and he closed the door behind him. He moved in front of her and walked slowly back towards the kitchen.

He turned around in the doorway. "Get you something to eat or drink if you need to. I'm going to go get changed and cleaned up," he said.

She nodded. "Tell me what you want, and I'll fix it for you for when you're done."

"Just whatever you find, Lori," he said. "Thanks." He moved off toward the back of the house.

She went through the fridge and put some seafood gumbo she found in the freezer to warm up on the stove and cooked up some white rice in the microwave. She didn't have a lot of trouble figuring out where things were—it looked like James ran the kitchen here just like he had when they were married. If his wife was sick as long as Mrs. Tyler said, he hadn't had much choice, Lori realized.

Moira said cancer, and when Lori found out James was in the waiting room at the NICU at Memorial, she could guess the rest.

He came back up front just as she was pouring the tea she found in the fridge. He looked more like himself in khakis and a golf shirt, but his face was reddened with some swelling around his eyes. She just handed him the glass and started tidying up from where she'd cooked as he ate.

The house was quiet. Lori could hear children playing outside next door as she cleaned. She couldn't remember the last time she'd felt so tongue-tied. *This was a mistake.*

"I do appreciate you thinking enough of me to come by," James said. "I'm surprised you do."

Lori turned to look at him. "Why wouldn't I, James?"

He looked up at her. "Because of how badly I hurt you."

Lori didn't quite know how to answer that. She sat down beside him. "That was a long time ago, James."

"In some ways it might be," James said. "But seeing you here makes it seem not so much."

Lori looked away. "I didn't come here to hurt you more, James. I'll see myself out."

"No, Lori—don't go. That's not what I meant," he said. "I was going to say you don't look all that much different from when I first met you." He reached for her hand. "It is good to see you."

"I didn't know how you'd react to me coming by," Lori said. "That's why I didn't come to the funeral yesterday."

"I understand," James said.

Find something else to talk about. Anything.

"Tell me about Jimmy," Lori said.

James talked about how much better he was sleeping and eating now, and how he'd actually gotten to hold him out of the isolette some the past couple of days. He lit up like a Christmas tree when he said they'd told him that day that Jimmy might could move to the well-baby nursery in a couple of weeks if he kept gaining weight like he was.

"Now what's his full name?" Lori said.

"James Saxon King, just like mine," James said. "Leilani and I decided to call him Jimmy for short."

Silence again—not as uncomfortable this time, though, Lori decided.

"How about we move into the living room?" James said. "Better chairs in there."

He led the way to the seating area and sat in the middle of the couch, while Lori sat in the nearest chair to it.

"What are you doing for Christmas this year?" James said.

Lori blinked. "I'll be in Mississippi at Mama's like always," she said. "What about you?"

James looked down. "Hopefully Jimmy will be out of the hospital then and I can take him to his grandmother's. Not sure about anything else."

She saw him biting his lip as his face turned red. "Not sure about anything else at all," he said. He turned his face away from her.

Lori had never felt so helpless in her life. "I don't know what to say to you, James."

"I don't know as there's anything you can say that I haven't already heard the past few days," he replied.

She got up from the chair and sat down beside him. She put her hand on his shoulders and felt all the tension he was holding in. *I know how I can help that.* She moved her fingers across his shoulders and began working on the knots in his muscles.

He let out his breath as if he'd been holding it in for days. "I wonder when I'm going to stop crying," he said.

"I think it's probably exactly what you need to be doing," Lori said.

"I made it better yesterday—she'd seen to that with what all she'd planned for the service," James said.

Lori kept working on his shoulders as he talked about hearing all Leilani's favorite gospel songs and the Bible verses Leilani asked to be read. "The last reading was of the Twenty-Third Psalm—when she wrote it all out for me, she said that she wanted me to read it so I would remember where she was instead of thinking about—what she'd been through." His voice trailed off.

"And she planned all that herself?" Lori said. James nodded, staring at the floor. "She sounds like she was a special woman," Lori said.

His face twisted suddenly, and he brushed at his eyes. Lori slipped her arm around his back, and he turned to rest his forehead on her shoulder.

She could feel how sad he was, but it wasn't the angry kind of tears she was used to from him. She'd seen him crying only a few times since she'd known him—the last time was when she'd seen him at Boyce Watson's office for their divorce. She moved her hand up and across his shoulder blades as she let him cry.

He pulled away from her and stared at the floor with his elbows on his knees. "Do you remember when I wasn't there when you miscarried?"

Lori nodded.

"And you felt like you couldn't forgive me?"

Lori nodded again.

He reached for her hand. "I don't know if I can expect you to now, either—but I'd like to ask you to."

Lori looked away. "I wasn't expecting this, James."

"I'm scared I won't ever have another chance to ask you, and I don't want to leave something like this behind me."

Lori looked up. "I don't like how that sounds."

"And I never expected to lose Leilani within three years, either. We're not promised tomorrow. When Leilani told me she was pregnant, I got scared," James said. "I told her what happened after the storm to us: Jack, our baby, everything."

He took a deep breath and let it out. "She said she was going to pray for me."

"And the next morning, it was like nothing ever happened, and that's when I learned what really being forgiven was all about," he said. "I can't go on with both you and her on my mind for what I've done. So I'm asking."

Lori sighed. "For a long time if I thought about you, I made sure I remembered how bad it got there at the end. But I could only do that to myself for so long."

She looked at James. "When Moira called me, I realized that I wanted to try to help you if I could because it hurt me to think about what you might be going through. I don't really remember how long it's been since the last time I thought about you. So I suppose I did forgive you a long time ago without even realizing it."

James reached out to her and brushed a lock of hair out of her face. "It was hard for me ask you that, Lori—but I'm glad I did."

He tilted his head. "Can you wait here a second? I'll be right back."

She nodded. He got up and headed towards the back of the house. Lori looked around the room and saw empty spaces on the walls where it looked like pictures were taken down.

But one small picture remained on the mantel, and Lori crossed the room to take a closer look. The lens caught a woman with blond ringlets, sliding down a big park slide, laughing, with her arms up in the air.

"That was taken before we knew she was pregnant at the park not too far from home," James said from behind her. "Leilani and I were there keeping her niece and nephew."

She turned. He was leaning up against the door frame. "That's my favorite picture of her."

He walked into the room, and Lori saw he was carrying a gift-wrapped package. She could tell from the wrapping that it was from Maison Weiss in Jackson, Mississippi. "I bought this awhile ago—when I was still in denial about how sick Leilani really was. I was saving it for her for Christmas." He looked down. "She left me a letter with notes about what to do with most of her things. But I don't feel right letting this go to Goodwill or anything like that."

He crossed the room and handed it to her. She looked at it, and then stared up at him. "Open it," he said. "I think you'd like it, and I want you to have it."

She moved back to the couch and sat down. The box felt bulky but light at the same time. She pulled the ribbon loose and started untaping the paper.

"Here, use this on the box," James said, unsnapping his pocketknife. "It's some strong tape."

She slit the box open and lifted the lid. She unwrapped the tissue paper and pulled out a short brown leather jacket with a fur collar and cuffs. She stared at it, then at James. "It's beautiful—James, I can't—"

"Take it, Lori," James said. "Please."

She stood up unsteadily and held it up to her chest. "I think it'll fit—it looks long enough."

James inclined his head towards the entry. "There's a mirror up there if you want to try it on and take a look at it."

She walked up towards the entry with James watching her. She pulled the jacket on—it was a little roomy on her, but the sleeve length was just right. She crossed her arms in front of her to see how it fit in the shoulders. When she looked up to the mirror, she saw James standing behind her with a smile on his face—looking like his old self again.

"You like it?" he said.

She looked at his image in the mirror. "I really do."

"That's mink on the collar and cuffs. I think you have to be really careful with storing it in the summertime—I guess you could call somewhere and find out," he said.

He put his hands on her shoulders and squeezed. "Merry Christmas," he whispered.

She turned around towards him. She could feel her throat closing up at the expression on his face as he looked down at her. She reached up and put her arms around his neck and hugged him. "Thank you," she whispered just before she touched his cheek with her lips.

She didn't know what he'd meant to say—all she heard was a low sound in his throat. But she wasn't able to pull away from him before he tightened his arms around her and turned his face to look at her.

"You beautiful girl," he said, staring at her.

He moved to touch his lips to hers. She didn't stop him.

As he kissed her, Lori wondered if she kept her eyes shut long enough, she'd open them and they'd be back in Louisville in their big house by the lake. Back when—

This is wrong.

Suddenly she choked up and couldn't breathe. She pushed on his shoulders and pulled back. He loosened his hold, and she turned her face away from his and rested her cheek on his shoulder. She could hear him fighting for breath himself as he held her.

He ran his hand through her hair. "Stay with me," he whispered. "We can try to start over—help me raise Jimmy. Please? I don't know where else to turn—Lori, please—"

"James, I can't," she said. "I—can't."

And she couldn't say anything else.

For a long minute, he didn't speak.

"Why not?" he finally said.

She squeezed her eyes shut. "It wouldn't be right."

"I think I'm past caring about doing right," he said.

She knew what a bad idea it was, but she also knew she hadn't told the whole truth. It had taken her so long to trust someone after she had divorced James. But she couldn't bring herself to say the words.

Finally he picked up her left hand and kissed the inside of

her ring finger. "That blue stone fooled me for a while. It doesn't read right without a diamond on it." he said.

She started tearing up. "It's a sapphire. He gave it to me on my birthday. I liked it better than I did the diamonds when me and Michael went to pick it out."

He let go of her hand, and she rested it on his shoulder. "You set a date?"

"We're looking at February."

She could hear his heart hammering in his chest up against her ear.

He started playing with the ends of her hair. "I hope he can be better to you than I was."

There was an edge to his voice she didn't like at all.

She shut her eyes. *What am I supposed to say to that?*

Finally he stepped back from her and put one hand under her jaw to tilt her face up. "Why did you come again? Just to remind me of everything I've lost?"

His eyes were empty—just like when he'd left for good.

"No!" she cried. "James!" She let a sob out without meaning to.

Suddenly James turned to the wall, leaning over and placing his hands flat against it.

She stood there staring. He was taking deep breaths, looking down at the floor.

"Thanks for coming by, Lori," he said in the same cold voice he had used when she miscarried.

"Are you going to be—"

"Goodbye, Lori."

She reached up and touched his shoulder, and he flinched. "Lori, please."

"I don't want to leave you like this, James!"

"Lori! You're not helping me now by staying!" he said through his teeth.

She opened her mouth to answer, then closed it. She looked towards the living room to make sure she wasn't leaving her purse behind. *I can't just walk out.* She looked up at him.

"Wait a second," he said.

She saw him reach for the drawer on the small table in the entry. It had two lovely vases on the tabletop.

She gasped and backed away when he pulled out his Glock. "Take this, while you're at it," he snapped.

She took another step back.

"Take it," he said. "Unless you want to be responsible for what I do with it when you leave."

She reached for it and took it, her hand trembling.

"Now, *go*," he said.

She realized she had to say something. "Take care, James."

She saw him turn away and make his hands into fists as he nodded his head with his back still to her. He started tapping the knuckles of his right hand against the wall.

Lori's eyes blurred. She walked over to the front door and fumbled with the knob before she got it to turn. She pulled it open, stepped out, and shut it behind her.

She cringed as she heard a crash from inside before she could even let go of the doorknob. She wondered which one of the vases wound up on the polished wood floor. She jammed both her hands in the pockets of Leilani's jacket as she walked to her car. She got in, threw the gun on her passenger seat, and sat in the front seat gripping the steering wheel.

"God, help him," she whispered. She crossed herself and whispered a Hail Mary as she started the car and drove away.

About the Author

Julie Liddell Whitehead lives and writes from Mississippi. An award-winning freelance writer, Julie covered disasters from 9/11 to Hurricane Katrina throughout her career. She writes on mental health, mental health education, and mental health advocacy. She has a bachelor's degree in communication, with a journalism emphasis, and a master's degree in English, both from Mississippi State University. In August 2021, she completed her MFA from Mississippi University for Women.

Milton Keynes UK
Ingram Content Group UK Ltd.
UKHW021308230824
R3667300001B/R36673PG447187UKX00001B/1

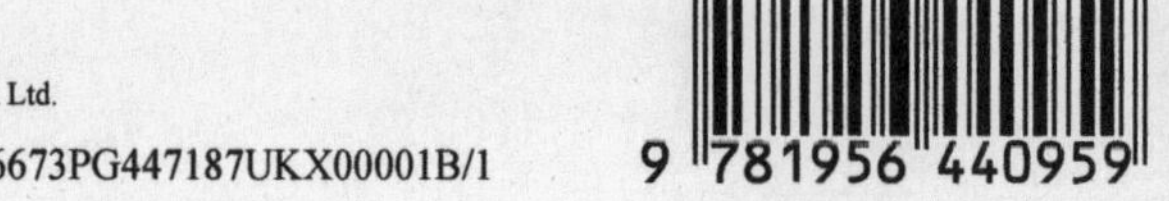

9 781956 440959